By Gayleen Froese

BEN AMES CASE FILES
The Girl Whose Luck Ran Out

Published by DSP Publications
www.dsppublications.com

GAYLEEN FROESE

# THE GIRL WHOSE LUCK RAN OUT

DSP PUBLICATIONS

Published by
DSP PUBLICATIONS

5032 Capital Circle SW, Suite 2, PMB# 279,
Tallahassee, FL 32305-7886 USA
www.dsppublications.com





Mass Market Paperback ISBN: 978-1-64108-398-0
Trade Paperback ISBN: 978-1-64108-383-6
Digital ISBN: 978-1-64108-382-9
Mass Market Paperback published May 2023
v. 1.0

Printed in the United States of America

To my personal private investigation agency, including novelist Laird Ryan States; Nero, Archie and Molly, the dog detectives; the Scooby Gang of monitor lizards; and Marlowe the tegu. You make our home messy but never dull.

In memory of Spenser and Dashiell.

Acknowledgments

I AM beyond grateful to everyone who read this book once, twice, or more as it developed. Thank you to Noreen, Tanya, Tyler, Deb, Tarra, Meshon, and Sarah.

Thanks, too, to Andi and everyone else at DSP for their good questions, hard work, and keen eyes.

My greatest thanks go to Ryan and Cori, whose support and advice was and is indispensable.

# About This Book

*When Ben Ames solved his first big case, a lot of people offered to tell his story for him. He heard from TV producers and reporters. Ghost writers approached him. No fewer than three production houses wanted to buy the rights and make a movie.*

*Still running a detective agency, he couldn't unlist his number and disappear. At some point he got so tired of those calls that he placed one of his own. To me.*

*I don't know why he chose me, except that I live in Edmonton. I didn't have the connections or the pull of agents in Toronto and Vancouver, but I knew things they didn't. I knew Calgary had paved roads and power lines and that not everyone there wore a cowboy hat every day. Anyone who has lived out West can tell you, that is no small consideration. So it is possible that was why he called my number and told me who he was and what he wanted.*

*"I want to tell this my own way," he told me. "I want to write a book."*

*He'd never written a book before. He asked was I willing to take on a guy with no idea what he was doing?*

*I would usually have told him to reach out again once the book was done, but I knew Ben Ames had a great story, and I liked his determination to stay in control of it. I told him I'd work with him and connect him to some friends who could give him advice along the way. I won't say it was easy for him, and there were a lot of false starts, but he found his way to the book you're reading now.*

*It's a bit of a mystery, a bit of an adventure, a tour of Kananaskis Country, and a kind of romance too. Ben and I hope you'll enjoy it.*

*Gayleen Froese*
*Literary agent for Ben Ames*

GAYLEEN FROESE

# THE GIRL WHOSE LUCK RAN OUT

# CHAPTER 1

THE CLIENT was talking, and I was stealing glances at the magazine on my desk, wondering about Jesse's eyes. Specifically, did they look better with the eyeliner or without? He was staring at me from the cover of *sCene*'s weekend edition, a close-up of his face, and the eyeliner was on thick. Maybe there was a sweet spot between thick and none.

Or maybe I should have been listening.

"People will surprise you," I said. Most of my clients came to me because someone had surprised them.

Lauren Courtney frowned, fine lines spreading around her mouth and eyes like cracks in spring ice. "Kim wouldn't do that."

I could still see Jesse's face from the corner of my eye. Dark, glittering green eyes, like the embodiment of jealousy. I didn't think he'd ever felt it. Cheekbones high and sharp. The make-up sliced into every contrast between his features and his bone-white skin. This was not a person you'd imagine in a ratty T-shirt and boxer briefs, eating dry Honeycombs out of the box while doing a crossword with his off hand. I could only picture it because I'd seen it so many times.

Jesse's expression, whatever it was meant to be, looked like judgement. Not kind judgement. I slid some flyers over the magazine.

"I apologize," I said. "You're here because your sister hasn't checked in for... four days. And she's never done that before. Well, people don't do things they've never done before... until they do. I'm not trying to dismiss your concerns. It's not uncommon for people to do something that their family or friends consider out of character."

She looked down at the bag on her lap. Her hair fell around her face in thick slabs of honey brown. She was every mid-thirties mother you'd see in the supermarket line, dressed politely in that season's chain-store clothes. Her nails were shiny buttons of beige, and her foundation was a little too thick. A look intended to convey irreproachable smoothness, but the illusion was breaking down everywhere, from a loose cuff thread on her white wrap sweater to the slight bulge above the waist of her pleated pants.

"Did you report this to the police?" I asked. "You can report someone missing anytime. There's no waiting period."

Her eyes narrowed. "Mr. Ames...."

"Ben."

"Ben. Please don't tell me to leave this to the police. They opened a file, but it's not like they're going to work on it. It's more like they'll know her if they find her. That's not good enough."

She was probably right that they weren't really looking. Definitely they cared more about a missing white girl than about, say, indigenous women. But a student who'd been gone less than a week? They'd ask a few questions, maybe, and then dump her file on a stack of about a hundred others representing all the adults who had wandered off and not shown up again. They'd assume that either she'd be back before they could even start looking, or she was already dead.

Expressing this to my client might be a mistake.

"And you've got posters up?" I asked instead. "Social media? Called local reporters?"

"All of that, yes," she said. "The media are about as interested as the police. A couple of them said, 'When she's been gone for a month, give us a call.' Do so many people really do that, disappear for weeks and show up again? Don't they have jobs and families?"

"Don't burn any bridges with the media," I advised. "Ideally you won't need them later. But in case you do…."

"I held my tongue," Lauren assured me. "I don't know how to explain this, obviously. No one understands. It's not just that she's never flaked out on me before. It's that she loves babysitting my daughter. My daughter thinks her aunt is the coolest person in the world. Much cooler than me. I mean, she doesn't think I'm cool at all."

"Not really your job," I told her. That melted some of the cracked ice on her face.

"Kimberly likes to swoop in and tell my daughter, 'Oh, don't listen to your mom, Emmy-Bird. Me and you are the cool ones,' or something like that. Emma and her aunt Kim are the cool people, and her mom and Grandma and Grandpa are, I don't know. Boring. Losers. Whatever the cool word is for that."

I was pretty sure *cool* wasn't even the cool word for cool, if you asked the kids of today. I didn't mention it. "How old is your daughter?"

"Eleven, going on twenty. She's almost old enough to stay on her own. Why does it matter, though?"

"I like to get the whole picture," I told her. "Ms. Courtney—"

"Mrs.," she said. "It's my ex-husband's name. Or Lauren is fine."

"Lauren, I charge one hundred an hour, and the first few days of a missing person investigation can be long days. Also, these cases can drag on, especially when someone doesn't want to be found. I bill for expenses on top of that. Some people will say you can't put a price on your loved one's well-being. What I say is this: paying me is not necessarily an investment in your sister's well-being."

Lauren's frown deepened. "What does that mean?"

"Most missing adults aren't missing. They met a new guy and went to Vegas on a whim. They broke up with some guy and went to Vegas with their best friends to drown their sorrows. It is Vegas a lot. Paying me to find that out may not do any harm, except to your bank account, but it doesn't do your sister any good."

"Her friends haven't seen her," Lauren said. "People do go missing."

I looked at the flyers on top of the magazine. I didn't have to see his face. I could imagine the amusement and, worse, the fond indulgence as he asked why I insisted on shooting myself in the foot. "It's called having a conscience," I told him silently.

"What was that?" Lauren asked. Apparently not as silent as I'd thought.

"If you want me to look, I'll look. I just wanted it to be an informed decision."

Before she spoke, I had her answer. Her hands were fiddling with the clasp of her purse. "Do you need a retainer?"

"Thirty hours." I grabbed a business card from the stand I'd gotten from my insurance company. It was plastic, fake wood grain, and a man with any style or money would have replaced it. "I'll check in at least once a day, and you can call me off at any point. If your retainer isn't spent, I'll refund the difference."

"That's fine," she said. "Is there anything else you need from me?"

I glanced at my watch. "I'll get started first thing tomorrow. What you can do tonight is send me an email with everything you can think of that might help. I'll need photos and a good, honest description. Where your sister lives, who her friends are, what her routines are. Does she have a vehicle? I'll need everything you can tell me about it. Does she have particular clothes and jewelry she wears often? Tattoos or piercings? Did she say or do anything unusual over the last few weeks? Also the name of the police officer you spoke with. If you wonder whether you should include something, include it. I'll still have questions for you, but this will save time."

"I'll do my best." Lauren made tidy notes in a pad she'd set on my desk, next to her cheque book. She carried a cheque book. Most people pulled a crumpled blank from the back of their wallet.

I saw her out, returned to my office, and settled in to stare at the cheque. Three days, with some room for expenses. I could deposit it now, but what if I found Kimberly Moy in eight hours? Or what if it turned out she wasn't really missing, just holed up with some guy? Kimberly complains about the invasion of privacy and

Lauren cancels the cheque. Clients had done similar things before.

I pulled the stack of files off the magazine. "What do you think?" I asked Jesse. He gave me a smouldering look. Me and everyone. And the photographer. Had he tried to pick up the photographer? Why was I asking a millionaire what to do about my pathetic finances?

I took out my phone and looked at the ticket: Jack Lowe. Show 8:00 p.m. Doors open 7:00 p.m. I'd shoot for eight o'clock. That gave me four hours to decide what to wear, how much to drink, and whether to go at all.

The phone buzzed.

I was sure it had to be the client, checking that she had the number right or telling me something she forgot. I nearly dropped the phone when I looked at the text.

*Do you want to meet before the show?*

*- Jess*

My hand went numb. My stomach, iffy all day, felt like a hedgehog was trying to get out. The screen went in and out of focus, and I remembered lying on a cold bathroom floor feeling this way, like I was going to die and wouldn't mind. Jesse laughing, calling me a lightweight, flushing the toilet for me and wiping my face with a damp towel.

Not Jack Lowe. Not the stage name Jesse had picked for himself before he ran off to be rich and famous. This text was from plain old Jess.

My shaking hand managed to turn off the phone without accidentally responding or sending a selfie of my gobsmacked face. I put the phone into my pocket and went to the back door. Frank had been scratching since the client arrived and I'd put him in the yard.

"Get in the house, asshole," I directed. Frank took it as a suggestion and lumbered past me without urgency. He'd rolled in dead leaves and looked messier than usual, which was bad for a dog who usually looked like a Rottweiler in a Wookie costume.

"You know Jesse," I said. Frank looked over his shoulder at me.

"Not personally," I clarified. "But when I'm talking to the computer.... *That* Jesse. What the hell do you think you're doing, Jess? You can do better than him, Jesse. Jess, Buzzfeed is not your friend. That Jesse."

There was no obvious connection between what I was saying and Frank getting dinner, so he lost interest and trudged to his food bowl. I followed, picking up the leaves he dropped.

"Do I meet him before the show? I haven't talked to the guy in seven years. He thinks he can text me out of the blue and I'll come running? How did he even get my number?"

Frank sat next to his bowl and tilted his head. Here we are in the kitchen. We both know this bowl is empty. We both know what needs to happen.

"If I don't go, I'll drive myself crazy wondering what he wants."

Frank nudged his bowl toward me with one huge, muddy paw.

"I'm not going to lose my mind and start following his tour bus. I remember what he's like. Yes, I will feed you."

While Frank chomped on his kibble, I looked at my phone. No new messages.

I could always walk away. If he said something that pissed me off. No law saying I had to stay.

No harm in sitting across a table from him for twenty minutes or whatever it turned out to be. We'd catch up.

*Where?*

I put the phone on the counter. Filled Frank's water bowl. Frank slurped up a mouthful and walked away without swallowing, leaving a stream on the floor.

I looked at myself on the side of the toaster. My hair was okay. It was always okay. It was a good medium brown and too short to misbehave. My face was all right for an off night. The rest of me was too tall and a little awkward, but at least I'd filled out since university.

As long as I wasn't competing with movie stars and pop idols, I did fine.

The phone buzzed, and the hedgehog in my stomach jumped again.

*The Baxter 5:00*

Not what I'd expected. The Baxter was a cavernous pub, a former warehouse, awkwardly sharing a corner of downtown with some of Calgary's best hotels. Nothing wrong with it, and the place filled up on weekends and late nights, but it wasn't where stylish ladder-climbers had after-work drinks. I wondered whether Jess knew that. Was he trying to keep his head down?

I glanced at my watch and figured I could make it.

*see u there*

"Look after the place," I told Frank. He was lying on the throw rug by the gas fireplace. The fireplace hadn't worked in two years, but Frank kept thinking it would come back to life one day. He raised his head for a few seconds before dropping it to his paws again. I took that for agreement.

I had my phone, my wallet, and a leather jacket that I didn't need for as warm as the September day had turned out. I grabbed my Jeep keys from the hook and I was good to go.

After walking into the Baxter, I waited for my eyes to adjust to the dim light. Little clutches of chairs and tables and booths took advantage of the huge empty room to allow for private conversations. Probably another reason Jess chose it.

I edged forward past steel tanks and wood crates giving the impression that everything from the food to the tables to the debit-card readers was handmade by an artisan in a back room. As my sight improved, I spotted a scruffy guy in a Baxter T-shirt, alone at a table with a burger in front of him. Probably staff on a meal break. Group of twenty-somethings having a jacked-up hair competition. And alone in a booth at the back, a small figure in an oversized grey hoodie, hood up and sleeves pulled halfway down the hands. I stepped closer and saw shadows on the fingers, what could have been black nail polish. Another step and I saw a wingtip of coal black hair peeking out from the hood just above the shoulders.

For a few fast beats of my heart, I was back in Toronto. Really, the wilds of North York. A bar much like this but with a band and a crowd. My boyfriend's band, the first time I'd seen them play. Jesse's voice, searing and huge like a forest fire. They were a new band, half the songs were covers, and no one had come here to see them, but none of that mattered. Everyone knew they were seeing a star.

I kept it casual. Ambled across the room. Nearly tripped on the uneven concrete floor. Caught myself before he saw. Slid into the other side of his booth as he looked up and smiled. The drop light over the table let me see him clearly for the first time.

"Ben."

"*The* Jack Lowe."

He shut his eyes for a moment. "Don't."

It really wasn't Jack Lowe in that booth. No eyeliner. No make-up that I could see. Far from dressing to piss off Peoria, he was hidden under his hoodie and jeans. The only dramatic things about him were his black nails and too-pale face and a strange glow to his eyes. And he was distractingly beautiful. Never anything he could do about that.

I glanced over my shoulder. "Anyone recognize you here?"

"The server," he said. "She's down-lowing it."

I gave a soft whistle. "How did you tip for that?"

"I tip well. How are you?"

Christ, how was I? I shrugged. "Okay, I guess." I gave him a big-tooth grin and made my voice as cheerily fake as I could. "What've you been up to since university?"

Jess sighed. "Can you not do that?"

"What do you think I'm doing?"

"It's weird seeing your ex." He paused for a few breaths. "It's weird for me too. Can you… not make it extra weird?"

I gave him the smile again. "Hell no."

Jess looked at his hands, which were wrapped around a coffee mug. Strange seeing him in a bar without a drink.

"Private investigator," he said. "You weren't a cop very long."

I wasn't trying to hide. But if he knew how long my shingle had been out, that meant he'd been Google stalking me for a while.

"I was asked to resign," I told him. "It was… they called it off-duty activities."

Jess raised his head and a suggestive eyebrow.

"These activities, were they anyone I know?"

Of course not, because he didn't know anyone in Calgary, but I knew what he meant.

"It wasn't like that," I said. "Not exactly."

He shrugged. He looked tired suddenly, and his eyes were sad. He'd always said it was stupid to join the police unless you were a thug who liked that kind of thing. Which I wasn't. I'd asked how he expected it to get any better.

"It wasn't everyone," I said. "Mostly just one guy. He outranked me by a lot."

"Sucks," he said. I didn't hear any "I told you so" in it. Also no questions about what exactly had gone down or why I hadn't gone to the union. "How's the detective thing?"

"Not like on TV. How's the rock star thing?"

Jess smiled, but his eyes were still sad. "It gets old."

He reached up to push his hair farther back into the hood. His hand was shaking. He seemed to have gone, in under a minute, from tired to exhausted.

"Jess?"

He grabbed the mug, and I realized that was why he'd been holding it all along. So I wouldn't see him shaking.

"It's nothing," he said. He shut his eyes again and breathed. Old instincts kicked in, and I put a hand over his. I think I expected it to be cold, like maybe he was coming off a drug, but instead it was papery dry and so hot it almost hurt to touch. His eyes opened as I moved my hand to his forehead, brushing the skin before he could pull away.

"What the hell, Jesse? Are you sick?"

He looked over his shoulder, then narrowed his eyes at me. "Shh!"

"What is wrong with you?" I asked, ducking my head toward him and keeping my voice low.

"Walking pneumonia," he said. "It's fine."

Closer to him, I could see the fever flush in bright patches on his face. "In what universe is pneumonia fine?"

"Walking," he said. "Got rid of the cough. I just get tired."

His eyes closed. It didn't seem optional. I put a hand on his arm, over the thick fleece of the hoodie. "Have you seen a doctor?"

He nodded. His eyes stayed shut. "Two days ago."

"You have been doing shows with fucking pneumonia?"

That opened his eyes. He looked horrified and glanced around the bar again. "Keep it down!"

I leaned in closer. "How the hell are you singing?"

"Just tonight and Van tomorrow. I'll push through."

The server hovered in sight. She was easily forty, with a shrewd weathered face. I liked the substantial look of her, the way her broad frame made the bar's short skirt and white tee uniform look like a cheap Halloween costume. She sized up the mood at our table from a good ten feet away and withdrew before Jesse even noticed she'd been there.

"No offence, Jess," I told him, "but it's a rock concert. It's not like there's one chance to blow up the Death Star and no one else can do it. You can call in sick."

Jess smiled. His "you're sweet but you don't get it" smile. I knew it all too well.

"It's a lot of money to cancel."

"You can afford it," I reminded him. I didn't know how much money he actually, definitely had, but it wasn't chump change.

"Not my money," he said. He took a few breaths to fortify himself. "I'm a cog in a big expensive machine."

"I don't really give a shit about—" I started.

He cut me off. "And we lost a lot on the tour before this, with COVID."

"That's not your prob—"

"And there's gossip," he said. "It's drugs. I'm a drunk. Can't just be sick."

Toward the end, for us, it had been drugs, and he had been drunk. That wasn't specifically what had done us in. I wasn't a puritan. But it hadn't helped.

"I thought drugs and drunk were your image," I said. "Aren't you supposed to be an Olympic-level sybarite?"

It was hard to tell in the dark, but he might have flinched. His voice didn't betray anything when he said, "My image and my reputation are different things."

I didn't know what he meant but decided to take his word for it. "Can't your manager take care of your reputation?"

"He would," Jess said, "if I hadn't fired him two days ago."

"Jesus," I said. "You can't get enough of the drama, can you?"

"He—never mind. It's me, my road manager, and a bunch of label people. It's okay. Two more shows."

"Shouldn't you be in bed at least?" I asked. "Until the show?"

His face responded with another expression I knew well. Guilt.

"I snuck out," he said.

I leaned back in my chair. "I don't understand. Why would you do that?"

Jesse gave me a one-shoulder shrug. "I wanted to see you."

"You could have—" I started, thinking he could have asked me to meet him backstage. But it wouldn't have been him that way. It would have been the rock star.

I stood, went to Jesse's side of the booth, and offered my hand.

"C'mon. Get up."

He raised his eyebrows at me.

"Jess," I said, "get up."

He slid from the booth, and I put a hand under his arm to steady him.

"Which hotel?" I asked.

"Ben...."

"We can talk when you're not swaying."

I released his arm for a second to make my point. He swayed into me, and I put my arms around him. He was wearing something with heels, probably boots, because the top of his head came to just above my shoulder.

It was unsettlingly natural to have Jess in my arms, like the years apart hadn't happened. I felt his arm move and looked down to see him taking out his wallet. I went back to the way I'd been holding him before, one hand carefully supporting his left arm. He used his free hand to take out a bright-red fifty and drop it next to his cup.

I resisted the urge to tell him I'd keep any number of secrets for him since it paid so well. He'd probably have handed me a grand, and giving it back would have been awkward.

"Your hotel?" I said again.

It was only three blocks, so I walked him there. Really it was walking and dragging and carrying, with Jess leaning hard against my side. He pushed his hood back as we reached the elevator, and I noticed his hair smelled the same, the grape Kool-Aid and honeysuckle of the cheap Aussie shampoo he used to buy. I'd have thought millionaire boy would have gotten himself more expensive shampoo. Then again, why mess with something that worked?

Inside the elevator, he swiped a card to light an extra row of buttons. Not for mere mortals, those floors.

He eyed my sour face. "People try to break into my room."

He had the elevator to lean against now instead of me. I looked him up and down. It wasn't surprising that no one had recognized him on our way to the hotel. Not because of the hoodie or that I'd tried to hide his face. He was too tired to project the charisma, the special something that had made him stand out even before he'd become famous. He was five six and always seemed breakable—that delicacy was part of the charm. But he usually carried with him a force of will, like he centered a tornado. Without it he was hardly there.

I opened my arms, and he humoured me by stepping forward and leaning against me, his face pressed to my chest. I held him and ran my thumb over the heated skin at the nape of his neck. I should have wanted him so bad it hurt, and I did, a little, but mainly I was worried about how he'd gotten this sick and why he was thinner than he'd looked in that interview last month. Things I shouldn't have given a damn about, considering.

I said, "Do they know your real name in that room?"

His real name wasn't a secret. He'd graduated from the University of Toronto as Jesse Serik, and he'd appeared on enough programs under that name. But the fact that his name wasn't a secret made it uninteresting to most people.

He was silent for a moment. "No."

"Okay."

He pulled away when the elevator stopped. The door opened not onto a typical hotel hallway, but into a lounge about half the size of the palatial downstairs lobby. A pack of hipsters clutched phones and paced, veering from one another's paths at the last second. Planning for the show that night and, most likely, trying to find their star. I didn't think I saw the band, though I wasn't certain I'd recognize them. Jack Lowe was a solo artist, and the band seemed to switch with every tour. I'd assumed he pissed other musicians off beyond tolerance and had to get new ones. Maybe that was unfair. I could ask him later what the revolving bands were about.

The pacing and buzzing stopped in a wave as the entourage noticed us. They stood still, like cattle in a field. Not aggressive or afraid yet, but open to either. I stayed a few feet to his side, far enough to be clear that I wasn't some kind of crazy kidnapper but close enough to see his face and to catch him if he fell. Or in the case of a hipster stampede.

"This is Ben," Jesse said. He drew in a breath, and his voice was different when he spoke again. Still his but with an edge. "He's an old friend. We had a drink."

A small woman in a black leather jacket and thick black-rimmed glasses approached at speed. Her hair embraced an impressive range of colours, none found in nature, and was messily piled at the top of her head.

"Jack, you cannot just leave. You threw off the entire schedule. You've got an interview in fifteen, and we can't move it because sound check is—"

"Can I hear this from bed?" Jess asked, with a tight smile that made it clear it wasn't a question. His tone wasn't kind.

He had, to be fair, gone truant on them. They probably had some right to be annoyed. I might have held it against him if I hadn't known how hard it was for him to stand upright, let alone square his shoulders and radiate control.

"Yes!" the woman said, unfazed. "The doctor said you're supposed to be in bed when you're not doing the show. Or the soundcheck. Interviews are to be done from bed. You have no business running around town meeting old friends. The label is fucking furious!"

Genuine anger flashed in Jess's eyes for a second. I wondered whether she knew him well enough to catch it. He'd always been good at dousing that fire before anyone could see.

"Of course," he said without much expression. He turned to me, and I saw he'd positioned himself so that when he faced me, his back would be to the room. So they wouldn't see his face soften, the weary affection in his eyes.

"Later," he said.

I stayed long enough to see which room he went into, then made my retreat.

# CHAPTER 2

I CHECKED my phone from the lobby. As expected, Lauren Courtney hadn't wasted time. She'd shared a Google Drive with me, a collection of facts about Kimberly. Things I'd asked for. Things I hadn't. She'd shared it with a few others, likely Kimberly's friends. I admired it a little. It was efficient to let everyone pour their leads and facts and "I remember thinking it was strange" into one document. She probably planned baby showers the same way.

She'd also set up a Facebook page for people to leave tips. Nothing on there so far. I didn't know how many college kids were on Facebook, but to be fair, anyone who wanted to leave a tip on TikTok would have to work out a dance routine first, and that was a big ask.

There was some traffic under #FindKimMoy on Twitter, but it was just Lauren and Kim's friends asking people to share information. A lot of surprised and sad emojis. Praying hands.

I took a moment before I started reading to call in a favour from a friend, then dived into the data.

Kimberly Moy was a second year Mount Royal student, pursuing a history degree with a minor in arts or, as her social media put it, an art history degree. She doodled constantly, putting herself through school with a scholarship and gigs as a Paint Nite instructor, teaching drunk people to capture the ineffable beauty of a sunset.

She largely went by K-Tel online. The disco glitter surrounding this identity gave a nod to the record label of the same name, something Kimberly should have been much too young to remember. Was this the kind of thing art historians studied these days?

I clicked through a seemingly endless collection of photos. Kim with her friends at school. Kim with her friends in restaurants and bars. Kim in her room, showing off the drawings she'd spread across the walls. She looked a little like her sister but played down the resemblance by dying her hair a glossy purple-black, slathering on a too-light foundation, and outlining her eyes Cleopatra-style. She wore dresses, mostly, and favoured rockabilly polka dots and ginghams with nipped waists and flared skirts. The overall effect was of Wednesday Addams starring in an Annette Funicello movie.

She had a tattoo because who didn't. Hers, at least the only one I saw in the photos, was a singing blackbird with the word "ME" across his wing. The bird perched on her left bicep, below where cap sleeves stopped. Of course she'd planned her tattoo in relation to her dress sleeves. From her look alone, the careful matching of shoes and make-up and nails and hair ribbon, it was clear she liked to plan ahead.

To her credit, the shots weren't a pouty parade of whatever look was considered sexy this month. In her expressions, the genuine-seeming laughter and weariness and surprise and disappointment, the unplanned person came through. She laughed a lot, if the photos were anything to go by. She didn't seem to mind looking less than perfect. She had intelligent eyes.

I could only see the public face of her social media. That wasn't ideal since I was looking for secret passions or appetites that might have induced her to leave town in a hurry. Probably she wouldn't put those things where anyone could see them. There could always be clues, though, so I scanned every photo and video and post as if it held the cure for cancer. I was so intent on the job that I nearly jumped out of my skin when something flicked the middle of my forehead.

"I hope you're not on a stakeout, Ames."

I dropped my phone into my pocket and looked up at Dr. Luna Fares. "It's your job to save people, not give them heart attacks."

Luna put her hands on her hips. Glossy red nails stood out blindingly against the dull green of her scrubs. "I could have walked right past you. Are you sure you're cut out for your job?"

I'd met Luna when I was a cop and a regular in the city's emergency rooms. She was addicted to glitter lip gloss and adrenaline and had once accidentally on purpose spilled cranberry juice into the wound of one of my detainees after she'd gotten fed up with the shit he'd been talking to us both.

"I'm not on the job," I told her. "I mean, I am, but this isn't it. This is… someone needs my help. Thanks for coming."

Luna glanced at her watch. "As you mentioned on the phone, I do owe you one. But I've only got about forty minutes, so let's get to it." The faint British accent she'd kept from her childhood was always stronger when she was hurrying. Or angry. Or excited. Or drunk. "Where's this someone?"

I gestured for her to follow and led her to the elevator. "It's more who than where. You know who he is."

"Oh yes?" She looked at her reflection in the closed elevator doors. Even under the cold fluorescents, her dark eyes and light brown skin made her look as warm as a firelit den. She raked her nails through her long hair, shoved a stray curl behind her ear, and sighed. "Is he one of your exes?"

"I… actually, yes. But that's not…." The elevator doors opened, and I hurried us inside before anyone could join us, then swiped the room key card I'd stolen from Jesse's pocket. "It's Jack Lowe."

Luna's mouth dropped open. She blinked. Then she slammed the heel of her hand into my chest, hard enough to hurt. "Fuck! Off! You called me down here on my dinner break for some stupid practical joke?"

"He and I dated when I was in Toronto. We were at university together. I promise I will tell you all about it some other time. Right now, he needs to see a doctor. He got a diagnosis of walking pneumonia in Winnipeg, and he seems… not good."

Luna was running one thumbnail across her lower lip. Back and forth, back and forth. "Oh my God. You aren't joking."

"I want an unbiased opinion. Can he push through this show and the show tomorrow night, or is he going to wind up in the hospital?"

"You'd like me to make that call clinically?" Luna pulled a stethoscope from her pocket and placed it around her neck. It was a simple gesture that changed something deep in her, from regular Luna to Dr. Fares. "With no labs, no BP. Lucky I've got an oximeter and thermometer in my bag. How long do you think I'll have with him?"

"Depends whether he cooperates," I said.

Luna's flat look of disbelief would probably have been followed by a lecture on the difficulty of treating unwilling patients at the best of times, but her speech was pre-empted by the opening of the elevator doors.

Luna didn't need to be told how to play things. She stormed off that elevator with an urgency and entitlement seen only in doctors and toddlers. I cut around her to direct her to Jesse's room. The entourage herd had thinned while I'd been downstairs, and no one stepped forward to question us.

Jesse's room was a suite, and we walked into a living room with a kitchen to one side, a sunken fireplace, a dining area, and a baby grand piano by the floor-to-ceiling window. The piano was probably the only part of the fancy set-up that Jesse had actually used.

Two staffers sat by the fireplace, one typing frantically into a laptop and the other into a phone. They looked up as they heard us enter, and Luna charged ahead of me.

"Is my patient in there?" she asked, pointing at one of the suite's closed doors.

The staffer with the laptop nodded as the one with the phone slowly got to his feet. "I'm sorry, are you—"

Luna didn't even bother to look at him. I hurried to keep up with her as she threw open the door to Jesse's bedroom and strode inside.

I saw Jess over her shoulder. He was dressed and on top of the blankets. Instead of sleeping, he was on his phone. Whoever he was talking to, he was doing everything he could to give them the impression that he was fine. Better than fine. Terrific. His face, pale and almost grey in the hollows, said it was a damned lie.

The woman with the dark-rimmed glasses was standing at the far side of the bed, watching Jesse talk. He had his own glasses on, a slight pair with wire rims, and that was another bad sign. Jesse had an oddball mix of near- and farsightedness that meant he could force his eyes to focus, unless he was exhausted. It wasn't a good day when Jess had to put his glasses on.

"…great to end the tour here in Canada," he was saying. "I've missed Vancouver—it's been a few years since I've been out west."

Whoever was on the other end began talking at him, and Jesse took advantage of the break to shoot questioning looks at Luna and me. His keeper glared at us and raised a hand for silence. Luna, not accustomed to being shushed, opened her mouth. I put a hand on her shoulder and shook my head. Jesse would be off the phone in a second. We could wait it out.

Whatever the caller had said made Jesse laugh.

"Oh, come on. Would you stop someone leaving the office on Friday and ask them what they'd be doing at work on Monday? I've been on the road a long time. I'm taking a break."

His keeper glared. The question had obviously been about what he had planned after the tour, and by the look on her face, I was guessing he'd gone off message.

When Jesse spoke again, his voice was quieter, and he was taking breaks to breathe. The performance was over. "Thanks, guys. I'll see you tomorrow at the show."

He hung up, dropped the phone to the bed, and surveyed the room. Before he could say anything, his keeper jumped in.

"Whatever this is," she said, waving an arm at Luna, "we can get to it in a minute. Just—what is so hard about plugging the ZZGold single? That was the deal, Jack. You sing, you plug it. When someone asks you what's next for you, you say the fucking single drops next week. How hard is it?"

Jess shut his eyes and sighed. "I forgot."

The back of my neck tingled. He'd lied. I'd never seen any particular tells with Jess, but I usually knew anyhow.

He opened his eyes and gave Luna a weary smile. "I don't think we've met."

"I'm Dr. Fares," Luna told him. She didn't seem starstruck. "I'll be your doctor today, if you'd like one."

"We don't have time for this," Jesse's keeper said. Luna ignored her.

"You look sick," she told Jesse. "Doctors don't say that to just anyone. I'd like to examine you. Would that be all right?"

"He doesn't—" the keeper started.

Jesse cut her off with a word. "Yes."

"Yes?" Luna asked. She pulled her crossbody medical bag forward and tugged at the zipper.

"Yes. Thank you."

"Jack, we do not have time for this," his keeper said. "You have soundcheck in half an hour. The doctor in Winnipeg said you were good to go. You told me you don't want to cancel."

She finally had Luna's attention.

"Could you step outside?" Luna asked.

"What? No!"

"Would you like some privacy?" Luna asked Jesse. "As my patient?"

"Gia, please wait outside," Jess said. "Okay? Please?"

She narrowed her eyes at him but turned and went, pulling the door shut behind her with a nasty snap.

"Are you a friend of Ben's?" Jesse asked.

Luna smiled. "Are you?"

"Ask him."

"Intriguing. Hold still a sec, please."

Luna took his temperature while I positioned myself near the door, ready to block it if anyone tried to come in.

"I know Gia must seem like the biggest bitch in the world right now," Jess said. "She's not. It's her job to keep things running, and—"

The thermometer beeped. Luna looked at it and frowned, then put her stethoscope in her ears.

"And?" she asked. "Please take your shirt off. You probably get that a lot."

"Right back at you," Jesse said. Luna laughed like a trumpet, and I was certain they could hear her on the next floor.

"I did say I wanted to do the shows," Jesse said between Luna's orders to breathe and hold and breathe. "It's better than the alternative. Gia knows that."

"Well." Luna half sat on the night table. She was digging for something deep in her bag. "That depends on the alternative. Oh. Here. Give me your hand."

She clipped something onto his index finger. Second later it beeped, and a blinking 93 showed on its small square screen.

"Ah," Luna said. "Are these gels?"

I didn't know what she meant, but Jess nodded. Luna took his hand and deftly peeled off the black layer on one fingernail.

"Hey!" Jess pulled his hand back.

"Show me your hand," Luna said. "Come on."

He did, and I could see what she was looking at. With the black polish gone, the nail had a distinct blue tinge.

"That's bad," Luna told him. "Your oxygen sats are bad. Not hospital bad, but this is not walking pneumonia anymore. You've graduated."

She flipped his arm over and studied the skin there as Jess rolled his eyes.

"I'm not on anything that wasn't prescribed," he told her.

"Your reputation precedes you," Luna said, sounding slightly apologetic.

Jess nodded. "I get that."

Jesse unclipped the device from his finger and gave it back to her, then pulled on the black tee he'd been wearing under his hoodie. He could have left it off, in my opinion, but probably this was better. Less spur to my memories of him in my bed, or our bed, in all states of dress and undress.

"Your fever is thirty-nine point five," Luna told him. "That's also not bad enough for the hospital, but I'd guess you're already on ibuprofen or something, and that's the reason it's not higher. What you've got is likely bacterial pneumonia. The good news is, antibiotics can help. The bad news is, a three-hour stage show will not help, and I say this as someone who has tickets."

Jesse lay his head back against the pillows and took a deep breath, or tried. "It's not like calling in sick. I cost people a lot of money if I cancel."

"Oh, do they have life insurance on you?" Luna chirped. "Because then, if you do the show and you die, they can get paid twice!"

"Aren't they looking past these two shows?" I asked. "If they're smart—"

Jesse made a noise between a cough and a laugh. "They do have life insurance," he said. "Look, it's not just the money. I told you, Ben. The internet gets mean."

"It's not mean now?" Luna asked.

Jesse rolled his head on the pillow to look at her. "You'll see."

She put a hand on his forehead and looked at him with sympathy. "You have to cancel. Tonight and tomorrow night. You are very sick."

"I can push through."

Luna shook her head. "Do you think you're the first performer I've treated? You're all demented, and you can push through a lot. If it was still walking pneumonia, I'd say you could do the show. Ben, here," she pointed at me, "wouldn't like it, and it wouldn't be my best medical advice, but I'd let you go ahead. I'm telling you no because this is something you can't do."

Jess shut his eyes. Luna took her hand off his forehead. His breathing was a strain, and he wasn't trying to hide it anymore. His hand was limp across his stomach, and the pale blue under his bare nail drew my eye.

"I'll help you tell them," I said. "And you don't have to stay with them. You can go to the hospital if you want, just in case. Or… you could stay at my place."

I didn't know I was going to say that until I said it. Jess opened his eyes halfway and regarded me without expression. Luna busied herself putting her equipment back in her bag.

Jesse kept looking at me. "Did you mean it? I have options. You don't have to."

I shrugged. "I have a spare room. And Frank could use the company."

He showed surprise at that. He didn't know Frank was a dog, so who was Frank? A boyfriend? A live-in boyfriend? I couldn't tell whether he cared. Why did I care whether he cared?

I looked at Luna instead. "What's the care and feeding for him?"

"Rest, mostly," she said. "He should eat. He probably doesn't want to. I'll give you a prescription for antibiotics. If his temp goes over forty or… oh." She fished the little clip from her bag and threw it to me. "That's a pulse oximeter. It measures his blood oxygen saturation. He's at ninety-three right now. If it drops below ninety-two, he needs to go to emerg."

"I'm in the room," Jess said. His eyes were closed and his voice was ghostly, so it wasn't convincing.

"Or if he seems a lot worse," Luna went on. "His colour gets worse. He can't breathe well enough to speak. Use good sense."

I opened the bedroom door and waved Gia back in. She offered me a glare as she swept by. "Well?"

"We're fucked, Gia." Jesse's smile was there and gone. He kept his eyes open, barely.

Gia's shoulders rose and fell as she breathed in a solid chunk, like concrete. "Just tonight?"

Jesse shook his head.

"Bacterial pneumonia," Luna said. "If he's singing again in a month, he'll be lucky."

Gia made a sour face. "I… fine. I'll throw the switch. There'll be fallout."

Jess shut his eyes. "I know."

"Are you going to the hospital?" Gia asked.

"I'm staying with Ben," Jesse said.

Gia looked at me. "What the hell?"

I didn't have a great answer. I knew because I'd been asking the same of myself.

"We're old friends," I reminded her. "He's not quite bad enough for the hospital, but it's close. I'm going to keep an eye on him."

"He'll stay here," Gia said. "The suite is paid until tomorrow."

"I'm staying with Ben," Jesse said again. "Tour's cancelled. Everyone can go home."

"He's not under house arrest or anything," I said. "Right?"

"No," Gia said, making it sound a lot more like yes. "Obviously. But I'm responsible—"

"You aren't," Jesse said. "Not if it's cancelled."

"I have to get everyone home," Gia told him.

"Not me."

"You know what?" Gia said. "Fine. You're an adult. Do what you want. I'll mop up here."

"Thank you," Jess breathed.

"It's the job," Gia said. "Do you understand the cancellation insurance won't cover this? Deciding to take a sick day is not an act of God. And we have been counting on this to make up the losses."

"I know," Jess said.

Gia's face softened. "Okay. Where can I reach you?"

"My phone," Jess said.

I stepped forward and handed my card to Gia. "My office is attached to my house."

She read the card and raised her eyebrows, first at Jess and then, seeing his eyes closed, at me.

"I'm not here in a professional capacity," I said.

"I am," Luna said and handed over a card of her own.

"Well, I have calls to make." Gia turned on her heel and marched smartly from the room.

"That woman is pissed," Luna observed.

"That woman has problems," Jesse said. "My fault."

"Do you need to pack?" I asked Jesse.

He shook his head and grabbed his phone from the nightstand. "There's a kit in the bathroom. Anything else I can have delivered."

I went into the bathroom and found a travel bag on the back of the door, large enough for the kit and some clothes. I threw some in. No sense going to trouble when this was just as easy.

Luna had Jess on his feet by the time I was done. He was shaky but seemed to want to walk. I was in favour of that, since a guy being helped to walk draws a lot fewer stares than one being carried from a hotel. I left him with Luna while I retrieved my car from the bar. As she and I were pouring Jess into the passenger seat, she asked if her tickets would really be refunded.

"If the venue doesn't, I will," Jess told her. "But also, stick it up your ass."

Luna laughed and waved. "Get well soon."

# CHAPTER 3

IT WASN'T even an hour before I had Jess tucked into bed in my spare room. His phone and charger and a glass of water were beside the bed, along with his antibiotics, the oximeter, and everything else Luna had told me to get from the drug store.

Frank was at the foot of the bed, having already decided he liked Jesse more than he liked me.

Jess had seemed relieved, maybe, when he'd found out Frank was a dog. It was hard to be sure because Jesse had melted into a soppy grin at the sight of him and declared Frank a "beautiful boy," which could only mean that Jess was delirious.

I settled into an armchair in the corner with my laptop and phone. Jess rolled over to look at me. "I don't need a babysitter."

I glanced at my watch. "You need your temperature and oxygen saturation checked once an hour. If you want me to leave, I will, but I'll be right back."

"No, I just didn't want you to think you had to sit here." It took him a while to get out all of those words. He added, "It's fine if you want to stay."

"Okay."

I opened a few news sites to start, in case something in the news cast some light on my case. The big local story of the moment was that Jack Lowe had cancelled the final two shows of his tour. Gia worked fast. There was a pile-up south of the city, despite ideal road conditions. Alcohol was believed to have been a factor. A winning lotto ticket had been sold in Calgary but not claimed. Every Wednesday was Winsday, as the ads used to say. Someone had been sitting on a fortune for days. The kid who'd fired off a flare gun at a frat party last year, killing one of his buddies, was going to trial tomorrow. The question was whether he'd known what a flare gun could do if you fired it next to someone's head. The answer was anyone's guess.

I went back to sifting Kim Moy's social media. It was a little Zen and a little frustrating, this stage of an investigation. Not knowing what I was looking for. Open to anything. Not knowing what I'd find. Was there something in the background of a photo that would tell me where she was and why she'd gone? Damned if I could tell.

The timer went off. I closed the laptop and saw Jesse sleepily reaching for the thermometer and oximeter.

"Don't get up," he mumbled around my thermometer, which was a mercury-and-glass museum piece that I'd borrowed from my parents' medicine cabinet during a nasty flu and never thought to return.

He held up the oximeter, and I nodded. His pulse was better. Sats were the same. He took the thermometer out and checked it. "Thirty-nine."

I nodded. "Okay. Good."

"Are you working on something?" he asked. I opened my laptop and looked at the screen full of photos, none of which had given me a lead or a clue.

"I guess," I said. "A case."

"Can you tell me about it?"

"Are you looking for a bedtime story?"

Jess smiled. "Something like that."

It sometimes helped to talk this kind of thing through. I usually did that with Frank, since Frank could keep a secret, but I didn't see Jess broadcasting this story all over town.

"It's a missing person," I said. I told him how I was hired and what little I knew.

Jess lifted his head from the pillows. "Shouldn't you be looking for her?"

"I probably shouldn't even have taken the job." I set the laptop on the floor. "Kimberly Moy is a university student. She's nominally an adult, and generally when adults disappear, it's because they intend to. Sometimes they want to drop off the map, for a while or forever. Usually, with students, they forget to tell people they've run off with some guy or whatever. They turn up eventually."

"Why wouldn't you take the job?" Jesse asked. "It sounds like detective work."

"If the client thinks I'm going to rescue her sister from a cult or pull her to safety from the bottom of a well, she's dreaming. It's not like that."

"What if she needs rescuing?" Jess asked. "She could be in trouble."

"Four days is too long. It's too late. If I find anything, it won't be what her sister wants me to find."

"But she'll know." Jess shrugged. "It's better, right? Than wondering?"

"If her sister's dead, the cops will find her eventually," I said. "The client reported this to the cops. Actually, they might even find Kimberly if she's alive. They'll circulate her photo and information. Sometimes that works. And it won't have cost my client a dime. Hiring a detective isn't cheap. But she insisted."

"Maybe she needs to know she tried," Jess suggested. "She hired a detective. She did something."

Like she'd paid to transfer her guilt to me so she could sleep while the fate of her sister lay in my hands.

Dammit.

"That could be," I allowed.

Jess looked as if he wanted to say something. I waited. Nothing came.

"I'm looking at her social media," I said finally. "It's a fishing expedition right now. I need to know where she might have gone and why. I was hoping for something obvious, like a new boyfriend, but nothing's jumping out."

"Huh." Jesse grabbed his phone from the night table. "Kimberly M-O-Y?"

"You're here to sleep, not to Google stalk my missing person."

"I'm resting," Jess argued. "You'll have to wake me to check my temperature in an hour anyway."

I sighed. "The client sent me a link to some info. I'll make a copy and share it to you."

Jess nodded. He was already typing and swiping.

"Artsy," Jess murmured. From him, it was probably a compliment. "Is she dramatic, then?"

"She does Paint Nites."

"Good reviews," Jess noted a few seconds later. "Fun… easy-going… patient."

"She does okay in school," I told him. "Mostly shows up to class. They might be covering up for her, but… I don't know. If they were—"

"They'd say she never missed school," Jess finished.

"I think her sister's right. This genuinely isn't like her."

A wry little twist turned the corner of his mouth. "No one would have said that about me, hey? At her age?"

That wasn't safe ground, stuck here together as we were. Jess had been a little older than Kimberly when he'd gone off the rails, one year out of uni rather than one year in. And it wasn't like he'd avoided drama during the seven years since. But that wasn't the point.

We looked at each other for a moment. Then Jess dropped his eyes, and we went back to work.

"Tell me if you see a new boyfriend," I said. "Or a new girlfriend."

"Is there no other reason someone would disappear?"

Jess seemed legitimately curious, as if he were asking about my long and storied history of finding missing people. All three of them. Most of my work was insurance fraud, divorce cases, and background checks. Especially background checks. The more of their lives people put online, the more everyone assumed strangers had to be hiding something.

"I believe," I said carefully, "that when most people do stupid, hasty, inconsiderate things, it is about a boy. Or a girl. There are at least a thousand other reasons, I'd guess, but this is the one I'd put money on most of the time."

"It could be passion for anything," Jesse said. "Um, or… fear. Or anger. Those all hijack people's brains."

"I'm interested in any of that," I agreed. "Shame works too. If she was the type to find pregnancy shameful, I'd wonder if she was pregnant. She might be mulling over an abortion or something. I can see a woman wanting privacy for that."

"You don't have to tell anyone you're pregnant," Jess pointed out.

"You do have to explain why you're not drinking," I said. "Or taking ibuprofen or eating soft cheese or drinking anything with caffeine…."

"How do you find that out?" Jess asked.

I shrugged. "Ask her friends. Or her enemies, if I can find any. That's my day tomorrow. Talking to college girls. And to the officer who opened the missing person report."

"I'm gonna search her image," Jess said, slurring toward the end. "Case she's using a fake name…."

"I can do that," I said.

"Does she have any friends-only accounts?"

"I do this professionally, Jess. During COVID, cyberstalking was practically my whole living. Go to sleep."

"No, I'm…."

Jess was quiet after that, and then he seemed to be asleep.

I took a few of Kim's photos—dressed up and in grubbies, hair up and down—and image searched them. Nothing turned up that wasn't already in her social media. For a university student, she was frustratingly above board. That didn't mean she didn't have secrets. It mainly meant that if she did, they were a lot darker than putting on the freshman fifteen or thinking Beyoncé was overrated.

I ordered a criminal-record check, but I didn't expect to turn anything up. All it would tell me was whether she *had* a record, anyway. The particulars wouldn't be in there. As a cop, I'd been able to look at all kinds of things—charges laid and dropped, traffic stops, public incidents. Mental illness sometimes. I'd check in with my old partner tomorrow, see what my former colleagues had turned up.

More photos, tracking her from one friend's Facebook to another's Instagram to the LinkedIn of someone who'd worked with her at a gas station in Manitoba.

Had she gotten into a fight with someone who'd scared her? Embarrassed herself somehow and been unable to look someone in the eye? Done something wrong and taken off out of fear that she'd be caught? I didn't see signs of any of that.

Got religion? Joined a cult?

If she was a nice, normal kid with no dark secrets, I had to face the possibility that leaving hadn't been her choice. And if she really was in that kind of trouble? I gave it one chance in a thousand, at my most optimistic, that this had any way of turning out well.

I kept digging long after I'd given up hope of learning anything new. Once an hour I woke Jesse to check his temp and oxygen, both of which were the same or slightly better as the night went on. A few minutes before midnight, my phone buzzed with a text from Luna.

*how's my patient?*

I gave her the numbers. Time checked. Pulse. Sats. Temp. Next time checked. Pulse. Sats. Temp. Next time checked. I hadn't even gotten to his 11:00 p.m. numbers when she broke in.

*Kk let him sleep I'll come before my shift tomorrow where r u*

I sent her the address. A few seconds later, she returned *SW* and a grimace. Not convenient to her downtown condo.

*You pay I'll move*

She sent back a grin and a time. *7ish*

That would come far too soon. I set the alarm on my computer and considered my sleeping situation. Go back to my room, the main attraction of which was my own bed. Stay here and sleep in a chair, ensuring a lousy night and a crick in my neck but available in case Jesse needed something. Take up the other side of the spare bed, which would be uncomfortable in deeper ways.

"What do you think?" I asked Frank. He was eyeballing me pretty hard, which made me think he must have an opinion.

"Fine," I said. "I'll be back in a few."

Frank watched me leave, his chin on his crossed paws. He watched me come back in a T-shirt and boxers, carrying the cushions from the living room couch. He watched me wrap a sheet around the cushions and throw a blanket and pillow on top.

"Enjoy the bed," I told him. He yawned. I made sure my laptop was plugged in and the alarm was set, then tucked myself in and tried to tune out the faint wheeze in Jesse's breathing. At least it was steady and quiet. At least he didn't snore.

TORONTO AGAIN, in the second-floor apartment of that Cabbagetown house. Jess and I had shared the place for about two and a half years. Standing on the broken lino of a kitchen that was somehow bare and messy at the same time, I had been asking him where his half of the rent was. In this moment, this time, I knew. The first time I'd only suspected.

I knew about the party he and the band had hit after the show. Everything they'd bought there. That he'd been celebrating because he was this close—this close—to signing with one of the last big labels standing. And it was a good deal, not one of those shitty indentured-servitude things he'd told me about in the middle of the night, back when he'd been committed to building indie cred.

He hadn't set aside anything he'd made at the gig. Probably hadn't even thought about the rent. Or me.

I heard myself saying that I needed the rent now, today, as if that were the most important thing. It was the most urgent, though, since my part-time security job didn't pay all the bills.

He said he was hungover, could we please discuss this when he wasn't, and I asked when he thought that would be. Next month sometime? Next year?

He shook his head and left, with his leather jacket and hangover and without paying the rent. This, too, was familiar. This happened. A page fell from his jacket pocket, and I remembered that too, seeing a list of crossed-out names and one at the bottom. Jack Lowe. I'd thought at the time that this Jack Lowe was an industry contact. Those were the only people he'd seemed to care about then. Musicians and influencers and club owners and whatever. It hadn't even crossed my mind that it might be another guy, that he might be leaving me for another guy. Where would he have found the time to two-time me?

The truth didn't occur to me either, though, because who assumes their boyfriend will leave them to become another guy?

Now that this was a dream, or a memory, there was a lot I could have said. Maybe nothing I could have changed, but definitely a few things I could have gotten off my chest. Except that I'd pissed him off, and the apartment door was hanging open because he was already gone.

He never did pay the rent. I'd pawned the one guitar he kept around the apartment, and that got us through for another month. Two years ago, I'd tried to make a payment on my student loan, only to find the loan had already been paid back in full.

He probably thought we were square.

WHEN THE alarm went off, I was certain I was back in Toronto. Lousy bed? Check. Crick in my back? Check. The sound of Jesse breathing and the smell of his shampoo? It all tracked. I opened my eyes and saw a stucco ceiling without 1970s sparkles and brownish water stains. Where was I?

Frank stuck his big jowly head over the edge of the bed. There was a clue. I hadn't had a Frank in Toronto. I rolled away to avoid drool and slammed the space bar on my beeping computer as I moved. Right. Guest room floor, on couch cushions, thirty minutes to Luna's arrival. I sat up and saw Jesse on his back, hair all over the place but his colour better than it had been the night before. He didn't seem to have heard the alarm.

He looked younger while he was asleep. He always had. He had young features—big eyes, a wide mouth, a neat bob of a nose—but his expressions were too clever and cynical for him to look innocent when he was awake. Dark brown hair dyed flat black, as it had been since shortly after I'd met him. The strands were straight now that he'd slept. He usually curved the edges to run along his jaw, a little lower than his chin.

I held my breath for a moment and listened for wheezing. That seemed better too. If I'd bought a fancy infrared thermometer like Luna had told me to, I could have checked his temperature without waking him. On the other hand, the way he looked right now, I could have had a high school marching band come in and check his temperature without waking him. He also didn't move when Frank gracelessly spilled from the bed and *oof*ed his landing beside my pillow.

Frank and I had our morning routine down to a cool fifteen minutes, so I had time to throw Jesse's stuff into the bathroom and get breakfast together for him. He hadn't wanted to eat the night before, and I'd had to withhold coffee until he'd downed a half cup of quinoa and veggies. Luna had been impressed when I'd texted her to let her know he'd eaten. She'd assumed I'd give him French fries and beer. She'd praised me for even knowing how to spell quinoa. She didn't know it came in microwave bags at the dollar store. They usually stocked it next to the Wagon Wheels, which was convenient since I always got both.

For breakfast I went with a bowl of oatmeal and half a banana sliced on top. I knew he ate both of those things, and Luna would think more of it than the bowl of Froot Loops he'd probably prefer.

The sound of coughing told me Jess was awake. Ugly, thick coughing, followed by the sound of Jesse stumbling to the bathroom. I listened for the thump of a body hitting the floor, but he managed all right and pulled the bathroom door shut behind him. It gave me a chance to clean up the bedroom and put his breakfast and pills in place. Water. No coffee. I wasn't giving up my leverage.

I heard the shower. Steam was probably the best thing for Jesse's lungs, but he'd have been in there even if it wasn't. He'd always been this way. More than happy to have a romantic fever and ghostly skin around me, but he'd be damned if he'd let me see him coughing up a lung. He'd even trashed the Kleenex he'd coughed into before dragging himself down the hall.

Frank barked from the living room, by the door. My early doorbell alarm system. He accompanied me to the door as I opened it for Luna. Without a word to me, she took a knee and put her hands on Frank's face.

"Oh my God, what a beautiful boy!"

"Don't say that," I said. "It'll be a let-down when he learns the truth."

"Don't listen to him," she told Frank. "Don't oo wisten."

I stepped back and opened the door wider. "Please, won't you come in?"

She smirked and sailed into the living room. "It's not a bad house," she pronounced, eyeing the floor-to-ceiling windows and patio doors to the yard. "Lots of light. Late sixties?"

"Probably?" I told her. "Don't know for sure. I'm renting. Your patient is in the shower."

"Oh good," she said. "Best thing for him. Do I smell coffee?"

By the time I'd hooked Luna up with her drug of choice, Jess had made his way back to the bedroom.

She followed him in, Frank on her heels and me a distant third with coffee of my own.

"Looking better," she observed.

He was, though his eyes were red from coughing. His hair was wet and brushed back, and he wore the white T-shirt I'd left for him next to the bed. It hung far enough down that I couldn't be certain he was wearing anything else, though boxer briefs were a strong possibility. I wasn't going to figure it out if I looked long enough, so I made myself stop.

"I feel better," he said. His voice was rough, and she nodded.

"Coughing," she said, with more approval than I would have thought that warranted. "That dreadful shit you were taking to stop the coughing must have worn off."

"I'm less excited about it," Jess said. He crawled into bed and poked his oatmeal with a spoon. He looked like he was trying to figure out what was clogging a sink.

"Eat that and you get coffee," I told him. He glared at me, and my stupid heart found it adorable. I didn't tell him it'd be decaf.

"You need to clear your lungs," Luna said. She aimed her thermometer at him and showed him the reading. "Much better."

He put down the spoon and clipped on the oximeter. Luna seemed pleased by that number too.

"You're on the mend, Jack Lowe."

He looked surprised for a second, as if he'd forgotten that he had a stage name. Then he smiled. "I guess I could have done the Vancouver show."

Luna pulled the oximeter off, letting it snap the end of his finger.

"Ow!"

"That's for being an idiot. You're better because you took antibiotics and slept and did not jump around a stage. If you continue to sleep and eat and take antibiotics, you will get well. If you insist on going straight back to work, you will get worse. You always seemed bright enough in interviews, so don't get stupid on me now."

He lay back and shut his eyes. I cleared my throat.

"What?" Jess asked, not looking.

"Breakfast. You want coffee, you eat breakfast."

"Okay," Luna said, "fun as it would be to watch this battle of wills, I'm on shift in a few. You've both got my number if you need anything."

Jess opened his eyes. "You came all the way here to check my temperature?"

"I wanted a look at you," Luna told him. "Eat your breakfast."

"Thank you," Jess said.

"You won't say that when you get my bill. Ben, walk me out?"

I did. As I opened the front door, I said, "You should actually send him a bill of some kind. He can afford it."

"But then I'd still owe you a favour," Luna pointed out. "I prefer it this way."

"You did owe me, but thank you anyway. Do I need to babysit him today?"

"No. So long as he takes it easy and takes his antibiotics, he should be fine. You've got a case?"

"Missing girl. Woman. Young woman. Oh, which reminds me—if someone wanted to get an abortion on the down-low, where would they go about that?"

"She's pregnant?" Luna asked.

"Just trying to think of reasons a university student would leave town suddenly and not tell anyone."

Luna stared at me. Frank snuffled at her bag, sensing she was distracted. She continued to stare at me.

"What?"

"Really, Ben. A woman leaves town, so it has to be about her womb?"

I managed not to roll my eyes. "It's usually about sex, Luna. For boys and girls both."

"Pregnancy. Honestly. Well, I'll stop in after my shift. But I turn around to nights tomorrow, so it'll have to be quick."

Despite the rush she was in, she paused.

"Is there something else, Luna?"

"Ben."

"Still my name."

"You know I think you would be quite the catch for any available man."

"You certainly set me up with enough of them," I said, as if she could have forgotten. Pairing me off was the first thing she'd ever sworn to do and not accomplished.

"I don't believe I'd have matched you with a glam rocker."

"I think he'd say dark alternative, but he does wear a lot of make-up on stage."

She gave me an exhausted look. "Not my point."

"I know. He wasn't even in a band when I met him. I worked part-time doing security during my first year at U of T. I worked at the music building a lot of nights. This little brat in the second-year music program kept sneaking in to use the pianos because he didn't have a piano in his place."

"Oh my God. You met him by throwing him out of a building?"

"That was my job," I said. She opened her mouth and made a protesting sound. I held up a hand. "I didn't do my job. I asked him what he was doing, and he said students weren't supposed to use the pianos for personal projects so he had to sneak in at night. He was writing songs. He figured he was going to be a rock star."

"And you could see it in him," she said. "Even then."

"Stop writing my life like it's a Harlequin. I thought he was very charming and very pretty. And yeah, talented, but a lot of people are. I didn't realize. Once he had the band and a whole show and I knew what a tenacious son of a bitch he was, sure."

"This is fascinating. Who asked who out?"

I leaned against the island next to the door, home to keys and letters and everything I'd left undone.

"This is why I didn't tell you. You get that, right? You want everything to be all roses and violins, and you imagine these big schmoopy scenes. I was bored, and he's overly friendly, so we started to talk whenever he came in. We got along, and there was, you know, chemistry, so we started hanging out together in general. Then we both needed a new place after spring semester, so we got one together. Around the time I graduated, we broke up. I haven't heard from him in years."

"The way you tell it," she said, "it's like it barely happened. But I should be going now."

Once I'd seen her off, I went back into the bedroom to find Jess making an honest attempt at the oatmeal.

"That's the spirit," I said. He gave me another one of those glares my heart liked so much.

"Coffee," he mumbled around the food.

"When you're done."

I sat on the end of the bed and waited. It was surreal. He smelled of my soap and shampoo now, and he was under my blanket, or at least my guest blanket. I couldn't fully commit to this as being reality. I'd play it out until I woke or came to my senses in an insane asylum.

He showed me the empty bowl.

"Very good."

"Thank you," he said. "I mean, seriously—thank you. This is…."

"It's okay."

"If you hadn't even answered my text, I would have understood."

I patted his leg. "I would have too."

He said nothing, just looked at me a while, then handed me the oatmeal bowl. I took it and went to the kitchen for his coffee.

He was on his phone by the time I came back, looking at something that had bled the life from his eyes. He dropped it, face down, as soon as he heard me.

"You okay?"

"Yeah. Go talk to college girls. I can stalk her on your laptop if you want."

"I can do my job," I told him. "You can sleep."

"I'll take the laptop," he said. "If that's okay. I can't sleep all day."

"Suit yourself." I tossed the computer on the bed. "Passcode's my Toronto number. Take whatever you need from the kitchen and… whatever. Have food delivered. Call me if you need anything else."

"Good luck."

I wanted to say it wasn't luck I needed, just good work, but that would have been a lie. Instead I nodded and left.

I checked the news on my phone as I went to my car. Not much had changed from the night before. Dead people were still dead. Burned down buildings were still burned down. No one had claimed the lottery win.

Thinking of Jesse's expression when he'd checked his phone, I went back to the article about him cancelling the shows and scrolled to the comments. Pneumonia? Bullshit. Everyone knew he had a drug problem. Someone swore they'd seen him drunk in a club roughly around the time he'd been eating quinoa in my guest room. Someone heard he'd lost it on the crew at soundcheck. That soundcheck hadn't happened.

And these were the moderated comments on a news site, which made them probably the nicest ones out there. To be fair, a few fans were leaping to his defence and hoping he'd get well soon.

It was a clear enough morning that I could see the mountains, or a suggestion of them, as I reached the crest of my street. That was something the hip kids didn't get in Toronto.

Jesse and I had talked about the mountains when we were in school. He liked snowboarding. I didn't, but it was something I could say about Calgary that wasn't rednecks and rodeos, so I'd played it up for him. Come visit. Come home with me for Christmas. The Rockies are right there.

Damn it, how did I keep winding back to Jess when I had a case to think about?

# CHAPTER 4

IT WAS too early to talk to university students. It was not too early to stop by the cop shop. The voice from the intake desk was Vedette Hodder, a fearsomely competent admin and self-appointed leader of the Calgary Police LGBTQ club. These facts endeared her to me in unequal amounts. I'd always thought a first-rate admin person was like gold.

Vedette looked the same as when I'd last seen her. Her slight overbite, narrow nose, and close-set eyes all gave the impression that she was straining to see something and not impressed by the look of it so far.

"What brings you by?" she asked, her Maritime lilt making it a cross between a greeting and a sea shanty.

"Looking for Kent," I said. "Is he around?"

Vedette folded her hands on the desk in front of her. "Is this a social call?"

People were starting to gather behind me, waiting to see Vedette, the gatekeeper to the locked floors for anyone who didn't have a pass card. I felt glares stabbing the back of my neck.

"It's business," I said, and she *tsk*ed me.

"You should visit sometime when you don't need something."

I sat on the urge to get pedantic about how many times I'd helped Kent versus Kent helping me, or how many times I'd dropped by to say hello. "Can you call him for me now?"

"You had only to ask," Vedette said. Was she trolling me? I kept my face neutral and nodded, once. Vedette picked up the phone. "Hey, it's me. Guess who's here to see you." She smiled and shook her head. "Nope. Nope. Not them either."

"Can you tell him—"

"…no, can you imagine that? That would be the day."

"Vedette…."

"It's your ex-partner, here to lick crumbs of knowledge from the thin blue plate."

"For fuck's sake, Vee."

She put the phone down, smiled, and pressed the door-release button. "Go on in."

"Thanks for that. All of it."

She kept smiling and pointed at the doors. "Get out of the way. I have people to see."

I went into the secured area, through metal detectors that would have picked up the gun I was not carrying. Since quitting the force, I rarely carried anything more substantial than a pocket knife. Even that I'd left in the Jeep today.

It started the moment I crossed. People saying hello, nodding my way, waving. Good to know I wasn't persona non grata with most of my old colleagues, but I wasn't up for socializing. I smiled back and waved. Friendly but not encouraging. I'd spent months perfecting that in the bars, back when every friend I knew had been dragging me out to get over Jess and I'd been pretty sure I'd throw up on the shoes of the first man to speak to me.

"Anyone seen Kent?" I asked the room.

The delight on the faces around me told me the answer before I heard his voice.

"Has. Anyone. Seen. Kent? He's got to be around here somewhere…."

I turned to see my ex-partner crossing the room. He looked the same as ever. Alberta beef-eating football jock, ten miles wide and twice as tall, with his dark-blond hair in a military fade and the start of a paunch pushing at the front of his uniform.

He greeted me with a rib-crushing hug.

"Ben Ames, private eye!" he announced. "First rule of private detection. Let the cops do your work for you."

"Hilarious every time," I assured him. "I'll be solving a case for you guys, so be sure to send a thank-you card."

"You don't have to act brave," Kent said. "You need help, all you have to do is ask."

"I was thinking more of an equitable trade."

Kent slapped my shoulder with a meaty hand. "You need coffee? I'm buying."

I did need coffee. I was already starting to bite back yawns, and my first two go-cups of the day seemed distant memories. I followed Kent out the back of the station to the Starbucks across the street. Kent liked to play good ol' boy, but I'd never seen him skimp on a cup of coffee, and he ordered his socks and underwear from a fancy place online.

Once we had overpriced coffee and a table in the corner, he opened with, "I've gotta say, you look like hell."

"Long night," I told him.

He laughed and slapped the table, making the coffees jump. "Ha! I bet! Old boyfriend in town… cancels the show…. Next time you need a better story than pneumonia."

I took a swig of coffee. It burned my mouth. I didn't care. "He does have pneumonia."

Kent's eyes widened. "Are you telling me you saw him?"

"He wanted to have coffee," I said. "Bury the hatchet, I guess."

"And did you? Bury your hatchet? Ben, if you nailed a rock star last night, I deserve to know."

"He was obviously unwell, so I had Luna take a look at him. That's it."

I'd mentioned Luna. Why did I do that? Kent would ask her about this the next time he saw her, because he loved gossip at least as much as he loved single-origin coffee, and she'd tell him Jess wound up at my house. Plus whatever romantic horseshit she was reading into the situation.

Kent raised his hands. "Just fucking with you. Sincerely, man. Your ex is Jack Lowe. I am not worthy."

"He was not a rock star at the time."

"Okay, it was before," Kent said. "So what? It's like finding out Vee bagged Lady Gaga or something. Even if it was back in the day, you'd be impressed."

I nodded. "If my sex life makes you happy, go ahead and enjoy it. But it's not what I wanted to talk about."

"I didn't figure it was," Kent said. "What's your case?"

"Missing person. Mount Royal student didn't show up to babysit her niece. The sister looked into it, and no one's seen this girl for a few days, so she hired me to find out what happened."

Kent raised his brows. "How many days?"

"Last seen Wednesday night," I said. To his wince, I added, "I know. I told the sister I probably wouldn't be a lot of help, but I guess she needs to feel like she's doing something."

My tongue curled behind the flow of Jesse's words coming from my mouth. Like dry wine, I couldn't tell whether I liked or hated it.

"Adults have the God-given right to fuck off," Kent said, as he had many times before.

"Yeah, exactly. But you probably BOLOed the car, so I thought maybe you'd found it. I don't have anything worth trading right now, but I'll spill when I do. Doesn't matter to me who finds her."

Kent pulled out his phone and a stylus. He always said his fingers were too big for the phone's keyboard. I thought he was just allergic to typing.

"Give me the deets and I'll see. If we haven't found it, I'll put a KOLO on it."

"Kent On The Lookout" I asked.

"It's like you read my mind."

I described Kimberly's car, a light purple 2015 Mitsubishi Mirage with a white flower decal toward the back on the driver's side.

"Alberta plates," I added and pulled my phone to text him the plate number. "I pulled her driving record last night, and it's pretty clean. Name's Kimberly Moy. The sister is Lauren Courtney."

Kent nodded, scribbling away with his stylus. "Anything else I can do for you?"

I shrugged. "The sister connected me to Kimberly's friends and social media, so I'm working on that.

If there's anything Lauren doesn't know—or doesn't want me to know—I'd be missing that."

"I'll see what we've got," Kent said.

"Thanks. I owe you."

Kent *pffed*. "I'm just glad you stopped by. Because now I can see your face when I tell you that, no word of a lie, I bagged an Outrider."

It was the height of achievement in Kent's book, nailing a local cheerleader, so it was natural he'd be proud.

"How'd you manage that?" I asked.

"They had a locker room theft at McMahon, and the rest is history."

"Very professional. Did you find the thief while you were searching that cheerleader?"

"I did not," Kent said. "Maybe I should search the rest of them."

I tried not to roll my eyes but couldn't entirely suppress it.

Kent grinned. "She was a grown-up lady, and she called me after the case was closed. All on the up and up. Turns out we weren't, ah, compatible. She was a nice girl, but a little kinky for my tastes."

"I don't need details on that," I told him.

"You know I'm an adventurous guy."

"I am not curious."

He sighed. "I bet you were more fun in university when you were having a cool sexy life with your smokin' hot boyfriend. When he dresses up like a chick?" Kent made a chef's kiss motion. I swatted his hand. "Get me drunk enough, I might try to hit that."

"He's not open to tourists," I said.

Kent made a faux-wounded face, then laughed. "Okay. This has been a pleasure, but I need to get back to it. Good luck with your case." He stood and started to walk away, then paused after a few steps. "Oh, and good luck with your boyfriend."

"I don't have a boyfriend."

"You have a guy living in your house," Kent answered.

I couldn't think of what to say. I didn't have to say anything, it turned out. My face, judging by Kent's bray of laughter, said it all.

"I know everything. Luna's been texting me," he said. "You think she was going to sit on something like this?"

Just fucking with me. The whole time. I took a sip of coffee while I thought about that.

"Did you tell her that you knew I used to date him?" I asked. "You tell her you've known for years?"

"Hell no. How pissed would she be if she knew I knew something like that and never told her?"

I pulled my phone from my pocket. "Should we find out?"

Kent's face fell like an avalanche. "No, man, come on. I don't need Lunes pissed at me. That woman is terrifying."

"That woman has a big mouth," I said. "She's lucky she just did me a favour."

"Brave talk," Kent said. "Hey, Ben."

"That's my name."

"No chick who was done with me ever invited me to crash in her spare room."

"Okay," I said. "Noted."

"Noted." Kent shook his head. "Like I said, good luck."

I stayed at the table, finishing my coffee and scanning social media for more opinions about Jess. It was the same as I'd seen that morning. Rumours. Speculation. Discussion about whether his label was going to drop him. That was new. From what I'd seen the night before, Jess might have been wondering about that himself.

What would happen if his label did drop him? Was it like getting fired? Did he still make money? I didn't know how any of it worked. I was pretty sure Jess had told me, one of those nights in the practice rooms of the music department, both of us cross-legged on the floor. Me ignoring the chatter of other guards on my radio and excusing myself every hour or so to make the rounds. Sometimes he came with me, like it was a game of cops and robbers.

My phone rang, actually rang instead of buzzing in a text. I looked at it suspiciously, and it told me Jesse was calling. Weird timing.

"Everything okay?" I said. "Are you worse?"

Jesse laughed, then coughed. It didn't sound too bad. "I'm okay. You're still a crepe hanger. Look, I have some information for you. I don't have any business knowing this, so don't ask how I got it."

"Go ahead."

"Kimberly Moy had a ticket to my show last night. She bought it with a credit card last month. One ticket, in the nosebleeds. She might have been planning to go with friends, but finding that out is a lot more work. Probably not worth it, right?"

I frowned. "So she had plans as of a month ago."

"Right," Jess said. "Not serious plans… like, she can't be that big a fan or she would have bought her ticket when they were released instead of last month. There weren't a lot left when she bought."

"She wouldn't have moved heaven and earth to be there," I said, "but she also didn't expect to be away."

"Not if she's as broke as most students," Jesse said. "The cheap seats were still about forty bucks. She probably doesn't drop that amount casually."

I was a little surprised that Jess still realized that. It had been years since he'd had to care how much anything cost. I didn't let that thought out since he was trying to help—maybe even legitimately helping—and so did not deserve me getting bitchy with him.

"You're dying for me to ask how you got this information," I said.

I could hear Jesse's smile as he said, "I am, but I really can't tell you. Are you at least impressed?"

"You're lucky she has no taste in music."

"You're lucky half of Calgary bought tickets to see me," he shot back. I heard the rustle of sheets and realized he was calling from my bed. Well, my spare bed. I wanted very, very much to be there.

"You should be sleeping," I said. My voice sounded rough. I gulped coffee, holding the phone away so Jess couldn't hear it.

"I'm bored," Jess said. No whine, just a statement.

"Too fucking bad."

Jesse's sigh was plenty loud, even through the phone. "I'm in bed. I'm not on stage. I can't look at my social media anymore. Let me Google stalk."

"Do what you want," I told him. "Just stay in bed."

"If I had a nickel for every…."

"Antibiotics in half an hour," I said with a glance at my watch. "If the doorbell rings around noon, it's food."

"Okay," Jess said. Like when we'd had coffee the day before, he seemed to have run out of steam as we talked. "Thanks. Seriously."

"Sleep," I told him. "Seriously."

KIMBERLY'S ADDRESS was an up/down duplex not far from Mount Royal. Probably the same age as my house but shabbier, like it hadn't been painted since the first time. Crumbling concrete steps and a metal railing along one side that looked ready to come loose. Not that any of that would have mattered to a couple of students, but it did make me wonder if the inside hadn't been fixed since the sixties.

She lived in suite A, the bottom one. The path to the door had cracks in the concrete every foot and a half, with sow thistle scraggling through. The doorbell's plastic cover was broken at the bottom, but I heard it ring deep in the suite below.

After a few minutes of cooling my heels, I thought I might have to call Lauren. Before I could grab my phone, I heard steps on the stairs. The front door opened a crack, a chain lock keeping it in place.

A dark-ringed eye blinked at me. "Yes?"

"I'm Ben Ames," I said. "I'm the detective Lauren Courtney hired to look for Kim Moy."

"Oh. Yeah. Right." The door closed. I heard the chain slide, then slide back. The door opened a crack again. "You got ID?"

I showed her my licence. I doubted she knew what she was looking for, but she seemed satisfied anyway. She closed the door for a moment and, this time, opened it wide. "C'mon in."

Purple-haired and dressed down in grey sweats and white runners, she was a match for the photos I'd seen of Siu Trinh, Kimberly's roommate. Siu featured in Kimberly's social media as a buddy and confidant, the sort of person Kim would tell before leaving town. Siu told Lauren that Kim hadn't told her anything, but confidants didn't get to be confidants by blabbing.

I followed her into a boxy suite with large windows and a pony wall ringing the wide living room. Mismatched furniture and piles of books and papers circled a screen and a few game consoles. A plate with the remains of Kraft Dinner was about to fall from a stack of folded T-shirts.

Still, it seemed to have been vacuumed recently, and the KD was the only food lying around. It wasn't a disaster area or a public health risk, just a student apartment. Siu waved me toward the room's sturdiest seat, a long low couch set against the back wall.

"Can I, um, do you… I was gonna make coffee," she offered.

"Don't let me stop you," I said. "But I'm fine."

"Right," she said. "Yeah. BRB."

I glanced around the room while Siu clattered in the kitchen. Maybe there were clues in the stacks of first-year textbooks or the IKEA framed posters of Matt Smith's Doctor—the last fuckable one—and Alexander Skarsgard vamping it up. Healthy young nerds, these girls. At least they didn't have a Jack Lowe poster, which was something I'd run across before. I never enjoyed it.

The place was small, just a doorless kitchen to my left where I could catch glimpses of Siu, an open door to a bathroom at the end of the hall, and two more doors to what I assumed were their bedrooms. If Kimberly had any of her personality on display in this place, that was where it had to be.

Siu returned from the kitchen and sat cross-legged next to the couch. She had a Snoopy tattoo on her shin and a handleless mug in her hands.

"'Kay," she said.

"All right?" I said. "Mainly I want to confirm the things you told Lauren. You told her that you last saw Kimberly at the Boston Pizza across from campus around nine last Wednesday night. Is that correct?"

Siu shrugged. "Yeah. You already know this stuff."

I nodded. "So what am I doing here, right?"

She shrugged again.

"Sometimes people remember more when they come back to a question," I told her. "And sometimes people aren't comfortable sharing their friends' secrets with their friends' families or other authority figures. For example, maybe you know something about Kimberly that would help me find her but that you wouldn't want Lauren to know or that you wouldn't want the police to hear about. That's why I'm here."

Siu shrugged again. "I saw her at BPs. I was picking up a pizza. She was having drinks with some people. She hangs with those girls sometimes, but I don't know their names or anything."

"Right," I said. "So you didn't speak to her?"

"Yeah. Like I put in the doc."

"Okay, like I said, I'm confirming. That's the last time you saw her?"

One more shrug. "Never saw her the next day, but she had a lot of classes, and I knew she had a Paint Nite Thursday night. I guess she gave that class away? That's what I heard. She has an early class on Friday, so I never see her Friday mornings, and I thought she was supposed to be at Lauren's Friday night to babysit, so I wasn't, like, expecting her home. I thought maybe she went straight there from school on Friday. But then Lauren called me, all, where is she because she was supposed to babysit, and on Saturday Lauren was asking people when they saw her last, and I guess Wednesday at BPs was, like, the last time. So Lauren called the cops, and then I guess yesterday she, like, hired you."

"She very much, like, hired me," I confirmed solemnly. Siu looked at me from under heavy lids. I could see piercing holes all over her face, things she'd reconsidered or didn't feel like adorning today. "Did Kim have a drink at BPs? Did you see?"

Siu frowned. "We're adults. We can have a fucking drink. It's not like, oh, she had a drink and she goes missing. Like, if she's even missing. But that's bullshit."

"I agree," I said. "But did she have a drink?"

"I saw her with a fucking beer. Okay? Is that fucking allowed?"

That likely meant she wasn't pregnant. Not one hundred per cent but close enough for me.

"You're adults," I said, trying to sound like I meant it. "Do you know why Kim might have left town? Say Kim had left a note on the fridge saying she was leaving town for a few days. What would your first thought be when you read that note?"

"That she was leaving town for a few days?" Siu said. "I'm not, like, her warden."

"You wouldn't think there was a place she'd probably gone? Someone she probably left with?"

Siu rolled her eyes. "I think it's her business, dude. She probably went somewhere to think about something. She's a thinker."

Interesting. "Did she have something in particular on her mind?"

"I don't know," Siu said. "She likes to mull stuff over. She doesn't, like, talk the shit out of everything."

"Okay," I said. "Is this her bedroom?"

I pointed at the nearest door. Siu nodded. "Lauren told me I had to let you in, so go ahead."

More abdication than invitation, but I didn't much care. Siu didn't bother to escort me across the room and showed little interest as I pushed the door open. She was not, it seemed, going to follow me around and watch over the silverware. Part of the abdication, probably.

Kim's room was thick with incense, perfumes, and scented everything. I imagined the various gases taking wispy forms and duking it out in the air. I didn't blame Siu for keeping the door shut.

Visually, it had the same lush overkill. I'd seen her room in the background of photos and videos, but they hadn't given the full impression. Christmas tree lights in white and blue were hung over the bed and along the longest wall. Scarves were draped over everything. The bed was half buried under throw pillows of every size, colour, and fabric. Clothes spilled from dresser drawers and down the back of the papasan chair in the corner.

The first impression was of chaos, but gradually I saw design in it. The colours of the throw pillows flowed smoothly from blues to greens to yellows and oranges. The clothes were draped, not bunched or dropped on the floor. The desk, a small wood knee-hole, painted white, was tidy. I saw where the laptop should have been and where her phone would dock. The dock and its cable were in place, but that didn't mean anything. She probably had a charger she carried with her.

What did mean something was the absence of the laptop's power cord. Those were bulkier, and if she threaded it through the hole someone had carved in the back of her desk, it would have been awkward to pull.

"Does she take her laptop cable to school?" I called.

"No," Siu said from the living room. "She has, I don't know, ten hours or something on the battery? It's super light."

"Any clothes missing?"

"No."

Of course not. To be fair, it would have been hard to tell. That laptop cable, though. That seemed like packing.

A vanity by the closet was piled high with makeup, mostly cheap, some better and sporting bright orange markdown tags. Tough to know in that jumble whether anything was missing. A K-Tel logo had been reproduced on cardboard and tacked to the edge of the mirror.

A few bottles of perfume, mostly knock-offs, sat along one side of the table, fronted by a bottle of what seemed to be genuine CK Euphoria for Men. I stuck my nose into her closet, and that was the primary thing I smelled on the clothes. Her regular, it seemed.

I called out to Siu again. "Does she keep money in here anywhere?"

I expected another no. Instead, I got Siu sighing and trudging her way into the bedroom. She went to the bed and picked up a throw pillow with a blue velvet background and green piping across it in waves. She gave it to me and gestured that I should flip it. The velvet was a cover, I saw, with a slit along the back so it could be taken off and cleaned.

"She keeps stuff in there," Siu said. She didn't seem curious as to whether there was money in it now. Had she already checked?

I slid my hand in and found nothing but pillow. "It's empty."

She shrugged. "'Kay. There's usually about fifty bucks."

I thought I saw something on the walls, some trace of lettering or art. Painted over, maybe, from the last tenant. Or… I looked at the ceiling and saw a dark purple bulb. Flipping the switch lit up the wall with designs. They were a collision of science and art, like Da Vinci studies. Drawings of buildings with arcs and numbers around them. A huge sea creature, like a giant snail, with the shell cut into segments and a number in each. A face with lines drawn through it, cutting it into thirds and thirds and thirds. One corner was given over to a K-Tel logo and a bird, like Kim's bird tattoo. A name on a banner was painted below it. ME Bird. I took out my phone and captured everything before the glow faded.

"Math," Siu said with a wrinkled nose. "She likes that stuff."

"Mulls it over, does she?"

Siu shrugged again. Damn it. She'd come so close to being responsive.

"Does she leave?" I asked. "Does she do this? Go away for a few days?"

"Sometimes. Couple days."

"But not five?"

"I guess not."

And per Lauren, she didn't flake on babysitting. Why was this time different?

"I have class in, um, right away," Siu said.

"I know," I said, and I didn't need the what-the-fuck look on her face to know how creepy that sounded. "Lauren has your schedule. Kim sent her a photo of the class list you keep on the fridge."

Siu nodded as if I had, for the first time, said something that made sense.

"Can I use your washroom before I go?"

"Whatever, dude."

I was always surprised when people let me use their washroom. Did they not know that I'd be going through the medicine cabinet and the trash? I found one toothbrush and tube of toothpaste. One stick of deodorant. One hairbrush. There was room for another of each of these things, even an empty glass where the missing toothbrush had probably gone. More packing.

I didn't see any medicine bottles or round marks in the cabinet where a pill bottle might have sat. That didn't mean Kim wasn't on medication. She might have kept it in the kitchen by the coffee maker or taken it everywhere she went. There wasn't much sense searching the apartment for it, since that was something else she would have packed.

I checked the trash for anything of interest. An empty pill bottle or a pregnancy test. All I saw was used tissue and a Q-tip.

Lauren hadn't mentioned the missing laptop cord or toiletries.

"Siu? Did Lauren say anything about Kim's toothbrush and laptop being gone?"

"Yes."

"And she said?"

Siu shrugged. "She asked, like, why is this stuff gone. I told her, you know. It's a thing."

I raised my eyebrows and waited.

"Like, if you have a late class and then an early the next day so you crash with someone in res," she said. "So you pack shit in case you wanna do that."

Then she looked into her mug, frowned, and scooped something out. A hair or bit of dirt, too small for me to see. She wiped her hand on her shirt.

"I bet we're very different people," I told her, "but I'd have been alarmed if my college roommate had gone missing. You do not seem concerned."

"I never said she was missing. So she missed babysitting one time. It's not a federal offence. Lauren needs to lay off the lattes."

"Lauren's overexcitable?"

"Lauren's overeverything. I bet Kim shows up, like, tomorrow. No big."

"It'll be great if you're right," I said.

Siu shrugged and showed me out. She left on my heels. I could have offered her a lift to class, but it wasn't far to Mount Royal. And also I didn't want to.

# CHAPTER 5

I'D MATCHED Kim's class list to a campus map and planned to do the rounds, looking for classmates and instructors. Other friends had offered their phone numbers. It would take a while to talk to them all. I looked at my phone, thinking. It was a big ask, but then again, he was using my spare room. And he'd said he was bored. He wasn't a detective, but he wasn't dumb. He could ask simple questions and take notes.

I called Jess.

"Hey," he said. He sounded tired but not unhappy.

"You up for some work?"

"I'm here half a day and already you want me working for rent?"

Very funny, considering rent was one of the things we'd broken up over. "Do you feel okay? I need someone to make some calls."

"I would love to."

Something occurred to me. "Do people know your voice? Will they know who you are?"

He laughed. It was a thick sound, but Luna had said that meant his chest was clearing.

"In context they might," he said. "If I'm on the radio being interviewed or something, people might know my voice. If it's some random phone call and I'm just a guy working for you? They'd have to be my actual biggest fan. It'll be fine."

It was tough for me to judge, knowing his voice as well as I did, but his speech wasn't nearly as distinctive as his singing. And who thinks a celebrity is going to call to ask about their missing friend?

"Okay," I said. "Can you call Kim's friends from that spreadsheet? I saw Siu, but I need someone to talk to the rest. I want to know who she had drinks with at Boston Pizza Wednesday night. And whatever else you can get—whether anyone knew she was planning to leave town, why she might have left, whether anything was new in her life… everything we talked about last night. But mostly find the people she was out with on Wednesday."

"How did it go with the roommate?"

"Some things are missing that Kim would have packed if she meant to leave for a few days. Her cash is gone. The roommate says she carries all that with her sometimes, in case she wants to crash with a friend in the dorms or whatever, so I don't know. Oh, and she decorated her room—I'll send you the photos."

"Is it a map of places she likes to hide?"

"Sadly, no. You'll just like it. It's a you kind of thing."

Jess laughed again. "I am dying to know what you think that is."

"Make sure you're not dying in general," I said. "Meds. Check your temperature. Check your sats."

"Jeez, Mom."

"If you die in my house it is going to look weird."

"I know you hate that," Jess said. It was another old argument, that I was apparently ashamed of being me and not comfortable in my own skin and a pile of related bullshit that mainly meant I had some standards for my behaviour in public.

"Fuck you," I said. Silence. More silence.

"Hey," I said, since I had another topic at hand, "I'm going to Mount Royal to find her classmates, see what people have to say about her. It's a fishing expedition, so feel free to call me if you turn up any actual leads."

"I feel like a Hardy Boy." I heard his smile.

We hung up because there was no reason to keep talking. I had work to do. I stared at the phone for a few seconds and saw my finger moving to hit redial. I had not told it to do that. I dropped the phone to the passenger seat, well out of reach.

MOUNT ROYAL would not appear in anyone's coffee-table book of the world's grandest universities. Concrete and practical, and even the occasional architectural flourishes looked as if they'd been picked out of a catalogue. Fair enough, though, since its students tended to be studying practical, unfussy things. Kim's cobbled-together "art history" program was unusually frivolous for the place.

Unlike the sprawling jumble of the U of T campus, it was easy to navigate and compact. Though Jess and I had technically gone to the same school at the same time, we had seen each other only deliberately. Kids here probably ran into each other all the time.

Word about Kim had made its way around campus. Most of the kids I stopped outside her classes knew she was missing, and I'd been surprised to see posters on bulletin boards, doors, and vending machines all over the place. They directed people to Lauren's Facebook tips page and gave the hashtag and offered a phone number for those who preferred to text. I didn't recognize the number, so I took a photo and sent it to Jess for follow-up.

*that was fast*, he texted back. *since when are students efficient?*

*kids these days*, I said. He sent back a smile and #findKimMoy.

The picture on the poster was one I'd seen in her social media. Black sweatshirt and, for some reason, a glittery bug-antennae headband. She was outside an escape room, a sign that said Failed in one hand, a thumbs up on the other, and a huge grin on her face. Having a good time, win or lose. I'd been way too into myself at her age to be okay with losing in public. Or private.

No one was going to say they disliked a missing girl, but I got the sense that Kim really was liked by her peers. The kids I stopped between classes seemed concerned in a distracted way, like I'd mentioned one of a hundred shitty things they'd learned that week and also they were late for their next class… but yes, it was weird and bad that Kim was gone.

The teachers had less to say, aside from the requisite comments about how disturbing it was and what was the world coming to. They said she was fine, a good but not great student. No trouble. For most of the teachers, I was pretty sure that I could have shown them a photo of any goth girl and they would have said it was Kim. Understandable. Once you'd seen enough university students, year after year, they probably did become types to you.

My phone buzzed as I was heading to her last class. Jess.

"Everything okay?"

He laughed. "I haven't died in the last half hour, if that's what you mean. Do you want to talk to the person who put up those signs?"

The cliche that criminals inserted themselves into crime investigations had some basis in reality. Always worth talking to the people who insisted on hanging around. "Same number as the poster?"

"Yes. Name's Katie Aland. I talked to her. She has a class with Kim, but they also know each other through Paint Nite. They're both instructors. Is that interesting?"

"Maybe. Thanks."

I ducked into an empty classroom and called the number. It barely rang twice before a woman with a strong, clear voice answered. "Katie speaking."

"I'm Ben Ames," I told her. "I'm a private investigator, and I've been hired to look for Kimberly Moy. Do you have a few minutes?"

"Yes, your assistant mentioned you might call." I heard a rustling sound, then nothing as she put the phone on mute. A few seconds passed. "Go."

"How did you get involved with the missing posters? I see it's your number on there."

"When Lauren reached out to Kim's friends, I volunteered."

"Are you and Kim close?"

"She…." The change from brisk junior executive to tongue-tied kid was startling. "We're friendly. You know, we both do Paint Nite, so I know her from there."

"You've gone to a lot of trouble," I said. I kept my voice neutral. I was pretty sure she'd find a way to read into it.

"It's not trouble," she said sharply. "It's really the least I could do."

I was worried about pushing her into hanging up, but there was definitely something here. "A lot of people would say the least they could do was nothing."

"I… didn't really think so."

Something told me to keep my mouth shut. After a few seconds, she went on.

"Kim called me Wednesday night," she said. "It was right after ten. There was a show I was going to watch, and then I was going to bed, so I noticed the time. I was… I didn't want a call."

"That's understandable."

"She didn't say she was in trouble," Katie said. "She didn't. She sounded a little upset, but all she said was that she needed someone to take her Paint Nite on Thursday."

"She didn't say why?"

"I should have asked her, right? Because she sounded upset?"

Obviously Katie thought she should have asked. I did not point this out. "Does Kim do this a lot?"

"Ditch Paint Nites, or call me during my show?"

"Either."

"She never ditched. She didn't call me a lot."

"Does she get upset a lot?" I asked. "You know, some people, every little thing…."

"No," Katie said. "Kim is stable."

The CEO tone was back. I thanked her again and deflected her repeated offer to meet and strategize. She sounded like an effective person, and her postering game was impressive, but I already had one more assistant than I was used to.

Which reminded me. I found a spot by the pond in the campus garden and called in a delivery for Jess. Soup and fruit juice from some bakery cafe. Soup was the thing for sick people, I thought. That done, I found a place that would sell me a decent sandwich and a monstrous coffee, and I fed myself.

Kim's class schedule was starting to wear on me. Asking dozens of strangers whether they've seen or heard anything is like a stakeout in some ways. It takes a long time, is mostly not interesting, and requires concentration to do well. A small hesitation or sideways glance could be my only hint that someone has more to tell me, and I'll miss it if I'm not alert. Worst of all, people would make up their own minds that they didn't know anything important, which was stupid because I had the big picture and they didn't, so how in hell could they tell what was important?

But there was no telling people that. All you could do was watch and try to catch the little omissions, and let yourself go cross-eyed with the staring.

My phone rang in the late afternoon. Jess again.

"First," he said, "thank you for the soup."

"Anytime."

"Second, I have found the people who were out with Kim on Wednesday night."

"Go on…."

"Allie and Hannah," he said. "They had drinks with her—they said the place was called BPs. Is that Boston Pizza?"

"Yeah," I told him. "We have one on every damn block out here."

"With your proximity to Boston. And with New England being known for Italian food."

"All of that," I agreed. "Are they willing to answer questions?"

"They are eager to meet you," he told me. "A real private detective."

I resisted the urge to bang my head against the nearest wall. "You're sure they saw her Wednesday? And they're not trying to get in on the excitement?"

"I think they might have been the last people to actually see her," he said. "I mean, of the people who know her. And not counting her phone call to Katie."

"Okay," I said. "Text me their numbers."

"I did better than that," he said. "They're waiting for you at the main gate, and they will walk over to the bar with you. Or the clam chowder pizza place."

"It's their specialty," I said. "Thanks."

"Anytime."

THEY WERE a matched set, nearly. One brown ponytail and one blond, in blue Mount Royal sweatshirts and black leggings.

"I'm Allie," Brown Ponytail said. Her friend was looking at her phone and barely glanced up. "Are you Ben?"

"I am. Thanks for meeting me."

"No big. We're at BPs all the time anyway. This is Hannah."

Hannah gave me a nod. She kept looking at her phone as we walked. She stayed a step behind Allie, and that was probably how she avoided walking into things. As long as a dim outline of a sweatshirt was in her peripheral vision, she was fine.

"Is there any news at all?" Allie asked. "Did anyone find her car?"

"The police are looking. They're much better equipped than I am to find a car."

And a missing person generally, but I didn't say so.

Allie led the way breezily through the restaurant's front doors and to a rounded corner booth in the lounge. "We sat here on Wednesday. If it matters."

Hannah slid into the booth and put her phone on the table, face down.

"She was normal until, like, nine," Hannah said. "Then she got weird."

Allie slid in next to her. I sat on the other side.

"What do you mean by weird?"

Before Hannah could answer, a server appeared and inquired as to what she could get us. And did we need menus?

"We're fine," Allie told her.

"Pop?" I asked them. "Beer? Coffee?"

"Harp," Hannah said.

Allie made an "oh, what the hell" face. "Same."

"I'll have a coffee," I told her. "Black. And is the person who served this table last Wednesday evening here today?"

"Huh." The server looked over her shoulder. She was a pale redhead with wavy hair exploding from a rhinestoned jaw clip. Her artfully faded T-shirt advertised a Gorillaz album that might have come out while she was a fetus. "I'll check. Was there a problem?"

"Not with the restaurant," I assured her. "I have a few questions. I'm a private investigator, and I'm looking for a missing person. Kimberly Moy."

"Shrrt," the server said. She took the pencil she'd been chewing from her mouth and said it again. "Shit. Was she here?"

Instead of answering, I showed her one of Katie's posters. The server's eyes widened. "You think something happened to her here?"

"This is the last place anyone remembers seeing her."

"Sure," the server said, like she understood. Her face said otherwise. "I'll check, and I'll get those drinks for you, 'kay?"

"Great," I said. "Thanks."

Once she was gone, I looked at Hannah. She was staring at her phone but put it down when Allie elbowed her.

"I was asking what you meant," I told her, "when you said Kim started acting weird."

Hannah had the sort of flat, immobile face that fed back whatever you were inclined to see there. To me, in this moment, she looked cagey. Probably she was not.

"I didn't notice anything," Allie chimed in. Hannah's eyes flickered. If she'd tried harder, they would have rolled.

"You were distracted," she said.

"You were on your phone the whole time," Allie responded. "Per usual."

"I pay attention," Hannah said. Her voice was pitched low and unemotional, as blank as her face. I wondered what she kept looking at on her phone. She didn't seem like a social media addict.

"Did Kim say something unusual?" I prompted.

Hannah shook her head. "She just got nervous all of a sudden. She was twitchy, and she tore up her napkin."

"Is she normally a fidgeter?"

Allie shrugged and looked at Hannah. Hannah said, "No."

"Did something set her off?" I asked. "A phone call? Did someone join your table?"

"Not right then," Allie said. Her brow creased, and she closed her eyes. I could see them moving under the lids, around the booth, looking at who had been there. "Some people left right before six, and some people came around eight. Not eight thirty. They were at a lecture until seven thirty, and they came straight here."

"Are you sure Kim's behaviour changed around eight thirty?" I asked Hannah. "Not eight?"

"It wasn't eight," Hannah said. "It wasn't because anyone sat down here. It might have been something someone said."

"I don't think so," Allie said. "I didn't notice Kim acting weird, but I would have noticed if someone freaked her out. I'm on the student union inclusion committee. I'm very aware of othering."

"I'm sorry, of…?"

She gave me a warm, pitying smile. I was old and didn't understand. "Othering. Making people feel as if they are the other instead of the supposed norm. Disinclusivity."

"If someone had othered her," Hannah said, "it would have been a whole thing."

Was that sarcasm? I couldn't tell, and by the look on her face, Allie couldn't either. The server broke the awkward moment by arriving with our drinks and a guy in his early twenties, maybe late teens. He was in jeans, hiking boots, and a grey T-shirt covered in red-checked flannel. He must have thought his shift was at a BPs on the top of Mt. Hood.

"This is Zach," our server told her. Her own name remained a mystery. "He had this table last Wednesday night."

"Totally," Allie confirmed. "Hey."

Zach nodded. A chunk of streaky blond hair flipped up and fell back over one eye. "Hey."

I showed him Kim's picture, and he nodded. His hair flopped again.

"Yeah, I remember her. She's missing, hey?"

"She is. Do you remember anything unusual about her? Did you see her arguing with anyone?"

"Yeah, no," he said. "No argument. But she was looking at her phone in the smoker's lounge, and she seemed kinda stressed."

"The smoker's lounge?" I asked, looking around. I was pretty sure that kind of thing was illegal.

Allie smiled. "It's the alley. If it's warm enough, they leave the side door open at night so people can smoke in the alley."

No one had suggested Kim was a smoker.

"Did Kim smoke?" I asked. Allie and Hannah both shook their heads.

"She wasn't smoking," Zach told us. "She was looking at her phone."

"Not on a call?" I asked.

Zach shook his head. "She had it, like, down here." He mimed holding a phone around stomach height.

"Did she say anything?"

"Not that I heard, man."

"Do you know what time that was?" Hannah asked.

"I was going on break. Eight forty-five."

Hannah's expression was easy to read now. It said, "Told you so."

It would have been great to have Kim's phone record, to see whether someone had texted her around eight forty-five. It would also have been great to know whether she'd done a Google search or visited any other websites. But unless I wanted to pay too much money to some very shady people, there was no way I could get that information. My police contacts wouldn't help—there was still no evidence that a crime had been committed. Hell, I still wasn't convinced there'd been a crime.

"She never said anything," Allie said. She looked put out by that.

Hannah shrugged. "So it was personal."

"Did she come back to the table after that?" I asked. Zach didn't know, but Hannah and Allie nodded.

"Yeah, she was here until nine," Allie said. "We walked out together."

"Do you remember anything else that seemed unusual?" I asked Zach.

"No, man. Sorry. Can I… do you need anything else?"

I told him thanks and he was free to go. Allie poured her beer into a mug. Hannah took a pull from the bottle. I didn't really want more coffee, but I drank it anyway since my day was far from over.

"When you heard Kim was missing," I said, "what did you think? What was your first thought?"

"That she was acting weird at BPs," Hannah said.

"That maybe she went back to Manitoba," Allie said. "Maybe one of her parents got sick or something. But it was her sister who told us she was missing, so obviously it wasn't that."

"No new boyfriend? No arguments with anyone? No… I don't know, sudden bad grades or disappointments?"

"Are you saying you think she killed herself?" Allie's voice hit a point midway between incredulity and outrage.

"I don't think anything," I told her. "I don't know Kim. You sound as if you think that would be unlikely."

"She wasn't depressed or anything," Hannah said. "She wasn't acting like she was."

"She wasn't on antidepressants or anything," Allie said. "I told her once that I was… I mean, I am… and Kim said…. I remember because it sort of pissed me off. She said she was normal."

"I doubt she meant it like that," Hannah said.

Allie flicked her fingertips against the frosted glass of her mug. "I don't know any other way to mean it."

"Lots of people take antidepressants," Hannah said. "But yeah, I don't think Kim… she likes to think things through, but she's not mopey."

"I'm not fucking mopey," Allie said.

Hannah sighed. "This isn't about you."

"No, it's not about you, and that's why you think it doesn't matter what you say." Allie pushed her beer away and looked at me. "Call me if you need anything else."

She stormed out as best she could, impeded by the tight fit of the table to the seat, the crush of people and tables between her and the door, and our server approaching from the kitchen. Hannah finished her beer.

"Drama," she said as she set it down. "I should probably go apologize or something."

"Let me know if you remember anything else," I said.

Hannah left, and I paid the bill, leaving a healthy tip and a handful of business cards. Probably the girls had the right idea. There wasn't anything else for me to learn here.

A sharp wind had come up while we were inside. We were barely into September, but I felt winter in it. Leaves fell like gusts of rain. I kicked them aside as I walked to my Jeep and tried to guess what Kimberly had seen on her phone at eight forty-five Wednesday evening. A threat? A nude photo she'd sent to an ex-boyfriend? An especially cute cat video?

As I walked, I texted Jess that I was on my way. Maybe he would have some ideas. It made no sense to me how natural that seemed. That Jess, whom I hadn't seen in years and who had never been to my house in Calgary, was waiting at home to talk over a case with me. Hanging out with Frank. Eating soup.

It wasn't as if I'd never imagined seeing him again, but it was always some big thing with fireworks. Either a lot of yelling or—not that I had ever so much as considered getting back with him, but sometimes I pictured a big movie scene. Rushing across a busy street or running to catch up to a train at the last minute. Music, orchestral or something bare bones that stripped away the noise and activity to frame this one connection as the center of… bullshit. Some bullshit. But you picture these things, or I did. As if I lived some enchanted movie life.

No scenario had included pneumonia or drinking with bitchy teenagers in a second-rate pizza chain. That was how I knew it had to be real.

# Chapter 6

I WAS met at my front door by Frank and by the smell of food from the kitchen.

"I ordered for both of us," Jesse called from the living room. That wasn't where he was supposed to be and did not contain a bed, but investigation showed that he was at least stretched out on a couch. He'd even dragged the duvet in from the bedroom.

"Your fireplace isn't working, by the way."

The couch faced the fireplace, and Jess was facing me over the back of the couch. I dropped my jacket on the half shelf between the door and the living room and patted Frank's head.

"I'm sorry the accommodations aren't to your standards," I said.

Jesse made a face. "I thought you might not know."

"Yeah, well. It's the landlord's job to fix it."

I went to the patio doors to offer Frank a visit to the yard. He ignored me. He'd probably had Jesse opening and closing those doors all day.

"Oh, you're renting." Jess didn't sound judgemental, just a little surprised. It was annoying anyway.

"No, I bought a fifteen hundred square foot house in Calgary working as a PI," I said. "Of course I'm renting."

He sighed. I could see him deciding not to say any number of things. "Why hasn't your landlord fixed it?"

"He pointed out that my lease does not mention a working fireplace and said it was a bonus that it worked the first year I lived here."

Jess nodded thoughtfully. "That man sounds like a dick."

"Probably because he is."

I went to the kitchen and found tall brown bags on the counter, so warm that they had to have been delivered only moments before. They were from a Vietnamese place a few blocks away, which suggested that Jess had ordered strategically as soon as he'd received my text. What place has food we both like and is close enough that the food might get here before Ben does?

"You still like Vietnamese, right?" Jess called from the living room. The last word was mauled by a cough.

"Yeah, it's good. I'll bring it in there."

Frank was at my heels, since I was looking at human food and standing next to his bowl, so kibble or vermicelli, either way he might be in luck. I gave him kibble and took the people food to the living room. Based on his order, it seemed Jess was feeling well enough to eat his usual favourites. Luna would be glad to hear it.

I set things on the living room table, and Jess scooched over to give me room on the couch. He was a little paler than usual, with circles under his eyes, but aside from that, he could have been visiting instead of convalescing. His eyes were bright, and his hands were quick as he arranged the food. We were still a machine at divvying up Vietnamese food. Fish sauce to me, chili paste to him, peanuts for him and none for me, all as if we'd last done it a week ago. Our hands brushed, and we stopped for a second at most, then carried on as if it hadn't happened.

"How was your day?" Jess asked.

"I learned a lot. And I have no leads."

"I thought it was supposed to be follow a lead, get a new lead, follow that lead, get a new lead."

I opened one of the beers I'd brought from the kitchen and slapped Jesse's hand when he reached for the other. "Not with your medication, sicko. You get water, orange juice, or decaf."

Jesse stared at me as if I'd suggested he drink from a puddle in the road. "Decaf?"

"You need your sleep. As for detective work, I don't know how anyone else does it, but I walk around talking to people and see what I find out. The information doesn't come in a neat line."

Jess grabbed a bottle of orange juice and shook it slowly—upending it completely, then back, then upending again. Like always. "So what did you find out?"

I told him, mostly. Things that didn't matter to the case, like speculation about my love life, were not included in my recap. He listened silently and intently, looking away only to get more food or take his pills. Frank trundled in and stood next to the patio doors. I let him into the yard and waited as he sniffed at leaves and circled a few spots, looking for just the place.

"When did you get him?" Jess asked.

"He sort of came with the house," I said. "I moved in a few years ago, and the guy who was moving out asked if I could look after his dog for a couple of days while he got settled in his new place. Like a sucker, I said fine, and of course the guy never came back. So I've got a dog. What is that look?"

Jess was grinning at me, but there was something strange in his eyes. It seemed dangerously close to sentiment. "You and strays."

I shrugged. "He wasn't a stray. He lived here first."

Once Frank was back inside and settled between us and the cold fireplace, I wrapped up my story with the meeting at BPs. While I chased that with the last of my beer, Jess packed up the leftovers and piled the dishes. He tried to get up to take it to the kitchen, but I gave him a look that suggested he shouldn't, and it was enough to keep him on the couch.

He did slip into the washroom while I was in the kitchen. Being a couple of beers in, I decided that wasn't a bad idea for me, either. We passed each other in the hall, and I watched him walk for a few steps. He seemed steady. If I hadn't known how fast he usually walked, he wouldn't even have seemed slow.

His shaving kit was on the counter, and it was about a third open, because why finish something when you can abandon it in progress? I glanced at it while washing my hands and thought about closing it and setting it on the shelf, to make a point. As I considered that, I realized I was looking at a couple of pill bottles. Amber plastic, not blue like the ones we'd picked up the night before.

My excuse, if I had one, was that detective is something you are, not something you do. I spun the bottle at the front to see the label. PrEP. I might have guessed. The second bottle was tucked behind, impossible to read, so I took it out.

Lexapro. Kent's sister took that for depression.

Some doctor in Toronto had prescribed it over a year ago, and Jess was on his second-to-last refill.

I put the pills back, left the shaving kit as I'd found it, and sat on the side of the tub. I was remembering this and that, so quickly that I barely recognized one thing before I was on to the next. The times Jess had gotten sick, I'd thought, or lazy, and hid out in the bedroom for days. The way he'd used drugs and booze like make-up, to bring out his eyes or plaster on the right kind of smile. How he would drink before going on stage sometimes, like not drinking would be the death of him.

I arranged my face before going back to the living room. Either Jesse hadn't meant for me to find those pills, in which case I had no right to bring this up, or he'd left the shaving kit there, open, with the pills in view, because he'd wanted to tell me but wasn't ready to actually say it. Jess was usually direct, but I didn't know every damned thing about him, did I?

Jess was looking at his phone as I returned. He heard my footsteps and set it on the table, face down.

"More hate mail?" I asked.

"I wish it was mail. Imagine that. People have something to say to me, they have to look up my manager's address, get a pen and paper, write it down, find a stamp, take it to a mailbox…."

"I don't think you'd bother to send a letter that said, 'Suck my dick, faggot,'" I agreed.

"You'd at least expand on your thesis," Jesse said. "Anyway, doesn't matter. Um, I borrowed a steno pad from your office. I hope that's okay."

"Since you were doing my job for me, I think I can let it go."

Jess grabbed a notepad and pen from the floor beside the couch.

"There's not much here, but now that I know what you found out, it's interesting how it lines up."

His phone buzzed. He didn't even glance at it. "I gave everyone I talked to your number."

"Got it," I said. "What did you find out?"

"Everyone said Kim wasn't a drama queen, so that tracks with what you heard. A few of them said Kim does go away to think sometimes, like her roommate said, but no one knew of any particular place she went. Anyone who saw her Wednesday evening said she seemed distracted and jumpy. And one person saw her at an ATM around ten thirty, so that would have been right after she called her friend to give up her Paint Nite."

"Interesting," I said and yawned halfway through.

Jesse laughed. "Yeah, clearly."

"Sorry," I said. "I had unexpected company last night. Kept me up. Anyway, Kim chose to leave town. She took out money. She gave up her Paint Nite. She took her laptop charger."

"So she saw something upsetting on her phone," Jesse said, "and suddenly decided to leave town. Maybe to do something or maybe just to think."

"But she wasn't back in time to babysit her niece."

Jesse sighed and dropped the steno pad on the table. "I mean, maybe she just… forgot?"

He looked genuinely upset, contemplating a girl he didn't know and a case in which he had no real stake. Still, he was not a client and wasn't going to be treated like one.

"I think she would have showed up to babysit," I said. "She and her niece were close. Or are close. She even drew her niece on that wall in her room. Well, not her, but the bird. The ME Bird."

"Yeah, it's the only thing that wasn't Fibonacci," Jess said. He picked up his phone, scowled at whatever was on the screen, and pulled up the photos I'd sent him from Kim's room. "See? Everything's a Fibonacci sequence."

"The blah blah blah are blahdee blah blah," I responded.

"Do you want me to explain," Jess asked, "or should I leave you alone with Wikipedia?"

I stretched my legs and put my feet on the coffee table. "Go ahead."

"This mathematician, Fibonacci, came up with a way of generating a sequence of numbers, like, you add the first two and get the third and you add the second and third to get the fourth and the fourth and the fifth to get the sixth. Like that. Which is, whatever, a boring math exercise, except that sequence is connected to how a lot of things grow, like the shells she drew here and this fern and this pinecone. It's weird how they all have ratios we can describe mathematically in this really simple way. And the other stuff? You see all these lines? They're principles in art. You divide an image up using these ratios and it'll be aesthetically pleasing. Or you build a house that way. And these art ratios are also connected to Fibonacci."

"That's it, then. She ran off with Fibonacci."

Jesse smiled. "I feel like you stopped listening about three or four words in."

"It's not relevant. Except what you said again, the niece matters and babysitting matters, so why didn't she show up to do that? Or at least call? And everyone says Kim's reliable."

"I get it." Jess sighed and put his phone back on the table. "I don't like it, but I do get it."

"Name of my autobiography."

"Name of your sex tape," Jesse returned and looked me dead in the eye.

My throat knew before I did that it was a pass. My throat was dry, and I could taste tin foil. But panic wasn't the only thing I was feeling. Being looked at that way, by Jess, tended to have an effect on people. I was people. I was also a guy who knew what that look promised.

And I was a guy who knew better than to start this. Not tonight. He was sick, if nothing else. I gave myself a few deep breaths, until I thought my voice would be steady, and politely said, "Shh… do you hear that? If it's very quiet, I can hear your cock wheezing."

Jesse blinked, a moment of surprise he probably had on every rare occasion when someone turned him down. Then he started to laugh. It turned into a cough that doubled him over. It sounded thick and messy, and he was hiding it from me as best he could, keeping a wad of Kleenex to his mouth and his head down.

I laid a hand between his shoulders and rubbed gently. His skin felt all right, not the dry fire of the night before. Between the rattle in his chest and the way his shoulders shook, it seemed like he could fall apart. I pressed harder to keep him together.

"Goddamned sexy," I said, and he laughed again, in the middle of the coughs, and flipped me off without raising his head.

We both jumped when Frank barked. A second later, the doorbell rang. Frank walked me to the door and sat as I opened it, his fringed tail sweeping the rug.

Luna was already in a crouch to meet Frank eye to eye. She'd pulled the edges of her hot-pink coat forward to keep them off the ground, so she hadn't lost her mind or anything.

"There's my handsome guy!" she said.

"Gee," I said. "Shucks."

She and Frank ignored me, lost in love. I headed to the kitchen.

"Show yourself in," I called over my shoulder.

By the time I went back into the living room, she'd shown herself all the way to the couch and was checking Jesse's vitals. His face-down phone buzzed, and he glanced at it and back, trying to look like he wasn't.

"…considerably better," Luna said. "How do you feel?"

"Uh, yeah, good. Better. I could dance night."

"Nope," Luna said cheerfully. "None of that. But you'll be back to walking pneumonia in no time."

"Yay," Jess said weakly.

Luna patted his head like he was a less-handsome Frank. "I don't recommend air travel or driving for at least another week. If you're really desperate to get away from Ben, being a passenger in a car is fine. Can you get an Uber to Toronto, do you think? I suppose anything is possible for the right price."

Jesse looked at me. "Am I calling an Uber?"

"I can stand a week if you can," I told him. "I could get used to having a secretary."

"I think you mean associate," Jesse said. "Extra detective."

Luna raised her brows at me. "He's been working for you?"

"I've been creeping some people online," Jesse said. "I made some phone calls."

"I suppose it must be all right," Luna said, "since you've improved. You will be straight to bed after I leave, of course."

"Do I get a story and a snack?" Jess asked. "Glass of water?"

"You must have been a delightful child," Luna said. "Oh, do tell me if you need me to testify for you or, I don't know, be deposed. I don't know how these things are done."

Jesse looked nearly as confused as I felt. "Testify?"

"Yes, to your illness. Because ZZGold is suing you for cancelling the show."

"Oh." Jess shut his eyes. His head fell back against the couch. "He's not. Probably. He's just bitching. He thinks I'm backing out on promoting the single I sang on, so this is how he's getting press instead."

"He's very convincing," Luna said.

Jess smiled but didn't open his eyes. "He's a performer. And," he added with some venom, "he can go fuck himself."

I sat on the arm of the couch. "He wouldn't happen to have a point, would he, Jess?"

Jesse rolled his head to face me and half opened his eyes. "Are you saying I'm not actually sick?"

"You sound like you would really like it if he went and fucked himself."

"You wouldn't like him either," Jess said.

There was a familiar pressure in my chest. Why did Jess insist on getting himself into trouble? "Does he know you don't like him?"

"He's not unaware," Jesse said.

"Goddammit, Jesse. Do you have to tell everyone everything you think at all times? What if he really does sue? What if your label drops you?"

"I forgot," Jess said. "All things should be borne in silence. If you see something wrong, say nothing. That's your policy, right, officer? I mean, former officer?"

"My goodness, is that the time," Luna said, running the words together. Not wasting a second, she grabbed her thermometer and stethoscope and threw them into her bag. "I must go. Jack—sorry, Jesse—you really do need to go to bed."

"Yep," Jess said. He picked up his phone and headed to the bedroom without looking back. He was humming something it took me a few seconds to recognize. "Sit Down, You're Rockin' the Boat."

"Sorry about that," I said to Luna.

She looked like she wanted to say something, but whatever it was, she swallowed it. "He's very much on the mend now. I won't come tomorrow unless you call."

"Goodnight, Doc."

She patted my shoulder. "Goodnight, Detective."

I let Frank see her to the door. I was tired enough to sleep, but it wasn't late enough, and besides, I wasn't done with work. I called the client. Lauren was up, unsurprisingly, and quick to answer her phone. No doubt she'd seen my number and hoped I'd report that her sister had been found, alive and well.

I told her what I'd learned and asked about whatever had surprised and upset Kim that night at BP. Lauren couldn't think what that might have been. Interestingly, she confirmed what Kim's friends said about Kim's nature and tendencies. I was willing to bet that the parents would have said their artistic, oddly dressed daughter was flaky or theatrical. That was the difference between parents and a big sister, even when the sister was in loco parentis. Siblings saw each other more clearly.

"She's a good kid," Lauren said. It sounded like a plea. Keep looking. She's worth finding. Whatever this is, it's not her fault.

If I'd been a tough guy in some old movie, I would have said it didn't matter. I'd keep looking as long as she kept paying. She'd hired me to do a job, not to care.

I wasn't a tough guy, particularly. I told her I believed her.

I didn't tell her that believing her made it worse. It would have been nice if Kim had been the kind of person to head to Vegas with some guy and forget about babysitting her niece. That kind of person, I would have expected to turn up alive.

# CHAPTER 7

I SLEPT in my own room since Jesse was doing better, and also, we didn't particularly want to look at each other. It was a good enough sleep that when I heard the doorbell, I thought I'd only been out for a few minutes and that Luna must have forgotten something. The sunlight that smacked me in the face was a surprise.

As it turned out, I didn't have to rush to throw on clothes and get to the door. I left my room to find Jesse up, dressed, and making coffee for Detective Kent Hauser. Jess was wearing a flattering plum-coloured T-shirt that I hadn't seen before and jeans that were a darker wash than the ones he'd had on the day before. Who knew what else he'd had delivered to my home in the one day he'd been there? Maybe there was a gazebo in the yard.

"You're letting random strangers into my house now?" I asked him with a nod to Kent.

"Detective Hauser showed me his badge. I thought it would be rude to leave your partner on the step." Jess gave me his nothing face. Polite, bland, completely unhelpful.

Kent, on the other hand, looked… guilty. Something like that. "Your new butler looks familiar."

"Ha," Jesse said. Didn't laugh, just said ha.

"What is it like," Kent said, "to know people are joking if they say they don't know who you are?"

"Not as great as you'd think," Jess told him.

Kent nodded amiably. I could see the shrewdness in the back of his eyes. The sizing up. He didn't know what he thought of Jess, but he was working on it.

"I have some unpleasant news," Kent said to me. "Police business."

My stomach clenched. There was only one thing his unpleasant news could be. I looked at Kent, who looked meaningfully at Jess. Jesse caught the hint before I did.

"Frank's taking his time out there," Jess said. "I'll see what's keeping him."

He handed a cup of coffee to me and went outside. Once the patio door was shut behind him, Kent raised his brows at me.

"Good-looking in person too," he said. "They're not always. Famous people. I saw Pamela Anderson at the airport one time, and I wouldn't have touched her with a stick."

"I'm sure she'd be happy to know it," I said. "Did someone find Kimberly Moy?"

"Under a waterfall in Peter Lougheed Park. She's dead."

I set my coffee down without a sip. "Dammit."

"Late Monday night, early this morning. Somewhere in there. The RCMP aren't saying much, but I get the impression they're thinking suicide. Not sure why it couldn't have been an accident."

"The RCMP," I said.

Kent pursed his lips and nodded. "Yup."

"Which detachment?"

"Kananaskis Village."

"Right."

Nothing against the world-famous Royal Canadian Mounted Police, but that detachment was beyond small town. It was basically a wilderness outpost, attached to a tiny resort village and covering parkland the size of a small European nation. I felt uncomfortable assuming they were on top of this.

"They might call someone in," Kent said, as if he'd read my mind. "If they're not sure."

"Yeah."

We drank coffee in silence, two men who had no business in the death of Kimberly Moy. I'd been hired to find her, and I had, sort of, done that. Kent was city police, and Calgary had not been invited to the party. The thing to do was to finish our coffee and get on with our days.

"Who identified her?" I asked.

"The sister," Kent said. "Your client. They had to pull the body out of the water. Might have had to hike in to do that. I understand this took a while. The body was taken to Calgary. No medevac, so it must have been pretty definitive when they found her."

"Well," I said, "if she fell off a cliff, down a waterfall…."

"Yeah," Kent said. "Messy."

I pictured Lauren's hands on the strap of her purse, the raw white and red of her tightly gripping fingers under the morgue lights. The raw red and white of the body.

"But they'll autopsy," I said. They had to, no matter what condition the body was in.

Kent leaned against the counter, trying to look casual. I knew that move. I was about to be interrogated.

"Did you turn something up that would suggest foul play? Get a bad vibe off the sister?"

"No, she seemed… like you'd expect. Why? Did you hear something?"

"No. You have a bad guy in mind for this?"

"No one. I wouldn't even call it a hunch." I looked out at the yard, where Jesse was throwing a ball for Frank. I didn't recognize the ball. I didn't know where he got half the toys I found in the yard. "It looks like something happened a few nights ago that rattled her. I have no idea what. She cancelled some plans, and her friends say she didn't usually do that. She forgot she was supposed to babysit for her niece, and everyone says she'd never do that."

"That all sounds like this could have been a suicide," Kent said. "Upset young woman, not acting normal, leaves town without telling anyone…."

I shook my head. "I get that on paper, but I'm not feeling it. Jess and I don't think she was the type."

Kent's face seemed to inflate with joy. "Oh, Jess doesn't think she was the type. I see."

"He's been helping me out with research," I said. I sounded defensive even to me.

"Isn't he supposed to be in bed with consumption?"

"He's supposed to be not on stage for three hours every night," I said. "And Luna's got him on meds."

"You might as well bring him in here," Kent said. "I'm not supposed to be disclosing this to you either, so one more person won't make a difference. Unless you think he's going to put this all over the internet."

I shook my head. "He wouldn't. Also, he's not talking to the internet right now."

"Yeah, he's getting kicked around," Kent said. "I was looking for some talk about Jack Lowe and his new mystery guy, but it's all bitching about him ditching the shows."

I put my coffee down and went to the living room to wave Jess inside. "You can see how people wind up collapsing on stage. There's a lot of pressure to go on no matter what. Jess kept saying it was a lot of paycheques—"

I stopped because Jess had noticed my wave and was following Frank's lead to the door.

"Do you wipe his paws or anything?" Jess asked, using his body to try to block Frank's entry. But he was a small guy and Frank was a big dog, so I didn't like his chances in the long run.

"Just let him in," I said.

Jess stepped aside, and Frank ran up to Kent as if he hadn't seen him in years instead of minutes. Kent ruffled his fur.

"Good man," he told my dog.

"You guys done with the secret police business?" Jesse asked.

"I told him you've been helping me with the case," I said. "Just remember, he's not supposed to be talking to either of us."

"I was never here," Kent said, moving his hands in a way that he seemed to think was hypnotic. He looked more like the Karate Kid. "I came by to tell Ben that his missing person was found dead last night."

"What?" Jess looked at me. "Kimberly's dead?"

He looked and sounded as gut-punched as if he and Kimberly had been friends for years.

"She was found in Peter Lougheed Park," I said. "That's about an hour west of here. Bottom of a waterfall. Sounds like the Mounties are thinking suicide."

Jess sat on the back of the couch. "That's really horrible. I'm sorry, Ben."

So now we were acting like Kimberly had been my old friend. Like I had any right to feel sorry for myself. "I doubt Lauren would have hired me if she hadn't thought I could find Kimberly alive."

"You never promised her that," Jess said. "All you said was that you'd look for her. You told me yourself the first night that she'd been gone too long and you didn't like it. She might have already been dead when you were hired." He looked at Kent. "Right?"

Kent shrugged. "Your butler's right. Either she was already gone or you didn't have the leads to find her. You're good. You're not magic."

"Will the RCMP investigate this at all?" Jess asked. He seemed to be directing it at both of us.

Kent and I exchanged glances.

"I don't know," he told Jess.

"Might depend on the autopsy," I added. "When the body has been outside and knocked around and in the water, it's hard to know what happened."

"Unless someone saw something," Jess said. "Or she talked to someone, or… will anyone even check?"

"I don't know," I said.

Jess didn't say anything, but he didn't have to. His face was clear.

"Look, you're not wrong," Kent said. "Could have been an accident. Or this kind of thing… someone could get away with murder. I'm not saying anyone did, here. You guys are the ones with dark suspicions. I guess I'd want to know why the RCMP is so sure it was suicide. I would probably start there."

"Have you seen her Instagram?" Jess asked him.

"No," Kent said. "I wasn't on the case."

"Well, it was really genuine. Not staged. She was expressive. She put what she cared about all over the walls of her room. Would she really not express it if she was that miserable? Also, do you call someone to cover your class when you're suicidal? Or do you leave town and say the hell with it?"

He said that last bit like he really was asking. Like it was driving him a little crazy and he needed to know what Kent thought.

"Some people are pros at faking good," Kent told him. "That's what the shrinks call it, when you act like you're fine. Some people are real convincing. Depression's not what people think either, you know. There's a lot to it. But I get what you're saying. I'd have questions."

Jess nodded. I realized, at that moment, that Jess had been forming an opinion of Kent while Kent formed an opinion of him. Wondering, maybe, what Kent's role had been while I'd been struggling on the force.

"It's not my case either," I reminded them. "I was hired to find her. She's been found. I have to go see her sister and close out the case."

"Oh God," Jesse said. "Of course you have to see her. I get it. It's just… that's hard."

I would rather have stuck a knife in my chest, in fact. "Not as hard as what she's going through."

"I'd go with you," Jesse said, "if I wasn't me."

I knew what he meant. Lauren probably wasn't in the mood to see one more sad-eyed stranger today, regardless, but showing up with Jack Lowe would have been like showing up with a dancing bear. Unexpected, inappropriate, and impossible to ignore.

"Did they find her car?" Jess said suddenly.

Kent shook his head. "It wasn't at the trailhead."

Jess stared at him. "Oh, come on. Is there a subway line to the trailhead? Did she ditch her car and take an Uber?"

Kent smiled a little. "Her car could be broken down somewhere, but I see your point."

Jess looked at me. "You'd drive, right? If you had a car?"

I could have tied myself in knots thinking up reasons not to drive, but they were all at least a little ridiculous.

"I'd drive."

Jess shook his head. "Anyway, man, should you call her sister? Is that... do you wait, or should you call now?"

"I should call now."

Jess put a hand on my arm and pressed gently. His hand was warm but not too warm. Not feverish. Mostly it was comforting, and it made me think about how comforting it would be to put my arms around him. He was good at that kind of thing, calmly staying there, not asking a lot of questions. Giving the impression that he understood.

I worked up some kind of half smile to tell him it was okay and I was okay. None of which was true. I took out my phone and went into my office.

Lauren answered on the third ring. She'd been crying, obviously, by the roughness in her throat, but she was calm and quiet now.

"Have you heard?" she asked.

"I'm very sorry."

She didn't say anything. It felt like blame, but I'd always taken the silence that way, even when I'd told people their child or spouse had died in a car crash.

"Do you want me to come see you?" I asked. "Whatever I can answer for you, any advice I can give, I'd like to do that. If you want."

More silence. I was about to offer my condolences again, tell her I'd call again later, when she said, "Yes. Please come. Did I—do you have my address?"

It was on the cheque she'd given me for a retainer. One more reason cheques were dying out. What woman wants to show her address all over town?

"Yes," I said. "I'll be there in… about half an hour?"

"Yes, that's fine."

From her dull, flat voice, I could have been asking if she wanted her coffee black or the receipt in the bag. I rang off and went back into the living room.

Jess was on the couch with a mug in his hands, the paper tea label hung over its side. Chamomile. Luna would have been pleased.

Kent was sitting on the back of the couch, and the two of them were so involved in whatever they were discussing that they didn't notice I was back until I said so. Jesse looked up, and his face was chalky white. Apparently he'd overdone it playing butler. At least he'd had the sense to sit down.

"Are you going to see her?" Jess asked.

"Yeah. I'll see if there's anything I can answer for her, or… I don't know."

"Tough one, man," Kent said. "Least you don't have to break it to her."

I nodded, though this didn't feel any better.

"She hired you less than forty-eight hours ago," Kent reminded me. "You walked in on the third act of whatever this was."

"What are you still doing up?" I asked Jess. "You look like hell."

"So do you," he said. "Ben, if she wants you to find out what happened, tell her the cost is covered."

I blinked. I hadn't considered that, the possibility that Lauren might want me to keep investigating. Because I'd done such a great job so far?

"I don't think she'll.... I don't think she'd ask me," I said. Jess's expression was odd, and I didn't know how to read it.

"I'll pay. Tell her it's no charge."

"I can waive my fees myself," I told him. "I don't need charity."

"I'm not offering it," Jesse said. "This is something I want. I think I'd have liked Kim. But I'll let it go if her sister wants it that way."

"I...." I didn't know what to say and couldn't look at Kent. I didn't know what I'd see on Kent's face, not at all, but I was still afraid to see it. "I never said I'd take you on as a client, Jesse."

He smiled a little. His eyes were sad, but the smile was real. "The sister would be your client. Or Kim would. But you're right—it's up to you."

"Right," I said. "I should go."

"Okay," Jess said softly.

Kent stood. "That's my cue to leave. Jack, it was good to meet you."

"You too," Jess said. They both sounded like they meant it.

LAUREN'S HOUSE was a tidy two-storey in Cranston, like the two-storeys on either side of it and the ones on the other sides of those. They had what were probably bedrooms perched above a narrow two-car garage, their front doors set safely back from the supposed noise and danger of the deserted street.

I'd made it in less than half an hour, despite construction on a few roads and the fact that I wasn't in a hurry.

The door was answered by a suitably solemn woman about Lauren's age with curly blond hair piled into a pink-and-green kerchief on top of her head. She looked as if she'd been crying but not bawling. Sad, or sympathetic at least, but not heartbroken. A friend of the family, maybe. She didn't say anything, just looked at me.

"Hi," I said. "I'm Ben Ames. I don't know if Lauren told you she was expecting me."

She watched me in silence for a few more seconds. Her eyes were the same green as her kerchief, and the lids were narrowed with suspicion. Someone had to be to blame when bad things happened, and here was the detective who'd failed to find Kimberly. Maybe I'd do. Eventually she decided against giving me whatever piece of her mind she had waiting and instead waved me past her into the front hall.

The living room was to the right of the door, and I could see Lauren there, sitting on the couch with her eyes fixed on a table of framed photos across the room. She was twisting tissues in her hands. Small pieces had already torn off and floated to the floor around her boots.

I was willing to bet she did not allow boots past the front hall when she was in her right mind. I took off my shoes before going into the living room and taking a chair next to the couch. All the furniture was too delicate and too short and too covered in rose-print upholstery, and I was a little scared as I sat that the chair would collapse and I'd drop with it to the floor. Even if I hadn't known Lauren was divorced, I would have guessed that no men lived here.

"I am so sorry," I said. The blond hovered between us and the front door, listening to make sure I didn't say anything wrong. I wanted to ask for a list of what those things would be. I sure as hell didn't know what I was supposed to say.

Lauren nodded. I waited.

Slowly, she turned her head to look at me. "They're saying she… that she did it on purpose."

"That's what I heard," I said. "I heard it second-hand. I don't know why the RCMP think that."

She gasped, a stuttering little breath over a trembling lower lip. "Do you think they're wrong?"

I made myself take a beat before answering her. It wouldn't have done her any good for me to charge in with my opinions when I didn't have all the facts. "I don't know what they know," I told her. "Knowing what I know, which is where she was found and that her car wasn't at the trailhead, I have a lot of questions. But I have to say again that I don't have any more information, and the RCMP do. If I knew what they did, maybe I'd agree with them."

Lauren didn't say anything. I wondered whether she'd heard me. Her eyes were unfocused. Slowly, she reached down and pulled her phone from her purse.

The photo she showed me was of a typewritten note, a few lines long. "I'm sorry," it said. "I've tried but I can't do it anymore. This is the best way. Goodbye." Beneath this was a written signature: Kimberly Jane Moy.

"What is this?" I asked Lauren.

"They found this at… the place," she said. "It was held down by some rocks."

"Is that Kim's signature?" I asked. "The way she normally would sign things?"

Lauren pressed her lips together.

"Does it look like—" I prompted, gently.

"Yes," she said. "It's her legal signature, the way she signs, I don't know, financial things. But she wouldn't do this. Someone must have made her sign it."

It was possible, though I thought someone as bright as Kim would have done something if she'd been forced to sign a note like that. Switched her signature up somehow so people would know. But people didn't think of everything when they were panicked, either.

"Is this it?" I asked. "Did they say anything else? I'm sorry. I don't mean to make you go through all of this. I'm trying to understand."

She had her eyes closed, but she nodded. "They showed me the note, but they still have it. They kept it."

It was a good sign, in a way. If they'd really been sold on the suicide, they might have given Kim's possessions to her next of kin. But I didn't know how the Mounties handled these things, and maybe keeping the evidence was their policy in all cases of unnatural death.

"Did they find anything else?" I asked. "Her phone? Her laptop?"

Lauren shook her head. "They must be wherever she was staying. They said—the constable said—her leaving her phone behind was the sort of thing a girl that age would only do if she meant to…. Because they never leave their phones. She said she'd seen it before, where a girl left her phone at home and went to a building…."

She stopped there, but she'd been tough. She'd gotten through it without crying, barely.

"I'm sorry," I said, leaving it open as to whether I was apologizing for her seeing that note or for the cops keeping it or everything, start to finish.

"I don't believe it." She opened her eyes and faced me. "I don't believe she would do this. I don't believe that—" She pointed at her phone, the note, with a shaking hand. "—would be her last message. Do you believe it?"

"Lauren, you're upset," the blond friend started.

Lauren jerked her shoulder back so her friend's hand fell away. "Fuck that," she said. The familiar words were shocking and ugly, coming from her. I didn't know why. "She wasn't some weirdo because she wore black clothes. She wasn't like that. She didn't do this."

The blond looked annoyed but stepped away without comment. That was probably for the best.

There had never been any question of bringing Jess along on this little field trip, as much as I might have liked the company. Now I saw it as a good thing, since Jess did wear black and was a weirdo and was probably also whatever Lauren meant by "like that."

"I don't know," I told her again. I didn't want to say what Jess had said about Kim seeming like the kind of person who wouldn't hide things. Neither of us knew that, really. And I was living proof that you could think you knew someone well and have no idea they had depression, so what business did I have making guesses about someone based on their Instagram?

"But they think they do know," Lauren said. She took a deep breath. "You don't think you know. That's the difference."

"Sometimes it's not possible to know," I said.

"But there are things you could find out," she said. She sounded frustrated. I couldn't tell whether it was with the cops or with me.

"There are," I allowed. The blond hovered, and I felt like the ambulance chaser she doubtless thought I was. I hadn't even brought up the existing bill yet, or my intention to keep the retainer and not worry about it. I had no idea how to get there.

Maybe I shouldn't. Maybe I should wait for her to come to me and complain about the money. If she didn't, I'd assume it was okay.

"Is there anything I can tell you?" I asked her. "What I told you last night is about all I learned, but I didn't go into details. I can if you want to know more."

"I want to know what really happened to her."

I nodded.

Lauren leaned forward. "Will you find out? I'll pay, of course I'll pay. I don't care."

"It's covered," I said. "If you want me to look into this, I will, and there won't be any charge."

From the corner of my eye, I could see the blond scowling, trying to figure out what my game was. I wondered how many guesses it would take her to get "shitty detective feels guilty, has expenses covered by rock star ex-boyfriend."

Lauren's face scrunched, and tears lined her eyes. The expression wasn't gratitude.

"I have your retainer. I'm retained. Okay?"

"Nothing is okay," she said. "But if you…. I can pay."

"No need," I said. "Just, please. I will do this."

She was looking at her hands again. Kneading a tissue. She nodded.

There didn't seem to be anything else to say. I gave her a little time in case she wanted to speak or change her mind or ask why the hell I hadn't found Kim before she'd wound up at the bottom of a mountain. She didn't. I put my hands on my knees and pushed myself up and out of the tiny chair. I thought about putting a hand on her shoulder, but then the moment had passed, and it would definitely have been weird. So instead, I left.

I'd almost made it to my car when I heard a voice behind me. Not Lauren's.

"You're the detective, right?"

The girl coming around the side of the house was familiar from photos. In real life, Kim's niece was not pretty, but she made an impression. She had a knife-thin nose and small dark eyes and an expression that said she knew things about me I'd never figure out.

"You must be Emma," I said.

She eyed me, unimpressed. Whatever she'd wanted the detective to be, I wasn't it.

"She never jumped," Emma said.

"Maybe not," I said. "You mom asked me to find out."

She leaned against the house. She was wearing a grey T-shirt, a little too big, and torn jeans. Her short dark hair was in two aspiring ponytails, each about two inches long. Her nails were as black as Jesse's.

"We were going to the zoo next week. For my birthday."

"I'm sorry," I said. Maybe I'd get it on a T-shirt and save some time.

"She wouldn't have said that and then gone away."

From where I was, I couldn't tell whether Emma had been crying. I assumed so, but maybe she was too angry for that. People got that way sometimes.

"When's your birthday?" I asked.

"Monday. Next week."

She didn't ask why. I couldn't have told her, except that the closer it was, the more I thought she might be right. That Kim, if she'd really meant to jump, might have waited.

"Okay. Is there anything else you can tell me that might help?"

"I don't know what you mean," she said, and she morphed in front of me the way pre-teens did, from sulky teen to uncertain child.

"I don't either," I said. "But if you think of something, it's Ames Investigations. Google me. I'm not on social media."

It was only half a lie. I didn't do social media in a professional capacity. And most of my accounts belonged to made-up people who were a little obsessed with my ex. I would take those handles to my grave.

"I have money," she said, "if my mom doesn't have enough. I got birthday money from my dad."

"It's covered," I told her. "Don't worry about it."

She straightened and took a few steps toward me. We were still about ten metres apart, as if she were keeping enough distance that she'd have the option to bolt. "Are you any good?"

Wasn't it obvious I was a failure? But she was intent on an answer, and I had to give her the best one I could manage. "I'm not the smartest guy or the dumbest," I said. "I worked for the cops, and I studied criminology. I know how to do the job. I try to be honest with my clients. I do the best I can."

It wasn't exactly "win one for the Gipper," but something in that mess seemed to have meaning for her. She came close enough that I could have reached out and booped her nose.

"Here." She pulled a loonie from the back pocket of her jeans and offered it to me. "You give someone a dollar, right? And then you're their client."

"That's for lawyers," I told her. "So things can be confidential. That doesn't work with private investigators."

"But I'd be your client," she insisted. "Right?"

I took the loonie. "You're my client," I told her. God help us both. I handed her my card, and she looked at it like I'd given her a chiselled lump of rock.

"Text me your number, and I'll report in once a day. Okay?"

"I walk my dog at six forty-five every night," she said. "If you call then, Mom won't know."

"Done."

She wanted to shake on it, so we did. Her hand was small and dry. Then she nodded once and slipped around the side of the house again. I went to my car thinking about whether I ought to be billing Jesse twice.

# CHAPTER 8

"HEY." JESSE greeted me when I got home. He was distracted, putting new clothes into a new bag. Packing. I felt like a guy I'd seen in a tarot card, lying on the ground with ten swords stuck in him. Because he was leaving? Because I'd thought he was going to stay? I was out of my goddamned mind.

I swallowed past the swords. "Hey."

He looked up and tucked hair behind his ear. He was wearing his glasses. Had he aged a minute since we'd been in school? I couldn't see it.

"You need to talk to Luna," he said.

I looked at my watch. "She'll be asleep. She's on nights, remember? Is something wrong?"

"She said she'd stay up." And then he handed me his phone, ready for me to press the button and place the call like I wouldn't have been able to handle it myself. I got by fine by myself. I grabbed the phone from him, more roughly than necessary, and called Lunes.

"Is he not home yet?" she said in place of hello.

"He's using Jesse's phone," I said. "Jess said I needed to talk to you."

Was it about him flying to Toronto? She'd told him not to fly.

"He didn't think you'd believe him if he told you what I'd said."

"Which was?"

"You're a charmer this morning, has anyone told you?" she said. Before I could unload more of my charm, she said, "I told Jesse it would be fine for him to go to Canmore with you."

What? Had he turned psychic at some point? I held the phone away from my face. "You asked Luna about going to Canmore?"

"In case," he said. "In case we had a case."

I put the phone to my face again. "He asked if it would be okay to go to Canmore?"

"It should be fine. He would have taken more elevation coming into Calgary in the first place."

"Why did he ask you about Canmore?"

"I'm a simple doctor," she said. "You would have to ask him. I did tell him not to climb any mountains. He needs to rest. No hiking."

She yawned loudly. Possibly milking it. Still, she was on nights.

"I should let you go to sleep," I said.

"If you insist."

She hung up immediately, and I turned to Jesse, who was leaning against the back of the couch, looking at me.

"Do you have a case?" he asked.

"Yes," I said. "Lauren hired me. I told her it was covered. The niece intercepted me outside my car and gave me a dollar, so she's hired me too."

"Okay, so we're going to Canmore? Or somewhere around there? I only know Banff."

"I'm going to Kananaskis," I told him. "You are welcome to stay here. I need someone to look after Frank."

Jess sank a little against the couch. He made it look casual, but I could tell he was flagging. He'd been running around, packing and making stupid phone calls.

"Luna said I could go with you."

"I don't work for Luna."

He shut his eyes and took a deep breath, or tried. I saw it catch. "Ben, how many times have your cases involved deaths?"

"When I was with the police?"

"You had a partner when you were with the police," he said. "Since then. How many times?"

"None," I said. "It's not like on TV."

"Didn't think it was," he said calmly. He seemed weirdly at peace. Might have been the exhaustion. "Luna and I don't think it's a good idea for you to go there alone."

"What the hell?" I bit off the next words, which would have been something about how Luna was my friend and he'd been in town five minutes and where did they get off having conversations about me? "You and Luna are both very good at your jobs, but you are not detectives. And I don't know what kind of help you think you'd be anyway."

"You mean if someone tries to murder you?" He was smiling a little with one corner of his mouth. No lipstick, but he'd put on gloss. Vain little son of a bitch. "I can call 911. I'll know where you went and who you talked to. I know I'm not your backup. I just… I don't want it to look like you could vanish and no one would know. Do you have a gun, by the way?"

"You don't like guns," I reminded him. His father had insisted he learn to shoot as a kid, somewhere in Switzerland, and Jess was torn about which—guns, his dad, or Switzerland—he disliked most.

"I like them," he said, "if they're keeping you from getting killed."

Some treacherous part of my brain was telling me that Jesse cared whether I lived or died and making that out to be meaningful when he'd been heartbroken that morning over a girl he'd read about online. And he was invested because of her too.

"It is illegal," I told him, "for me to carry concealed or to use a gun while working. If I ever got into a situation where I needed a gun, I would already have fucked up. I have never needed one, and that's how it should be."

"Okay," he said. "I agree with that."

"I am a professional."

He shrugged. "I think I'll come anyway. Just in case."

"Do I look like the manager you fired for probably no reason? Do I look like a teenaged girl with your face on my phone case? What makes you think I will do whatever you tell me to do? You need a reality check."

"I'm trying to help," he said. His tone was aggressively even. Nope, I was not getting a rise out of him.

"You think it's helpful for me to show up with Jack Lowe?" I asked. "You know what happens when you walk into a room. Everything is about you. I guess you've come to believe it."

That shot landed. I could see the hurt in his eyes and around them, the way the skin tightened. The same part of my brain told me I should feel bad. I told it to shut up.

"It won't be Jack Lowe," he said. "I can hide when I need to. You'll see."

"I did not invite you," I told him. "You're sick and you're distracting. Again, because you do not seem to be getting it: I'm not your road crew, and I'm not whatever guy you're dragging around this month."

"I am," he said, the funny twist at the corner of his mouth again, "very aware of that."

He looked at the shirt in his hands and threw it into the bag, much harder than was necessary.

"You're going there because you think she didn't jump," he said. He looked at me, and his face was so intense it made me feel imaginary. "You think someone faked a suicide note. Unless this is some fucked-up *Weekend at Bernie's* shit, which I highly doubt, that means there was a murder, and it follows that there was a murderer, and you're going to the mountains to poke into his or her business, which is probably the last thing they want. You really think it's a good idea to do that alone?"

"I really think that you are not a detective."

His eyes were bright with tears. "I'm not telling, I'm asking. Please let me come with, for whatever good that will do. You were a cop. You must know it's safer, and I'm not going to get better pacing your house wondering whether you've been thrown off a mountain."

His voice broke on the last word, and he pressed the heel of his hand to his eyes. He looked as scared and amped up as I'd ever seen him, and maybe there was something in what he'd said. Anxiety had never been good for him. Especially bad had been all the ways he'd tried to drown it.

I stared at him as he stared at me, and the look in his eyes made my own nerves raw.

"I still need someone to take care of Frank," I reminded him.

Jesse smiled like a kid. "Kent said he'd be happy to."

LESS THAN an hour later, I was packed, and I'd caught Jess up on everything Lauren and Emma had told me. We were heading west out of Calgary, making good time in light weekday traffic. Jess was holding forth on the ridiculousness of the police not caring about Kim's laptop or her phone or her car, stopping occasionally to bark out a thick-sounding cough.

"Easy," I told him. "I get it. I agree. The first thing I want to do is find her car."

He nodded, catching his breath. A sign for Cochrane caught his eye, and he pointed at it.

"Aren't your parents there?"

I was surprised he'd remembered. He'd asked about my family a few times when we'd been together, and I'd waved him off. I'd mentioned growing up in Cochrane once, maybe twice.

"They moved to BC."

He had the sense not to ask whether I missed them or ever visited. Of all the criminology programs that had accepted me, he knew I'd chosen one four thousand kilometers from home for a reason.

We'd never talked much about his family either. We were only children, so there were no brothers or sisters, no Emmas to take to the zoo. And for one reason or another, our families had never felt much like home.

"Will you find out about the autopsy?" he asked, changing to an arguably happier topic. "Will Kent?"

"Maybe, depending on who does it."

"Will they look for drugs or anything?"

"Probably. University student, wore a lot of black. They'll probably assume things."

Jess drummed his black nails against the dash and gave a quick, sour laugh.

The polish was missing where Luna had peeled it off. He frowned as he looked at his nails and began stripping off the rest of it.

"Jack Lowe wears polish," he said as he dropped the bits into the cup I kept between the seats for trash. "Gotta say, it does not break my heart to not be him for a few days."

That made me wonder how his online character assassination was going. He'd told me once, over half-price drinks in some Front Street bar, that everyone had thought Loretta Lynn was a drunk because she'd had migraines. I'd sympathized like I'd thought he wanted. Said people were always ready to assume an artist was drunk or high. He'd tilted his glass and watched the vodka slosh around.

"It's not that unfair," he'd said.

That had been about six months before he'd gotten his recording contract and about six months after he'd started coming home from gigs spectacularly fucked up, when he'd come home at all.

"Can they trace her phone now?" he asked. "Since they know she's dead?"

It wasn't a bad question. "I don't know, Jess. This stuff gets complicated. And they don't think there was a crime."

"Can they get her internet provider to check her browsing history? She might have looked up hotels."

I stared at him for longer than I should have, considering I was driving. "Jesse. What did I say?"

He dropped his head back against the headrest. "Sorry. It's frustrating. There are so many things it would really help to know."

"Yep."

It was coming up on the hour. Maybe Kim's death had made the news. I turned on the radio, and we sat quietly through provincial politics and the local speed-limit debate and the unclaimed lottery jackpot and a hit-and-run in Airdrie before the announcer mentioned that a nineteen-year-old woman had been found dead in Peter Lougheed Park. They named the trail, at least, which was more than I'd gotten from Kent or Lauren.

The report ended with a comment that the police were calling the death "non-suspicious."

"That's code," I told Jess, "for suicide. If they'd meant accident, they'd have said it."

"Are they committed to that, now that they told the media?"

I shrugged. "They can walk it back if they find new evidence. It does suggest they won't be looking that hard."

"Right."

I left the radio on. It was one of those "hits of the past five decades" stations, the furthest possible thing from cool, but I didn't think Jess would mind. However he might have acted in public, the truth was, he approached most music with the uncritical joy of a Labrador throwing itself in a lake.

"Did I do an interview with this station?" he said, more to himself than to me. "I'm not trying to sound like an asshole, but it seriously gets to be a blur."

"The living nightmare of wealth and fame," I sighed, and he swatted my arm.

"You would hate it," he said. "I promise. You in particular. You'd be having a meltdown on YouTube inside of a year."

"I'd be Harrison Ford cool," I told him. "Off on a ranch somewhere building artisanal chicken coops."

"And kidding yourself that people wanted them because they were so well built."

I smiled, but it was probably only half a joke. To get the attention of a label, Jess had needed to gin up a following.

He'd done outrageous. He'd done whatever it took to get those fans, and as that snowball grew, he'd started to wonder about people. Why were they being nice to him? What did they want? He'd had a paranoid fit about it in our apartment one night, telling me he couldn't trust anyone. Always the sensitive guy, I'd thrown a Mars bar at him and told him to lay off the pot. What I hadn't said was that he was disappearing from my life into the arms of thousands of worshippers, and he had a hell of a nerve bitching to me about it.

I'd told him, "You'll always be nobody to me."

"It must be hell," I said, "having movie stars lining up to date you."

I hated myself a little the moment it was out of my mouth. Jess did not need to know that I'd spent all three months of his relationship with Matt Garrett drunkenly yelling at the internet, between bouts of ordering sacks of burgers from Harvey's and hitting things at the gym.

Something strange crossed his face. I couldn't place it before it was gone and he was raising his brows at me. "Did you think that was for real?"

I didn't know what my face looked like, but he got a laugh out of whatever it was.

He put his hand on my arm, where he'd swatted me, and gave me a little shove. "It's okay. People were supposed to think it was real. That was the point."

What was important was not letting on how much this meaningless news cheered me up. "I obviously do not understand this celebrity bullshit."

Jess laughed again. "Oh, it's definitely bullshit. You will not fucking believe this. You know how I was living the whole rock star thing, one-night stands, new guy in every town…."

"Yep," I said, trying not to convey an opinion in my tone.

"It was never as crazy as the press made it sound," he said, as if I'd clutched my pearls. "I think it would be physically impossible to have as much sex as the media made it sound like I was having."

"And *you* made it sound like you were having," I said. "To be fair."

He grinned. "The image is part of the job, you know that. But okay, so I had the rock star image, and then some PR company the label hired decided I could pick up some fans in Middle America if I softened my image, so they wanted me to date somebody. But somebody famous so it would get attention."

"Mission accomplished," I said. That year, Jack Lowe had put out a few hits around the same time as Garrett's latest popcorn flick had been number one at the box office. Stories about the happy couple had been unavoidable. I was certain no one knew that better than I did.

"Yeah, we put on a good show," Jesse said. "It's funny because I thought at first they were going to say I needed to date women or something, like I could just… not be gay anymore. And they said, 'No, gay's fine. Gay's having a moment.' I just needed to be family friendly gay."

"You… what? What is that?"

"Have a boyfriend. Get some photo shoots making Thanksgiving dinner together. Ideally, we'd get married and adopt a kid. Then you're adorable instead of a threat to civilization."

"Huh," I said.

He nodded. "I like to think I was always adorable."

"Your mileage varies. So, if you were supposed to do cozy holiday photo spreads with your fake boyfriend, why did you fake break up with him?"

He got that look again, this time for long enough that it seemed fair to ask. "What's that about?"

"He's not like people think. I found that out pretty fast. And he had this idea that the fake boyfriend relationship should include actual benefits, and I wasn't into it. My manager told me Matt could ruin me and to suck it up, so I told Gia it wasn't working, and she got me out of it. She seriously puts up with a lot."

I stared at him long enough that he pointed at the road ahead of us.

"You're driving."

"You're insane. You could have been having sex with Matt Garrett and you didn't? Has anyone ever turned him down before?"

He sighed and looked washed out again. "I honestly don't know."

"What is he like?"

"Christ, do you want his phone number?" Jesse said. He seemed genuinely annoyed, not teasing. "You want me to set you up? I don't think you'd like him either."

I raised my hands from the steering wheel for a second. "Just asking. Anyone would be curious."

He lay back, and his hair fanned against the leather headrest like it had been spread out for a photo. "Sometimes it's better not to meet people."

His eyes were endless and sad clear through. I wasn't prepared for the way he was looking at me, like I shouldn't even bother trying to help because he'd drowned a year ago and he was just staring up from under the water now.

"Jess, are you sure you still like your job?"

He smiled. "I love how you say that, like I could just quit."

"Can't you?" I forced myself to look away, back at the road. "Money's not a problem, is it?"

"No. I hold my publishing. And I've sold songs to other people that you probably don't even know I wrote."

"I've read your Wikipedia page," I told him, and he laughed. I added, "If you're set for life, then quit. If you want."

"Someday when we're talking at the bar, remind me to tell you all the ways in which being on a label is like being in debt to the mob."

So he figured we'd be shooting the shit at the bar one day.

"Maybe they'll drop you," I suggested.

He laughed, and I could hear the thickness in his chest. "I told you, man, I make them too much money."

He went back to drumming on the dashboard, a habit he'd always had. Not that either of us had driven in Toronto—I was pretty sure he'd taken on his bass player because the guy had owned a van—but he'd drummed on tables and desks and his own legs and sometimes mine.

"Where are we going first?" he asked after a mile or two.

"The Mounties," I said. "As a courtesy. I'm not sure they'll tell me anything. Technically, I'm a private citizen and not the next of kin, so they don't owe me anything. But we'll see."

"You need the one cop who goes against the grain," Jesse said. "The rebel who thinks a little more and a little differently. He's too much justice for the law."

"I will drop you by the side of the road," I said. "You're not too sick to hitchhike."

"Is it weird not being a cop anymore?" he asked. "You used to be on the inside."

"I was too much justice for the law," I told him. He snorted. We drove in silence for a bit. A white-tailed deer watched from a roadside ditch, unconcerned, as we flew past at twice her top speed. Did they understand what cars were at all? Or did they think we were strange giant deer?

"I don't know," I said. "It was easier to have… a mandate, if that's the word. You're tax funded. There's this general idea that you have a job to do. As a PI, you have to work with people's curiosity or goodwill or personal interest, which the cops do too. But when you're a PI, it's all you have."

"So, as a PI you're just some guy? Can you arrest people?"

"I can," I said. "So can you. Make a citizen's arrest."

"I thought that was like some Wild West shit we couldn't do anymore." He blew a piece of hair from his face. "Now I'm sad. I could have been arresting people all these years."

"You have to catch them doing something unquestionably illegal," I told him. "It's not enough to think someone's been watering down your drinks."

"Well, damn."

"Exactly. And it's worse for me because, unlike the average citizen, I'm not allowed to call someone a greasy cunt while I'm doing it."

"I think society says you shouldn't be doing that anyway," he said. "Seriously, though, why bother having a licence?"

"Because people shouldn't hire an investigator who doesn't have a licence," I said. "That's just hiring a goon."

He smiled at me like the past several years had never happened. "Nah, you're not a goon."

The mountains appeared around us the way they always did on clear days, like they were an animation instead of reality. First the white-chalk outlines against the blue sky, then a hazy brown fill, and finally the definition of trees and patches of snow. The tallest mountains were still sketches, down the road inside the national park. There were some decent peaks to the south, though, and those were nearly upon us. The turn-off for the Kananaskis Trail was a few miles out, and I could see it if I squinted.

"The detachment is down that road," I said, pointing. "You can look around the parking lot while I'm in with the Mounties."

He nodded. "Yeah, okay. I brought masks."

I raised my brows at him. He shrugged.

"If I don't want people to recognize me, I put on a mask and a ball cap and pretend I'm sick."

"Okay, two things. First, you are sick."

"Yeah, but I'm not mask-level contagious. You'd have to tongue swab me like you were testing for COVID, and even then you might not catch anything."

"Every now and then," I said, "I wonder why you've never been asked to host the JUNOs. And then you speak."

"Me and Anne Murray. She swears like a trucker."

"Second thing. Not a lot of people around here mask up over a cold. This isn't Van or Toronto."

"So I'll look like I'm from out of town. As long I don't look like Jack Lowe, we're golden."

It was strange hearing him talk about Jack Lowe like he was some other person. I'd always thought of Jess and Jack that way, a little, but I wasn't the guy who put on the Jack Lowe persona every night.

"I really don't know, Jess. You were on the cover of *sCene* last week."

He laughed.

"Was it that shot with the insane smokey eye? I looked like I went ten rounds with Mike Tyson. Notice I'm not wearing liner today?"

"Okay, maybe most people don't see past the make-up, but some people are going to make you for Jack Lowe."

"It's not just ditching the eyeliner and the nail polish. Jack is a performance. You'll see."

I slowed for the turn to the Kananaskis Trail, and Jess pointed at the area to our left, an oversized parking lot with a two-storey building, a restaurant, and a gas bar. "What's that?"

"Nakoda property," I told him. "There's a casino and a hotel. It's res land, so I think they can get around some of the tourism fees."

"Can you turn in there? Can we talk to them?"

"I don't think this is the kind of hotel she could have afforded," I said as I made the turn. "But we can swing around the lot and look for her car."

"Maybe she stopped for gas," he said. "Or directions or something. It's a last-chance kind of place, isn't it?"

That was a dramatic way of characterizing the start of a paved all-season highway through resort country, but people did stop there, not knowing how far away the next cup of fancy coffee would be.

"Fine," I said. "You can come in with me, but I'll ask the questions."

"Shit. I need a name. Do you think Jesse is okay?"

"You do not need a name," I told him. "But Jesse is fine. If someone is a big enough fan to know your real name, you're already busted."

"We'll see."

Jess tucked his hair behind his ears and put on a plain black cotton mask, then pulled on a ball cap. It wasn't flashy or ironically hip, just a dark-blue cotton weave that said nothing about anything. It was good, and a little surprising, to see that he wasn't trying to blend in with the westerners by wearing a John Deere cap or whatever Torontonians thought we wore. But he'd travelled a lot, and he'd had years to learn how to keep his head down, so it was possible he knew what he was doing.

"Do I look okay?" he asked.

"You look like some asshole from Van."

Even with the ball cap, I'd have offered to buy him a drink if I'd seen him in one of the bars I never went to.

"People really drive pickup trucks around here," he said offhandedly. "Big ones. I hardly ever see them in Toronto. I'm mostly downtown, though."

The lot was about 80 per cent SUVs, to be fair, but I knew what he meant. In Toronto, every time I'd seen a pickup, I'd had a moment of dizziness when it hit me how far I was from home.

There were no Mitsubishis with flower decals in the parking lot. A few sedans, BMWs, and Audis. Nothing close to Kim's Prosecco-mobile.

"What do hotels go for around here?" Jess asked, as if he'd been pricing out the vehicles around us. Maybe he had. I pulled into a spot beside the convenience store and faced him.

"I thought you'd been to Banff a few times."

"Banff Springs once, and the other time I stayed at the Centre for the Arts."

So with the Calgary show in 2019, the one the year after we'd broken up, and two trips to Banff, that was four times he had been in or through town and not called me. Not that he was obligated. And not that I was counting.

"You can get a room for something like one twenty a night in the shoulder season," I said, "if you're not looking for anything fancy. Shoulder season starts around now. If you want something fancy or it's summer or ski season… I don't know. What does the Banff Springs top out at?"

"A grand I think?" He shrugged. "I wasn't paying, so I don't know for sure."

"Like I said, it's getting to be shoulder season, so there are probably some deals, but there would also be a lot of places that haven't dropped their rates yet."

"That is rich for a student. Okay." He unclipped his seat belt and put his hand on the door handle. "Let's go detect."

It was funny how fast a guy went from "I want to look out for you" to putting on a deerstalker cap and roaming the moors. I shook my head and followed him in.

# Chapter 9

"Oh yes, she was here Thursday! I remember the day because we talked about how it was supposed to rain and it hadn't."

The girl behind the counter was like a person-shaped sunbeam. Her round cheeks were pushed up by a friendly smile, and her eyes were bright behind blue-rimmed glasses. The brown hair in two loose pigtails was blond on top, like it had been painted by the endless summer light.

Jesse was standing a few feet away holding two coffees he'd picked up. Sunbeam hadn't asked who he was, and I hadn't said. She also didn't seem to recognize him.

"Was she staying here?" I asked.

"She asked, but we were full up. I said we could give her a deal later in the month and that, if she wanted. She said she was up from Calgary, right, so I thought maybe she could come back."

Kim's face looked at me from my phone, which was resting on the counter between Sunbeam and me. I swept the phone into my pocket. "What did she say?"

Sunbeam shook her head. "She wanted a room for the one night. That Thursday night. We had a show at the casino, and people stay over instead of driving and that. We were totally booked."

I glanced at Jesse and saw a glint in his eye. Here we were picking up clues like a pair of real detectives. I couldn't decide whether it was more endearing than annoying.

"I hope you find her," Sunbeam said, and I thought about telling her the truth, that I was looking for a girl no one was going to find. But she'd find out soon enough through the grapevine, and telling her now wouldn't improve her day.

"So she only meant to stay for one night," Jess said once we were back in the car. "Like her sister said."

"It sounds that way," I said. "But Kim could have been lying, or she could have changed her mind. We don't actually know."

He said nothing to that, just pulled the tabs off the lids of the coffee and handed mine to me.

"Do I have to be a coffee cop?" I asked him.

"It's decaf. I'm behaving."

"If you were behaving," I pointed out, "you'd be staying in the car."

"Yours is also decaf."

"Fuck you."

He nodded. "Fair."

THE FIRST few miles of the highway ran alongside a ranch of some kind, with horses lazily picking at wild grass and flicking away flies. A few summer foals were in the mix, knobby and awkward and nearly as tall as the mares. Jesse watched them with his head against the window and his eyes half-closed.

By the time we hit the turn-off to Kananaskis Village, he was asleep. In keeping with his doctor's advice, I decided to leave him be. I took it easy on the winding road to the detachment and got out of the car as quietly as possible.

The low brown building, roof peaked for mountain snow, looked more like a house than a police station. There were rules about how everything in the park should look and no exceptions, even for the RCMP. It made for a pretty picture anyhow, with the smaller tree-covered mountains behind it lined up before the taller grey peaks, like they'd been asked to pose for a class photo.

There was one person inside that I could see, a woman in the standard RCMP get-up sitting behind the counter and looking at something on her computer screen.

She would have been a disappointment to any international travellers, in her grey-and-bluc regular uniform. The Mounties generally kept their red serge for special occasions.

She lifted her head as I approached and did not smile, though neither did she look hostile. "Can I help you?"

"I hope so," I said and showed her my PI licence. "I'm Ben Ames. I've been hired to look into the death of Kimberly Moy."

"Oh." She looked appropriately sad and nodded. Her blond hair, put up in tight French braids, did not stir. "Not much to look into. We're calling it non-suspicious."

"Well," I said, "you know how families can be about that kind of news."

"Yes" was all she said, but the look on her face suggested that Lauren had spoken with her already, and it had not gone well.

"No harm in looking into it," I said. "Just to confirm."

A more experienced cop would have been glaring at me by this point, correctly assuming that I was there to investigate my own theory or the client's, and certainly not to confirm what the RCMP had said. But this one was a constable and looked young even for that. It was surprising she'd landed a posting in somewhere as desirable as Kananaskis, not even an hour outside of Calgary in the middle of the mountains, and, hell, an English-only detachment on top of it all. The nearest bilinguals were down the road in Canmore.

"Did Kimberly's suicide note stay with you?" I asked.

"It's in the evidence lock-up," the constable told me. Constable McKay, if the nameplate at the desk was hers.

"You figure you'll be releasing that today? My client would like to have it."

"We'll release it to the next of kin."

"And you'll give the autopsy report then too."

"Hasn't been done yet," she said. Since she didn't seem to mind talking with me about things that were none of my business, it was worth taking a swing at one more.

"Can you tell me something? Why did you put this one down as a suicide?"

She frowned. I shouldn't have started with "Can you tell me something?" That had opened up the question of whether she could or should. I thought she was about to kick me out, but she surprised me. "I know the sister is your client. She told me she hired you. You can ask her what I said, if you haven't already."

"It's tough with the family," I said. "You can't say everything you want. They might not be ready to hear it."

"We have our reasons," she said.

"When you called my client, you described Kimberly as a goth," I said. "I'm not convinced that goths are more suicidal than the average young adult, but she wasn't one. She was—what do they call it—rockabilly. Like a derby girl."

"She wasn't mainstream. That's tough on kids."

I wasn't sure about that either, but I didn't see the point in arguing. "You didn't happen to find her car?"

"No," Constable maybe-McKay said. "She probably left it somewhere safe with her belongings. Suicides will leave things somewhere safe for their families to find. She probably got a lift to the trailhead. There's a lot of traffic on this road."

There was. I'd seen it, even on this Tuesday in September.

"It's lucky the note was found," I said, "left out in the open like that."

"Yeah, the weather's been good," the constable said. "Little windy, but she put rocks on the corners to hold it down."

"We had some wind in Calgary yesterday evening," I said. Making conversation. Nothing to see here. "When was the note found?"

"Last night. A couple went up around midnight. The trail was closed, but they went over the gate. They said they wanted to look at the stars."

"Uh-huh," I said. "People look at the stars in some interesting places."

That got a dry laugh out of her. "Anyways, they came back down and told us, but they never saw the body, so we had to go looking and then retrieve the deceased. Takes a while sometimes."

"I can believe it," I said. "Well, I'd better look around a little and earn my pay. I'll leave my card in case you need to get in touch with me."

She took it, read it, flipped it and found nothing on the back. Double-sided cards had cost nearly twice as much.

"Do you know where you're staying?" she asked.

"Why? Do you have a recommendation?"

"No." She set the card down next to the landline, creating a small museum of things nearly gone forever.

"I can call and update you," I offered. The constable shrugged. I would have taken it badly if I hadn't been so pleased that she didn't care. Having the cops not care what you're doing is a blessed state for a PI, and I didn't want to do anything to ruin it. Carefully, I thanked her and watched my steps as I made my way out the door.

JESS WAS awake when I got outside. He was talking to himself, seemingly. Or talking to a phone. Kent had said once that, with everyone having wireless headphones, it was hard to tell who was crazy and who was on a call. Of course there was no reason it couldn't be both.

I got into the car and discovered that he was on speaker, not earphones. A woman with a familiar voice was saying something about promoting a single while Jess wrinkled most of his face in distaste. It was the woman from his hotel room, I realized. The one who'd seemed to be calling the shots. Gia.

"Gia, you know why he's doing this, and—"

"I do," she cut in briskly, "and I said no. But this isn't going to help with dog piling."

"Dogs gotta pile," Jess sighed. "I thought you were all about me pushing the single."

"In interviews," Gia said. Her frustration was clear, even through the phone's small speaker and however many miles were between us. "Not standing next to him. That's endorsing him, not the single. Endorsing him is short-sighted."

"I could blow him up," Jesse suggested. He was talking directly to the phone like it was on Facetime, though it wasn't. He'd probably realized the sight of him in the mountains, rather than a bed, would not improve the conversation.

"Let Ava blow him up if she feels like it," Gia countered. "MeToo and HerToo are different things."

"Good point," Jess said. "Okay. You handle his people. I'll do some social. I don't know what to do about Mr. Big Mouth Bass Player, though. The guy fucking hates me. If he just didn't like me, I'd get it."

"He's a prick," Gia said, the way you'd say the sky was blue.

"I didn't do myself any favours on this tour."

"You were professional," Gia said. "That's all that's required."

"I'm professional? High praise, Gia."

There was a pause. I hadn't had much exposure to this Gia person, but I was already pretty sure pauses weren't usual from her. She seemed to have an answer for everything, immediately.

"If I don't say anything," she said finally, "you are all right."

From the look on Jesse's face, she might have presented him with a dozen roses and an ode written in his honour. "Check back if you need anything."

"Did you want someone here to do your socials?" Gia asked.

"I should probably do them myself."

"You are probably supposed to be asleep."

The call ended there. No goodbyes. He plugged his phone into my charger and glanced at me. I nodded. My phone was good for a few hours.

"Find anything out?" he asked.

I told him what I'd learned, which was mainly that the RCMP didn't know a lot more than we did and that they were being oddly stubborn about their weak suicide theory.

"She's not goth," was the main takeaway. "Wasn't goth. You were pretty close with derby."

"You and I are the same age," I told him. "Not sure why you think you're a youth-culture guru."

Jess sighed. "So are we going to the trail next, or checking hotels?"

If the RCMP had been investigating, I'd have said they were in a much better position than we were to check hotels. They weren't investigating, though.

"You can call hotels while I look around the trail," I suggested. "Or you can take that nap you have pencilled in."

"I didn't want her to know she woke me. She would have felt bad."

"The Terminator has feelings?" I said.

Jesse threw his empty coffee cup at me. “The Terminator did have feelings.”

“I thought she was your road manager.”

“She does whatever. My management company knows I like her, so they assign her to me a lot. God help her.”

“What was that all about, anyway? MeToo?”

Jess shrugged. “Should we look around this place for Kim’s car?”

“We can do that while you talk,” I said. “Unless you don’t want to tell me.”

“The reason I don’t like ZZGold is that I saw him get grabby with one of the backup singers. I got in there and broke it up, and I told her to let me know if she wants to go public.”

This was normally where I’d have given him hell for not being able to mind his own business or play nice. But in this case, I could see his point.

“Anyway,” Jess said, “he does like money, so he wants me to do promo. Also… it’s a power game.”

“The gay-and-female-friendly world of rap music,” I said. Jess made a face.

“That’s not fair. This is the first time I’ve seen this kind of shit. I will say, anyone who hates gay people enough that they won’t be in a room with me is someone I’m never going to work with, so that screens out some of the assholes.”

I backed the car out and started a slow crawl of Kananaskis Village, which looked at least as much like a military base as a resort centre. Everything was practical and tidy and enclosed, because snow and bears were not things you could keep out with a bylaw and a sign. The roads curved around the few buildings and rose and fell a little where the ground beneath had been too stubborn to move.

"Now my bass player is piling on with some shit about how I'm too stuck-up to talk to my band," Jess went on. "If I were ZZGold, I'd be worried about being seen with me."

I'd slowed to take a closer look at what turned out to be a Beetle, so it was easy enough to pull over and put the car in park. Once we'd stopped, I turned in my seat to face him.

"What are you talking about? Why would this guy say you were stuck-up? Since when was there anybody you wouldn't talk to?"

"Since recently," Jess said. He took a few breaths and shut his eyes. "I can't right now, okay? Can I tell you later?"

"You can tell me never if you don't want to," I said. "It's up to you."

I went back to circling the lot. Jess kept a sleepy eye out for Kim's car until we were back on the main road. Then he grabbed his phone and started typing. I assumed it was the social media he'd promised Gia, judging by the way he was scowling at his phone and how often I saw him delete and start again.

I would have offered to write it for him, but "Go fuck yourselves" was all I could think of, and no doubt Gia would say it was off-brand.

Finally he got something he seemed pleased with, or at least not disgusted by, and he dropped the phone onto his lap.

"What will we be looking for on the trail?" he asked.

"You'll be looking for the second half of your nap," I told him. "I don't know what I'll be looking for. I'm just going to poke around."

He laughed until he coughed. "Remember how we used to come home from parties," he said, "and you'd tell me what was in all their kitchen cupboards and in the closets and under the bed?"

"Are you calling me nosy?"

"I admire how you've turned a hobby into a career."

I flipped him off before turning up the feeder road to the trail. It was a mix of sharp mountain gravel and rutted dirt that required full attention. I did take a second to glance at the yellow metal gate that was swung back into the trees on the right-hand side of the road. That must have been the gate the stargazers had hopped over to access the closed trail at night.

The road led to a few trailheads, and I decided to check out the small parking lots at each since Kim could have parked at one and walked to another. Jess was flagging again and didn't ask what I was doing or whether I'd gotten lost. There wasn't anything worth sccing in any of the parking lots, a truck here and an SUV there, but I doubted he'd have noticed if a grizzly in a hat had strolled by on its hind legs, swinging a cane. I was starting to regret not bringing a pillow and blanket for him.

My car was the only vehicle at the trailhead to the falls. There was room for a few more, maybe six or eight, in two lines leading to a green-roofed outhouse, a trail map, and a bear-proof garbage bin. I slipped out of the car and studied the map. It showed a loop trail, about three kilometers. You could take the longer part of the loop along the river to the falls and the more direct one back to the parking lot, or go the other way and see the falls first, about a kilometer in. Or if you were solely interested in watching the stars by the rushing water, you could take the short route to the falls and back without ever using the loop along the river.

The map suggested taking the river loop first but didn't say why. A sense of drama, maybe. The two-kilometer build-up to the falls, and then the big show and a spray of water to cool you off before you took the last leg back to the lot.

I checked the trail's colour against the legend and saw it was considered intermediate, whatever that meant. Not the easiest or the hardest, I figured, being the Sherlock Holmes that I was. The map did note an elevation gain of a couple hundred feet, peaking at the falls.

I looked back at the car. Jesse seemed to be asleep again. I figured I could do the short route to the falls and back in about an hour, giving myself time to look around on the way and to take a good look at the scene of the crime. Jess was a grown-up, and he should be fine in a locked car in a nearly empty park in the middle of a sunny day. He had a charged cell phone. We were maybe three hundred metres from the main road.

The car keys were in my hand. I didn't have a spare set to leave. But I could always knock to be let in. I went to the passenger side and opened the door. He didn't even move. I put the keys on his lap, next to his phone. I pulled a strand of hair back from his face and tucked it behind his ear. Back in the day, I'd have kissed the top of his head or maybe his face, along the cheekbone.

"I'll be back in an hour," I whispered, and locked the door.

# CHAPTER 10

IF I'D been looking for chipmunks or irritated squirrels, I'd have considered the hike a success. The former tore across the path at the sound of my footfalls while the latter chittered at me from the trees. There must have been birds too, but they were keeping a low profile, and suggestions of them were all I saw. A shadow moving through the green or a branch bouncing back from a quickly lifted weight.

The ground was damper than in the parking lot or the feeder road. The trees would have caught the moisture from the river and the falls, keeping the earth from drying out as quickly as the exposed dirt outside the woods. Even the air was humid, particularly for the mountains.

I couldn't hear the falls at first, but I caught the roar after a few minutes.

From Kim's point of view, the trail would have been a little tough, maybe, especially if she'd taken the short route to the falls. From her posts, she hadn't seemed like a sporty type or a gym rat. But the sound of the falls made it seem like they were around the next corner, and the trees lining the trail made it impossible to see how far away they really were, so the psychology was right to keep people moving along.

Had someone convinced her to walk down this path? Just a little farther and we'll be at the falls?

Or had someone carried her, unconscious or dead? She'd been a solidly built girl, and the trail was full of roots and rocks that could trip you up if you dragged your feet under the weight. And wouldn't someone have seen that on a short and not-too-tough trail to a waterfall? It had to be popular with weekend hikers.

Hell, with how many people must have been on the trail last weekend, how had her note gone unseen? Had she died on Monday? But if she'd been alive on Friday, wouldn't she have gone home to babysit, or at least called Lauren to cancel?

It wasn't making sense, and I made a note to myself to talk to the park rangers. Maybe the trail had been closed on the weekend for a bear sighting or testy elk. There had to be an explanation.

About twenty minutes of taking it slow brought me to the falls. There was a small guard rail between the trail and the cliff that oversaw them, enough to stop a toddler or a toy dog. For the rest of the world, it was a reminder that moving any closer would be a bad idea. This was reinforced by a sign next to the rail that showed a cartoon person falling off a cliff and announced danger in three languages.

It wasn't just that nothing was stopping you from pitching over the edge of the cliff. It was the soil, slick and silty. Any grit that might have come from pine needles or little rocks had been washed away by the constant spray from the falls. It would be easy to put a foot wrong and have it slide out from under you. If you fell on that wet, smooth surface, you could go right over before you even had time to reach for a branch that might save you.

Despite how obvious the danger was, people were people, and so of course there were a few footprints in the damp soil beyond the rail. All from the same pair of shoes, it looked like. I took out my phone and got a few shots of the tread, gone mushy at the edges from the water but still clear enough to match to a shoe. No guarantee the prints weren't from a cop or even one of the stargazers who'd found the note, but maybe I could be a storybook detective for once and solve something with an elegant clue.

I moved to the edge of the guard rail and looked down at the falls and the surroundings. No obvious trail led to the foot of the waterfall, though one might have been hidden by the trees. I could check the maps later. The river past the falls was fast and shallow, with grey rocks sticking up from the water and little white boils where other rocks hadn't quite hit the surface. It didn't seem like the kind of place someone would bring a canoe. I couldn't be sure what would happen to a body at the base of the falls, but it didn't seem impossible that the body might get caught on some rocks and stay in place, waves washing over and over it like a GIF of someone splashing water on their face.

There was no reason to think anyone had seen anything from below.

It was a hell of a spot to murder someone, a place where you were unlikely to be heard or seen. Interrupted, maybe, if you went at the wrong time. I wondered whether the killer had known this place and known when to go there. Did he—or she—come out here most weekends? Did they live in Canmore or one of the hamlets sprinkled between Calgary and Banff?

Had they known Kim before this weekend, maybe come out here with her? Or had she met the wrong person at a gas station or on a trail? Maybe she'd picked up the wrong guy in a Canmore bar.

Spray covered my face and dripped from where it gathered on the trees. Jess would have liked it. It was nature's humidifier.

I took a few more photos for reference, then made my way back to my car.

JESS WAS still asleep when I got to the parking lot. I didn't like the idea of waking him, so I spent some time taking shots of tire tracks. They weren't nearly as good as the footprint, the ground was packed and much drier in the lot, but I got a few that were clear enough to use. Not that it would prove much if I showed someone had been here in the past few weeks, because so had a few thousand Calgarians. It would be icing if I found a suspect I liked and could show their vehicle had been at the scene of the crime.

Once I'd taken every picture worth taking, I thought about what I needed to know and who might be able to tell me.

Lunes might know more than I did about what you could learn from an autopsy on someone who had fallen down a waterfall. She'd be asleep, though.

Lauren would know when her parents would arrive, taking her place as next of kin. She might also know what their attitudes would be about this supposed suicide, though I'd learned sudden deaths could make people unpredictable. None of that was urgent, and I didn't want to bother her if I didn't need to.

If I could figure out when Kim had been killed, I could ask whether anyone from her social circle had been out of town at the time. But I didn't know enough for that to be productive now.

That left one person who might know something useful and welcome a call from me. I checked my phone, saw a few bars, and made the call.

"Why it's high-roller Ben Ames, vacationing in the Rockies with celebrities," Kent said, his tone sparkling with wonder.

"It's a life you can only imagine," I told him. "Thank you for looking after Frank."

"He eats pizza, right?"

"One of you should have dog food for dinner. You can decide who gets what."

"You and your boyfriend shacking up in Canmore?"

"I do not have a boyfriend. I may wind up in Canmore for a few days. Do you know anything more since this morning? An estimate on how long she's been dead would be particularly helpful. Or I'd take the names of the people who found the suicide note."

"No word on the autopsy," Kent said. "I think I'm frozen out on that one. I went on a few dates with one of the ME's assistants last year. Didn't end well. I'll be honest—it didn't start well. I'd say—"

"How many times," I interrupted, "did I tell you never to—"

"Dip my pen in the company ink?" he interrupted back.

"But especially the ME's office," I said. "For exactly this reason."

"Buddy, this is what happens when you leave me unsupervised. You quit, and the new guy never says a word about my sexual adventures."

"I envy the new guy," I told him. "What else do you have? Name of the ranger on duty last night? And seriously, the people who found the note. I have a footprint, and I want to find a match."

"Like Prince Charming," Kent said, "in a fairy tale about withholding evidence."

"Per the Mounties, this was not a crime. And they know I'm running around out here. They didn't even ask me not to."

He didn't have to say things would get tricky when or if I did manage to convince them there'd been a crime. Cops liked a good evidence chain, where they knew when and how something had been collected and every place it had been since.

"The couple who found the note are summer workers at a boat-rental place on Upper Lake," Kent said. "I don't have their names, but you could hire a PI or something to find that out."

"Maybe I'll do that."

"You could put your assistant on it."

I looked at the car as if speaking of the devil would wake him. Jess was still out.

"Did you give him your number?" I asked. "Or did he have Luna call you and ask you to look after Frank?"

"We exchanged numbers," Kent said. "Don't be jealous, Ben. He's cute, but he's more your type than mine."

"You're both adorable," I said. "Don't get attached. In a week or two he'll be back in Toronto."

"Hmm. We'll see."

I took the phone away from my ear and counted down from five. Do not ask him why he said that. Do not ask him what he and Jess talked about when I was in the other room calling Lauren. Do not ask why they exchanged numbers.

"Do you know," I asked him, "whether anyone has found Kim's car?"

"Not that I know of," he said. "But we're not looking for it anymore. Maybe the Mounties still are, but I doubt it."

"I'll keep looking."

"I'll see what else I can turn up," Kent said. "Give your assistant my regards."

I'D WOKEN Jess with a rap to the passenger window. Since then, he'd been splitting his bleary attention between his phone and the scenery as we headed for Upper Lake. He hadn't even asked where we were going, though he had asked about whether I'd found anything interesting on the trail. I'd shown him my footprint photo, and he'd been suitably, if quietly, impressed.

"Go back to sleep," I suggested.

"I'm useless," he said. It was tough to hear him since he was resting his head against the window and his voice was low. "You were on that trail alone, and I was asleep. I didn't come along to sleep the whole time."

"You're sick, babe."

The endearment slipped out before I could catch it. If Jesse noticed, he gave no sign.

"Do you need a doctor?" I asked. "We can go back to the city anytime. Or Canmore."

"No," he said. "I'm just tired. It's gorgeous out here, by the way. Why does no one ever come here?"

Oh, the people of Toronto. I laughed.

"Do you mean why have you only ever heard about Banff and maybe Jasper?"

"Kept meaning to get to Marmot Basin, but there was always a tour coming up, and the tour insurance forbids 'high-risk activities.' I haven't been snowboarding in years."

"Seriously?" I glanced at him, and he nodded. "You have a list of shit you can't do when you have a tour coming up?"

"Or while I'm on tour. Yeah. What were you saying before about glamour?"

"Jesus. We both have terrible jobs."

"Yeah."

"Yours pays considerably better."

"What's that Elvis Costello line?" he said. "'Things haven't really changed that much, and one of us is still getting paid too much.' I feel bad about it, if it helps. I don't think it's fair."

"I don't even know where to start with things that aren't fair," I said. "But if it helps you, I don't think I would do what you do for any amount of money. I mean, if anyone wanted to hear me sing. Which no one does."

He gave my arm a gentle shove. "You're not that bad."

He turned on the radio, which I'd turned off to let him sleep. They were playing Fleetwood Mac, and Jess drummed the dashboard for a few bars, then started to sing. His voice was as strong as ever, and I shivered from hearing it so close instead of through a speaker. I'd missed that.

"I don't know how the hell you can sing like that with pneumonia, but I bet it fucks up your voice."

He shrugged but didn't argue. Upper Lake was about a kilometer ahead, according to the sign we'd just passed.

"Imaginatively named," he commented.

"You see that?" I asked, pointing at a nearby peak. "That is Mount Indefatigable. Does that suit you better?"

He grinned. "Shut up. It is not."

"It is," I assured him. "Half of what you see around here was named after boats in the Battle of Jutland. World War I, Brits and Germans off the coast of Denmark."

"That," he said with plain delight, "is so weird! How did the *Indefatigable* do?"

"Blew up," I said. "Never get cocky when you name a boat."

He had a good laugh at that and finished it off with, "Oh man, I have missed you."

Thank God we hit the turn-off before I could do something stupid, like asking him whose fault that was or telling him I'd missed him too.

WHEN I'D told Jess that a PI licence didn't give me many advantages, it had been true but not the whole story. I could see him figuring that out as I quickly showed my ID to a couple of Australian summer workers at the boathouse—they blurted out their colleagues' names without hesitation. People did not have to talk to private investigators, but for some reason, a lot of them thought they did. I was bound by law not to pretend to be a cop, but there was no law saying I had to educate them on how not a cop I was.

Jess hung around behind my shoulder, staring at the lake. I didn't blame him. It was a painting of the peaks around it, nearly perfect except for a ripple here or there. The sky was a deeper blue in the water's reflection, but the clouds looked lighter somehow. Jess seemed caught by it, barely aware that a conversation was happening next to him.

I don't know who or what the Aussies thought he was. They didn't ask.

I thought I might leave him behind when I went looking for the stargazers, but he stayed at my heels, head down and cap in place. They were at the docks, the other workers had said, cleaning out some canoes that were going into storage for winter.

I found an aggressively healthy-looking couple in brown cargo shorts and white tank tops, with deep tans they'd regret later in life. The girl was a sandy blond, and her boyfriend had darker hair, but aside from that, they could have been siblings.

"Chloe McDonald and Thomas Brown?" I asked, like a cop would. They looked at each other and got up from the canoe they'd been crouching in. Thomas stepped forward and offered an uneasy smile.

"That's us," he said. In the corner of my eye, I saw Jesse blink and realized he'd been paying attention well enough to note that everyone around us seemed Australian. If he'd spent more time in Banff, he wouldn't have been surprised. Half of Australia drifted through the Rockies every summer.

"I'm Ben Ames," I said, and flashed my licence. "I'm investigating the death of Kimberly Moy. I understand you found a suicide note last night?"

"We already told the police," Chloe said. She moved forward to stand beside Thomas.

"I just have a few questions."

Thomas nodded, but Chloe looked unsure. Her eyes flicked to Jess, and she frowned a little, like she was trying to figure out where she'd seen him before.

"I understand you found the note around midnight. Is that right?"

Thomas kicked at the ground with a brown hiking boot, a kind of aw-shucks gesture. "I know we weren't supposed to be there."

"Did you go past the guard rail at the top of the falls?"

"Yeah, Tom did," Chloe said. "I told him it was stupid. Why?"

She looked from me to Jess and back, her blond ponytail swinging. Jess kept very still, like that would turn him invisible. I'd told him he should stay in the car.

"Are those the shoes you wore last night?" I asked, directing the question to Thomas. They were both wearing hiking boots, but hers were too small to be a match.

"Yeah," Thomas said. "Is there a problem? It's a tragedy and all that, yeah? But I thought that woman had killed herself."

"I'd like to be sure there wasn't anyone with her."

I pulled out my phone and showed him the photo I'd taken at the falls. "May I see the tread on your boots?"

Chloe was shifting her weight from one foot to the other. It was the sort of thing that people mistook for guilt, that kind of tension and fidgeting. It could be and sometimes was, but more often it was regular nerves. People didn't like being close to death. They didn't like cops a lot of the time. And some didn't like being interrogated by a stranger.

Thomas, on the other hand, seemed eager to atone for his sin of sneaking onto the trail after dark. He toed off a boot and handed it to me. I turned it over and compared it to the photo.

Dammit.

I took a photo of Thomas's boot and returned it to him. "Thank you. That's a match."

"What does that mean?" Chloe asked.

"It means he made that print," I said. "If it hadn't matched his boot, I'd be wondering who else had been there last night."

"We only went because we're leaving at the end of the week," Thomas said.

"Thought it would be special," Chloe said, her mouth twisting down on the last word.

"Bad luck. Is there anything else you can tell me? Were you able to drive into the parking lot and jump the barrier there, or was the feeder road closed too?"

That was pushing it, and I saw suspicion in Chloe's eyes again. Why didn't I know that already? Wouldn't the ranger have told me if I really was a cop?

Chloe, Chloe. I never said I was a cop.

"We drove in," Thomas said.

"Did you see any other vehicles on the road?"

He and Chloe shook their heads.

"But you know what's odd?" Thomas said. "What you said about us jumping the barrier—we didn't have to. It was hanging open. We just walked in."

"It was strange," Chloe agreed, seeming relieved.

"If you think of anything else, please give me a call."

I handed my card to Thomas. Chloe read it before he pocketed it and narrowed her eyes. I pretended not to notice and told them to have a good day.

"THAT WAS a waste of time," Jess said once we were back in the car. "Unless that guy is the murderer and also the best actor I've ever seen."

"Sometimes you need to rule things out. Do any of these prints seem different?"

I showed Jess the photo again, and he gave it a good look before handing my phone back.

"It's all the one guy," he said.

"Right. But we know someone else was there Monday night."

He cocked his head.

"Well… Chloe was. But she stayed behind the guard rail."

"Someone didn't," I said. "If you jumped off that cliff, you'd have to go past the guard rail to do it. If Kim killed herself, there should be a set of size six footprints by the edge of the cliff."

Jess stared at me. "And if someone pushed her…."

"There should be two sets," I said. "Or if someone threw her over, there should be one. Or none, because if someone killed her, they could have wiped out the footprints before they left. The only thing that makes sense here is if someone carried her there or went up there with her, pushed or threw her over the falls and wiped out their prints. Then the lovebirds came along and Thomas went right up to the edge, leaving his prints. That's why his prints are the only ones still there."

Jess nodded. "That's good. That shows she didn't go up there alone and jump. She couldn't go up there, jump, and erase her own footprints. Or could she? Could she have knelt right by the edge?"

"Too slippery," I said. "If you knelt right at the edge and tried to erase your prints from there… first, why would she do that? But say she did. She would have fallen before she got done. Thomas is lucky he didn't fall when he went past the barrier. Someone else was up there with Kim, backed away, and erased their prints from a safe spot."

"You can tell the Mounties that, right? And they'll reopen the case, or whatever they do?"

"They should," I said. "But they can argue it. They could say, I don't know, that she jumped on Friday or Saturday. Her prints were washed away in the rain."

"Why couldn't it have been Friday or Saturday?" Jess said. "Will the autopsy show that?"

"I don't know," I said. "Lunes might know. She might even know someone at the ME's office. But that note. I know I only saw a photo of it, but I didn't see the kind of dirt or water stains you'd expect. Running ink. I don't think that note sat there for the whole weekend."

Jess shut his eyes, not like he was tired but like he needed to look at something drawn on the insides of the lids.

"So, if you believe the note was left Monday night, you also have to assume someone killed her. Because otherwise there would be more prints past the guard rail. If you think the note could have been left earlier, the lack of prints doesn't mean anything."

"That sums it up," I admitted. "It's not enough to take to the RCMP."

"It's no 'if the glove doesn't fit, you must acquit,'" Jess agreed.

"We need to find out what happened when," I said. "And we could use a suspect. Which might be easier if we can find her car. But we have to talk to the rangers first."

"Why's that?" Jess asked.

"Because of Ben's Law of Coincidence."

"You have a Law of Coincidence?"

"I do."

"And it is?"

"When something that never normally happens did happen on the same night and in the same place as a crime was committed… it isn't one."

# CHAPTER 11

JESS GOT out his phone and went to work finding the ranger who'd checked and locked the trail barrier the night before while I took us back the way we'd come. There were no hotels in the area we hadn't already seen, and I doubted Kim had thrown a tent into her car before heading west, so we needed to leave the park and start looking at the surrounding towns.

On the way, we passed Mounts Indefatigable and Invincible. That ship, I told Jess, had gone down like a rock after being hit by three German torpedoes. He laughed, then explained to someone on the phone that he wasn't laughing at her.

"So what time are the trails closed at night?" He was talking to someone at the visitor centre, getting whatever he could from the front desk while they sorted out who, exactly, had blocked the trail on Monday night. "Is it always 8:00 p.m.?"

I gave a thumbs up to that. It always helped to know what was usual, what people expected. Jess gave me his unguarded little-kid grin. The guy had music awards from a half-dozen countries, but apparently being good at assistant detecting made his day.

"And that's a change since Labour Day," he said. "How is the gate locked?"

Labour Day had been a week ago. Did the average visitor know that the trail closure times had changed? Did that matter?

A huge antlered beast cut across the road about a hundred yards ahead. Jess watched with delight and gave me a questioning glance once it had vanished into the trees.

"Elk," I said softly.

He mouthed, "Wow," then said to the phone, "What number can I reach him at?" I pointed at a notepad and pen tucked over the passenger side visor, but Jess shook his head. "No, I don't. Can you do that? That's amazing. Thank you."

I was starting to see why Jess had done so well with Kim's friends. Put simply, and I'd known this about him from the start, he was fearless. A lot of people would get nervous and stiff as soon as they had to ask questions of strangers. They tensed up in expectation of being told to go to hell. Jess obviously didn't figure being told off would kill him, so he could relax and talk to everyone as if they were his new best friend.

"Yeah, hi," he said. "Did Alex tell you what I was looking for? Okay, great."

Now he reached for the notepad. He flipped it open with one hand and balanced it against his knee as he wrote.

"Not trying to question you, but did you check the time, or do you normally—yeah, exactly. Yep. Okay, and do you know whether anyone checked the gate after that?"

I took the Texas gate at the head of the park as easy as I could, but the bump still knocked Jess's pen from the page to his jeans and earned me a quick glare. It didn't help that he probably didn't know what a Texas gate was or that you couldn't help taking some bumps when you drove over one.

"And how are the gates locked?" he asked as he got the pen and pad back into place. "Yeah, let's say both."

Traffic was still light on the Trans-Canada. I was able to take the interchange easy and still slip onto the main highway without much trouble. Jesse was given no further reason to stink-eye me.

Jess thanked the person he'd been interrogating, turned off his phone, and tossed it into the glove compartment. "I don't need to see Twitter right now."

"No one does," I agreed. "What did you find out?"

"From Victoria Day to Labour Day, any trails that are open are open until dusk," he said. "After that, they're closed at 8:00 p.m. When it snows, some trails get closed for the winter." He looked at his notes. "The gate on Quartz Falls trail was closed at 8:05 last night. The ranger writes down the time after each gate he closes, so he's sure of that. He says some of the gates have a hasp that can take a padlock, but that one doesn't, so they wrap a chain around it. The rangers didn't see that the chain was cut until after Chloe and Thomas reported the suicide note."

"That's a lot of trouble to go to," I said, "when you can hop over the gate."

"Yeah, and the ranger said the chain was pretty thick," Jess said. "So you'd either have to be the kind of person who goes everywhere with bolt cutters, or you'd have to know the chain was there and be planning to cut it."

"Are you getting the sense this person was a local?" I asked. "I mean, someone who works around here, at least. I could buy a weekend visitor knowing the trail would be closed after 8:00 p.m. or happening to have bolt cutters, but this person did everything right. Like they knew what to expect."

"Does that also violate your Law of Coincidence?"

"It's more like the law of no one being that lucky."

"So you think Kim came out here and happened to meet the wrong guy?" Jess said. "Something like that? Doesn't even matter why she was here?"

It didn't sit right, but it was how things were looking so far.

Jess pointed at a road sign to our left. "What's Exshaw?"

"Company town, basically," I said. I didn't bother to point out the cement plant, also to our left, because there was no missing it. "I don't think they have hotels."

"Okay. What about… oh my God. Is there really a place called Dead Man's Flats?"

"Barely," I told him. "And I heard they changed the name in the eighties to rope in tourists, so don't get too excited about it."

"Then they'd have hotels."

I steered for the exit. Jess was rooting through the glove box for his phone, probably so he could find out whether I was lying about how the town had been named. I wasn't.

The main street was as I remembered it from my last visit, when I'd needed a washroom and hadn't wanted to wait for Canmore. It was three blocks long and featured a gas station, two restaurants, and three hotels. It was not precious like Banff or Canmore. It was also a lot less expensive, and one of the restaurants, a Brit-style curry joint, wasn't bad.

I pulled in at the gas station, thinking I'd fill up the car and show Kim's photo to the attendant. Jess got out as soon as we stopped, and I figured he'd be on my heels, but instead he wandered off, still looking at his phone. Needed a private talk with Gia, I supposed.

I topped up the fuel and wiper fluid and washed the windows before heading inside. I was the only customer, and the spiky-haired kid behind the counter was taking advantage of the quiet to watch something on his phone. He glanced up when I came in, but not long enough to actually meet my eyes.

I picked up a few snacks and some iced tea, since I hadn't had breakfast and since people who worked in shops tended to be more forthcoming when you bought something from them. Quid pro quo.

The kid finally looked me in the eye when I put an armload of food on the counter. His eyes were red. Had he been crying over the tragedy of youth suicide in general? Allergic to some fall mountain flower? Astronomically high? Or had he, maybe, known Kim?

"Hey," he said. He didn't sound like he'd been crying. "That everything for you?"

I told him about the gas on pump four, then set my phone next to the card reader, with a picture of Kim on the screen. "I'm also looking for anyone who saw or spoke to this woman over the past few days."

He leaned in for a better look at the photo. "Oh," he said. "Oh shit, man."

"You've seen her?"

"Are you with the cops or something? Is this about that suicide thing last night?"

"I'm a private investigator," I told him. "Do you recognize the woman in this photo?"

"Yeah, totally," he said. "She came in here last Thursday. We got the fuel delivery on Thursday, and she had to wait for me to get done with the guy."

I nodded. "What time did you get the fuel delivery?"

"It's usually around ten."

So between this and the girl at the convenience store, I had to fill in about four and a half more days. "Did anyone come into the store with her?"

"I didn't see her with anyone," he said. "Do you think someone, like, did something to her?"

"Her family wants to know."

"Oh yeah, man, I get that," he said. "She seemed pretty normal. Like, she didn't seem sad."

As he spoke, an outdoors type in a short puff jacket and low-rise hikers came into the store. She headed directly to the coolers at the back and didn't seem interested in anything beyond finding her brand of iced coffee.

"Did you see her on Friday? And did you work the weekend shift?" I asked. The attendant moved his head, a cross between a shake and a shrug.

"Didn't see her Friday. There was another guy on the weekend, though. I can ask him."

"I'd appreciate that," I told him. I had more questions, like what she'd bought and how she'd paid and whether he'd seen her car, but all of that amounted to a fishing expedition, and he had a customer to look after. I could come back and throw my line in later.

I left the store to find Jess sitting on the hood of my car looking extraordinarily pleased with himself.

"Get off my car, punk," I said. He hopped off and came to me with his phone held out. He was showing me a picture of a light purple Mitsubishi Mirage.

"Well, fuck me," I said. When he opened his mouth, I held up a hand. "Where did you take that picture?"

He led me up the block to the Heart Creek Hotel, a small L-shaped two-storey building with motel-type units along the ground floor and a lobby and pub at one end. Hanging flower baskets outside the lobby and a few wide planters around the lot suggested that someone was trying to elevate the place.

Parked in front of one of the ground-floor units was the Mitsubishi, complete with flower decal. Jess tilted his phone toward me, and I saw he'd photographed the licence plate too. It was a match.

I took a picture with my own phone and sent it to Kent, letting him know he could call off his personal hunt for the car. I did not mention that Jess had been the one to find it.

"So," Jess said, "what now? Do we talk to the desk clerk?"

I handed him the bag from the store, along with my car keys. "You go back and move my car away from the pumps before some guy in a semi moves it for me. There's food if you're hungry."

He looked into the bag, then back at me. "Have you eaten anything?"

"I'll live," I told him.

He scowled and handed me a banana. "Nothing is going to change in the time it takes you to eat this."

He actually stood there and watched while I ate the banana. I half expected him to give me a pat on the head once I was done, but instead he tossed one of the iced teas at me and headed back toward the gas station.

The lobby was brighter and busier than I'd expected, with doors leading off to something called the "business centre" and a pool and hot tub room. Arches opened to the rooms on one side and the pub on the other. Two people stood behind the front desk, a man and woman not much older than I was. They bickered about who had forgotten to put the towels in the wash and didn't notice me until I was a few steps from the desk.

The woman slapped the back of her hand against the man's arm, and he stumbled forward. "I am very sorry about that. Can I help you?"

He had dark skin and an accent I couldn't place, which said nothing other than that I remained bad with accents. The impression he gave was of tidiness—he was small, smaller than the broad-shouldered woman, and his polo shirt and khakis looked as if they'd been steamed. Even the way he moved was precise and neat.

I laid my licence on the desk. "I don't know whether you've heard, but a young woman was found at the base of Quartz Falls last night."

The man and woman glanced at each other. If they'd heard about it, they weren't going to say.

"Her family asked me to look into what happened," I said. "I think she may have been staying at this hotel."

They both looked like someone had kicked them in the worst possible spots. A death was rarely good for business. The man recovered faster and put his hands on the keyboard and mouse of his computer. "Certainly, we can check that for you."

"Her name was Kimberly Moy," I said. "M-O-Y."

"Here it is," he said. "She stayed… Thursday night to Monday night."

"Do you have a photo?" the woman asked. I showed her Kim's picture, and she nodded. "Yes, she had a bird on her arm. Not a real bird. A tattoo."

"Was she staying alone?"

The man checked the computer. "It says one guest."

I put my licence away and regarded the probable couple before me. The story of a girl who stayed with them for a few days and killed herself on a mountain in another park was a sad and unappealing one, but the stain of it would scrub off their hotel's reputation soon enough. The story of a girl who stayed there and wound up murdered, though, that could stay with a place, especially in resort country where people expected untroubled relaxation for their dollars.

I felt bad for the hoteliers, but I often felt bad for people, and it was funny how rarely it made any difference.

"I need to talk to your staff about what they might have seen or heard over the past few days. I also need to see Kim's room."

"You say you are working for her family," the woman said.

"If you like, I can have Kimberly's sister give you a call. She's the one who hired me."

"No, no, that will not be necessary," the woman said. She seemed horrified. My suggestion that she bother a grieving woman may have been the reason. She added, "You can speak to our staff, but they are not all here now. They work shifts."

"I can talk to whoever's here now and come back later to talk to the rest."

"I can show you the room," the man said. "Since our guest… will not be returning."

He took a card from a machine next to the computer, then came around from the back of the desk. I offered him a hand to shake. "I'm Ben Ames, by the way."

"I'm Dan Diallo," he said as he accepted the handshake. "This is my wife, Marie."

"Good to meet you," I said. Marie nodded and smiled. I thought that was pretty gracious of her, since it was objectively not good for them to meet me.

Dan led me outside, and I realized the interior access was only for rooms on the second floor. Like the pool and hot tub room, the second floor had probably been added on long after the place was built.

I caught a glimpse of dark purple at the end of the lot. Jesse's T-shirt, disappearing around the side of the building. Whatever he'd been doing, it looked like he'd seen us coming and decided to make himself scarce. Dan didn't notice.

Dan stopped outside the room closest to Kim's car and used the key card on the door.

I had a moment of nervousness, the way I always did when I was getting close to a serious crime. I started to feel like something would grab my ankle when I walked by a bed, or skitter past me on the ceiling like a horror-film monster.

The door swung open on a perfectly normal motel room. There were two beds, each barely a double, against the north wall, and a doorless closet against the south wall next to the door. The back wall of the room had a door half-open to the washroom, a narrow table with two chairs, and a jumble of appliances the hotel's brochures would have called a kitchenette.

Before I saw any of Kimberly's things, I caught her scent.

The room was in order, more or less. It hadn't been ransacked unless it was by the tidiest ransacker in the world. The bed was made. I turned to Dan, who was in the doorway shifting back and forth on his feet like he needed the bathroom.

"How many days did she book?"

"One to start, but she was renewing," he said, and pointed to a card on the nightstand. I picked it up.

It was a cardboard slip, about the size of a postcard, with a place to write in the room number and boxes to check for maid service, extra towels, and "stay one more night."

"They check the box," Dan said. He took one step into the room cautiously, like he also thought there might be a monster under the bed. I guess neither of us knew there wasn't. "They put the card in the mailbox. If there is no other reservation, they can stay."

I looked around. "What mailbox?"

"Outside the office."

I'd look for it later. While I was at the nightstand, I sorted through the rest of what was on it. A card with the hotel's Wi-Fi password and instructions for using the Bluetooth printer in the business centre. A phone charger with no phone attached. A laptop charger with no laptop attached. Both had been plugged into the socket behind the nightstand. The lamp had been unplugged to make room.

"When someone stays multiple days," I said, "does the maid change the sheets?"

"Only if the guest asks," Dan told me. He was still one step in from the door and showed no interest in changing that. He pointed in the direction of the kitchenette, and I saw a card with a picture of a tree on it that said eco-something or other.

I pulled back the bedcovers and gave the sheets a good look. Dan turned on the overhead light, which helped. The room was a little dark even in the midday sun and with the door open.

There was nothing odd in the bed. No blood or body hair or rips in the linen. Nothing suggested she hadn't been alone. There were a few long black hairs with dark brown roots, a good match for Kim's newest social media pics.

The garbage can between the bed and the kitchenette had been emptied, of course. There was nothing in the fridge. A small chair held a sagging overnight bag, black leather, or probably vinyl, and covered in big-eyed cartoon cats. It had been left open and held a black poodle skirt and black-and-white striped henley, both very much Kim's style. A pair of socks and those folding shoes that women brought to bars. A Hellblazer T-shirt and grey fleece shorts that were worn from washing and looked like something she'd have worn to bed. Panties, two pair. No bra. No gum wrappers or pens or receipts or any of the little things that would suggest she was using this bag as her purse, so I had to assume a purse was around somewhere.

Maybe there were more clothes in her car, but I thought there weren't. Booked for one night. One outfit in the bag. Everything said she'd planned to be back in Calgary by Friday night.

I gave the clothes a once-over and saw no tears or stains. They smelled freshly washed.

There were a few things by the sink that looked like Kim's. Make-up. A hairbrush with the kind of hairs I'd found in the bed next to a half-empty tube of gel.

Toothbrush and toothpaste. The make-up was like the stuff I'd found in her room, mostly marked down and with the post-apocalyptic branding that seemed popular these days. Toxic bloodbath lipstick or whatever the hell.

A rumpled towel was lying in a heap by the sink, and a slightly used bar of soap sat in the soap dish. No bath towels had been used. The hotel-supplied shampoo and conditioner and lotion were lined up on the counter, untouched. They might have been used and replaced.

Now that I was done looking for whatever there was to see, I gave the room a good search for what there wasn't. Car keys. Hotel room card. Purse. Laptop. Phone. I went through every drawer and even popped open the microwave. Nothing. Nothing. I would have loved to see the room before the maid had cleaned it. As long as I was wishing myself back in time, I wished I could have been there when Kim showed up on Thursday, to ask her why she'd left Calgary and escort her safely home.

They say you always find something in the last place you look, and generally I'd call that a motto for quitters who find one thing and stop looking. In this case, though, it was the last place I looked that turned up the prize. I half closed the door to see what was behind it and found a folded piece of paper below the coat hook, where it might have fallen from a pocket. Dan couldn't see me, so I carefully picked it up and slid it into my jacket. Plenty of time to look at it later.

"I'd like to speak to the housekeeper who's been cleaning this room," I told Dan. He nodded.

"She is working today. Her shift begins at four."

"I'll stop by," I told him. "Thanks."

I followed him out of the room and watched him lock it behind us. He had a pensive look.

"Do you have a question?" I asked.

"Yes." He pressed his lips together and breathed in hard through his nose. "We heard about the young woman at the falls on the radio. They did not say her name. We thought it might have been our guest, but we were not certain, so… she is passed on, you say."

"Yeah, the cops say it too," I said. "She's been identified."

"This room, then…."

Oh. I could see his problem.

"I don't know what to tell you," I said. "The police are calling her death a suicide. Legally, I think you can rent the room. Her things—I can take them or you can keep them for her family. I don't think you have to do that either, but maybe you'd want to."

"Of course," he said quickly. "Of course. But you are investigating."

"I am. Depending on what I find out, the cops may show up here and want to see that room. You don't have to keep it empty and wait to see what happens. On the other hand, there could be DNA or even fingerprints in there that I can't find but the police could. If I find out her death wasn't a suicide, maybe what's in that room will matter. They might want her car too. I honestly don't know. It's your decision."

Dan didn't look thrilled by that, but he squared his shoulders and shook my hand again. "I will discuss it with Marie. We will see you later."

# CHAPTER 12

I STAYED by Kim's room, next to her car, on the theory that Jesse was watching from somewhere and would show up as soon as Dan was back in the office. He did not disappoint.

"So this is what it's like to have a stalker," I said.

"Ah, no," he said. "It's not. Did you find anything?"

"Maybe. I'll tell you later."

I told him about everything except the note while we circled Kim's car and looked in the windows. I tried the doors, but no luck there. Of course I could break in and claim she'd left a door open, but I'd leave that option until I was really stuck for something to do.

"Sometimes people put things under the seats," Jess said as he halfway climbed onto the car's hood and peered through the windshield. "Damn. I can't see anything."

"Might be nothing to see," I told him. "I'd bet her purse and phone and laptop are all in the same place, and this isn't it."

He slid off the hood and leaned against the car. "When do you think she died?"

"I don't know," I said. "She didn't show up for her babysitting gig. She had one set of clothes in the room, unworn. Like she checked in and never came back."

"You think it was Thursday."

"Yeah." I pointed toward the office. "That box to the left of the doors? I think that's the mailbox Dan was talking about. Those cards don't have a room number on them. They don't even have a spot for a signature. You could take a card from another room, swipe them off the maid's cart, take them from the office, whatever. Someone could have done that, filled one out every day and put them in the mailbox, and no one would have known that Kim had been gone for days."

"The maid would have noticed," Jess said.

I shrugged. "They clean a lot of rooms, and maybe they don't think about it that hard. We'll see."

We went back to looking in the car windows, but there really didn't seem to be anything worth looking at. A crushed coffee cup on the passenger-side floor. Another in the cup holder between the two front seats. A plush big-eyed cat, similar to the ones on the overnight bag, sat in the back with a box of Kleenex and a folded grey blanket. Sunglasses were hooked around the driver's side visor. It couldn't have been more normal… or less help.

"What now?" Jesse asked.

"Lunch," I said. "Get a hotel room, maybe. We could go back to Calgary, but Canmore is more convenient. You're paying, though, so it's up to you."

"We're not getting a room here?" he asked, wide-eyed.

"Are you serious?" I said. "Have you not realized that whoever killed her has been here? They know how this place works. They know about the cards."

"I know! We're on to something! Doesn't that mean we should stay?"

"Call me crazy, but I prefer to sleep at a remove from murderers," I told him.

"Anyone could be a murderer," Jess said a little sulkily, but that was all he said, and when I headed for my car, he followed.

As we turned onto the highway, I handed him the folded paper.

"Found this on the floor. Didn't get a chance to look at it."

He opened it quickly and spread it across his lap.

"Whoa."

I glanced over and saw hotel letterhead. Below that, drawings, unmistakably Kim's. The ME Bird would have given it away even if I hadn't recognized her style. I tried for a closer look, but Jesse flipped the paper over and pointed at the road.

"They're lined up in two blocks. Maybe columns? Hmm."

The art kept him occupied on the short drive to Canmore, where he raised his head long enough to warn me off picking the best hotel in town. Middle of the road was better.

"Staff in fancy places pay too much attention to the guests," he'd said. So I'd pulled in at a nice but not too nice place on the northern edge of town, set among the few big-box stores clustered there, and left him in the car while I talked the staff into setting aside a room despite their check-in time being a few hours away. They'd needed some time to clean it, and so Jess and I had gone downtown for lunch.

Canmore was quieter than I was used to seeing it, but that made sense. I was usually there on weekends in the peak season, and this was neither.

The downtown consisted of a few streets, each a couple of blocks long, with an endless supply of musk-ox wool sweaters and hand-painted boots. Everything you could want if you were a rich woman who considered herself down to earth, or a middle-class woman pretending to be rich but down to earth for the day.

There were a few of the souvenir shops that were everywhere in Banff, crowded to the rafters with toy polar bears and tiny bottles of maple syrup, as if either could be found anywhere near these mountains. Generally, though, Canmore took aim at a better-heeled crowd.

We picked a chalet-framed brew pub that looked as if it might have a quiet back corner and had ourselves seated there. I did the talking, and Jess stayed behind my shoulder with his mask on. So far it seemed to be working. He kept the mask on at the table and looked at the drawing. The menu was shoved back at me with "You know what I like."

He didn't even bother to double the entendre. The waiter came, and I ordered for both of us. Jess kept his eyes on the paper. Finally he turned the drawing around and let me look.

"So," he said. "Interesting."

He sounded like I would also find it interesting. I tried, but it looked like doodling to me.

"Interesting how?"

"You see this?" He pointed at some leaves and a building. The ME bird sat in a tree outside. "Ivy. The building has ivy on it. Ivy league, maybe. And that's the niece sitting outside. Can she get in? Uncertain. And here, this hot air balloon…."

"I feel like I'm getting a tarot reading."

"The hot air balloon is going past mountains, an ocean, I think it's going around the world. Like *Around the World in 80 Days*. Maybe that's why it's a balloon and not a plane. And look at the balloon pattern."

"It's a spiral."

He looked at me like a teacher whose slowest student had made a breakthrough.

"Yes! She's got them all over—there's a pine cone under this tree, and this beach has a shell on it. Fibonacci is in play, but what does it mean to her? Universality? Fate? A guiding hand for creation?"

"Did you learn to overthink doodling as part of your art wank degree?"

He actually had a BFA in music, which was not something he yelled during concerts. "Hello, Chicago! My Bachelor of Arts and I are here to rock this town!"

"These things had meaning for her," he said. "Look, this is her head from the back, and that looks like a mirror—you can see make-up on the table below it—but you can't see her face in the mirror."

"She's a vampire now?"

"I don't know. A monster of some kind? Here she's walking through a forest, and there are eyes on her from the trees. Maybe she felt lost and in danger."

"Like she might have come here to avoid a threat."

"Yeah. Maybe it wasn't a local. I don't know. This is about her niece going to college, travel, her identity, her safety… that's big stuff. And she's got it lined up with all the happy thoughts over here and the scary ones here, like it's—"

"A list of pros and cons?"

He shrugged. "It's like she's wrestling with her future."

"Sure you're not projecting? Since you're getting tired of your job?"

He looked surprised, then laughed. "Man, every time I finish a tour, I feel like I got paroled."

"The horror of being driven everywhere," I sighed. "Having meals brought to you… not paying for anything…."

"Oh, I pay for it," Jess said. "And I can't stress to you enough that you would hate it. You like rules, but you don't like being micromanaged."

"You don't know what it's like to be a cop," I told him. "Everyone who sees you has an opinion about what you should be doing."

"Why'd you quit?" he asked. Just like that, blunt and looking me right in the eye.

"I already told you," I reminded him. "I was asked to resign."

"Yeah, you said that basically one guy was harassing you about being gay. You could have fought that. You spent four years getting a degree so you could climb the ladder and change the system from within, and then you quit over one guy?"

I was regretting my decision to order iced tea instead of beer. Not that beer would have been enough for this conversation either. "He was up the chain."

Jess made a face. "You knew it wasn't going to be perfect when you got there. You had plans."

"Yeah, well. So did he."

Jess didn't look impressed. He said nothing.

I leaned forward. "Okay, what I'm going to tell you, you tell no one. Ever."

He blinked. "Oh my God. Do I have to sign anything?"

"Do you want to hear this?"

"I don't know. Do I?"

"I'm serious."

"I see your serious face."

"Fine." I paused while the waiter stopped by to refill our drinks, then leaned in again. "He hired people to follow me. Not cops. PIs, ironically. That's how he knew about the off-duty activities. They followed me into a club."

"Did I miss something?" Jess asked. "Did they re-criminalize sodomy in Alberta?"

"Well, technically," I started, then made myself stop. This was not the time for a side trip into the grey areas of Canada's vice laws. "Doesn't matter. I wasn't doing anything illegal, but the same couldn't be said for everyone in that club."

"So?" Jess waved a hand at the next table, not boldly enough to draw attention. "That guy could have an illegal knife for all we know. It's nothing to do with us."

"Cops are never off duty," I said. "You're always an officer of the court. That's the argument he used when he told me to resign."

Jess sat up straighter, and I wanted to warn him. Keep your voice down. Stay in the shadows.

"That's bullshit! Before pot was legal, how many cops went to parties where people were smoking it? There's no way he could make that stand up."

"Yeah, I know," I said. "The CPS LGBT club said the same thing."

"Jesus, Ben, why did you resign?" he asked. "I mean, I think you're better off getting away from that bullshit, but you wanted to be there, right? This isn't 1960. You could have fought it."

"My being an officer of the court was his reason," I said, "but it wasn't his leverage."

He'd been watching his hand, his fingertips lightly drumming the table. The motion slowed. Stopped. He looked at me. "What the hell did he do?"

"His guys got dirt on everyone but me. He had proof there were some underage kids in the club that night. Sixteen-, seventeen-year-olds. The fines alone would have been enough to shut the place down. He was prepared to go to each of those kids' homes and tell their parents where they'd been. Maybe the parents would have been cool, but I don't know that. He had photos of some people doing coke. That doesn't necessarily stand up in court, but he found out where those people worked."

Jess's mouth opened slightly as he stared at me. "He was going to fuck with the community?"

"Whoever was there that night," I said. "But he was willing to send his guys out again. And people at work too, obviously. Even Kent, for being my friend. Either I quit or he fucked up everyone in sight."

"That is pure evil," Jess said. I could tell from the glint in his eyes that he was thinking of what he could do about this guy. I put a hand on his wrist.

"Remember how I said you couldn't tell anyone?"

"He can't get away with that!"

A few people looked our way. Some even turned, elbows bumping the tall glasses on the small round tables.

"Shh," I said. "And yes, he can. And he did."

"But it ends his career too," Jess insisted. "Right? He was harassing you. He singled you out. You could ruin him for that."

"Yeah," I said. "So that's a wash, if you're not worried about all the people whose lives he was planning to ruin. But see… that would have worked for him."

Jess looked confused, and that was understandable. This wasn't his world.

"He has political ambitions," I explained. Before Jess could protest that wanting to go into politics only made it *worse* to look like an asshole, I added, "For the Conservatives. Sure, they'd disavow him if he pulled something like that while he was officially running for them, but they'd love it if he fucked over me and half the community now, laid low for a few years, and then joined up. *That* would work for him."

Jesse looked suddenly miserable, and I felt swamped by nostalgia, dragged under to where I couldn't breathe. The quickness of his misery and his joy. How fast his weather could turn.

"That is fucking horrible," he said.

I sighed. "I know."

"But how do you win?"

I wanted to put my arms around him. He looked so lost. "Baby, sometimes you don't."

He kept looking miserable, and I couldn't take it, so I went on to tell him the other thing I'd never told anyone. Something I'd planned, in particular, never to tell him.

"I didn't love being a cop. Like you always said back in school. Okay? You were right. The internet is a little fucking over the top on this topic, but *you* were right."

That made him look a little less sad and a lot more skeptical. "You always said you might not like being in uniform. You were prepared for that. It was about what you'd get to do once you were in charge of something."

"It's not… I don't think it matters," I said. "Yes, I would have liked major crimes or homicide better. But it's still this endless cycle of running in the same people, and I know there are major criminals doing brutal shit in the office towers all over downtown, but I'm never going to deal with any of them. I'll just show up when they call to complain about some homeless guy sleeping on the sidewalk out front. It really is a fucked-up system. And it sets you up to punch down."

Jess sighed. He was running his fingertips along the side of his glass. "You didn't want to go into policy work?" Jess asked. "Or social work?"

"I needed some time to… do my own thing, I guess."

"And you like it," he said. It wasn't a question, but it also wasn't judgement about my choice of career. If anything, he sounded pleased.

"It's mostly not exciting," I informed him. "Stake-outs and internet searches."

"Yeah, but you like it. And you're good at it."

I shrugged and hoped like hell I wasn't blushing. "I like it."

A dark wing of hair escaped his cap and fell forward along the side of his face. I had to close my eyes for a second and collect myself. I had memories on memories of his hair slipping from a quickly thrown-in tie, fanning as he brushed it, falling forward as he leaned over me.

"I'm sorry anyway," he said. I opened my eyes to see him looking at me, steady and still. "I'd always kind of hoped you'd prove me wrong."

"I didn't pick the easiest place," I admitted, and he grinned.

"Redneck capital of Canada."

"We didn't elect an actual murderer as our mayor," I pointed out.

Jesse's eyes widened. "Dude. You're probably kidding, but—"

"I'm not," I said firmly.

"As soon as the conversation is about whether a guy does his own hits, maybe don't vote for him. Maybe the question itself indicates that someone is not a good choice for mayor."

"Speaking as an expert on rednecks," I told him, "I think some people are a little bit proud of anyone who gets away with it."

Jess covered his face with his hands and shook his head. "It's all such a shit show." He took his hands away. "How did the world get like this? Was it always this way and we didn't realize?"

While I tried to think of an answer, he pulled a bottle from his pocket and set it on the table. Antibiotics, I realized. He laid one white horse pill on the table, then dropped a few familiar blue gels beside it. Painkillers. He saw me watching him and pointed to a spot below his right lung.

"Hurts along here," he said. "Apparently that's a thing? I don't know. The doctor in Winnipeg said it was normal. Luna said so too."

"This Winnipeg doctor is a negligent quack who should be run out of the profession for encouraging you to keep doing shows," I said. "But I trust Luna."

Jesse laughed, coughed a little, and took his pills. Once he'd washed them down, he said, "I wasn't as sick in Winnipeg. And saying I probably wouldn't die is not encouragement."

"It is to you," I said flatly.

"When do you think Luna might know about the autopsy?" He said it as the food arrived, and I saw him stifle a laugh as the waiter pretended not to have heard. I casually picked up a fork and got to work, like everyone talked autopsies over lunch.

"She might be able to find something out now, but I don't want to wake her yet. I don't think it's urgent."

Jess considered that. "Except if the autopsy shows she died by strangulation or that she died three days ago. What then? The cops show up and we go home?"

The main point of that was not him referring to my place as home. Focus, Ben. "I ask Lauren and Emma what they want. I'll stay on if they want me to."

"Would the cops let you?"

I stole a couple of fries from his plate. He grabbed a stand-up drink-specials menu and stuck it between us. No danger of him going for my salad, so we were probably at some kind of stalemate.

"There's no law against asking people questions. If I did something stupid, like… I don't know, say it was an active police investigation, and I knew that, and I found her phone and didn't tell them. They might find something to charge me with."

"We found her car," Jess pointed out.

"Yeah. That's something I would probably tell them."

"And then they'd reopen the investigation?"

I shrugged. "Or they'd ignore me. A lot of people like to share their ideas with the police. Believe me, you get to a point where you've heard enough of them."

He started to say something but abandoned whatever it was and instead made a comment about the song on the radio. It had been produced by a guy Jess had worked with and had a few stories about, and it was like old times, kind of, or maybe like a date. It was hard to say because Jess and I had never really dated. We'd gone from hanging out in the music building at night to hanging out pretty much always to getting an apartment, and I don't remember us talking about what we were doing even once, the whole time.

AFTER LUNCH and dropping things off at the hotel, it was time to head back to Dead Man's Flats to meet the maid. I'd tried to convince Jess to stay in the room and sleep, but he'd said he might as well have stayed in Calgary if he was going to sleep in a motel in the next town over. We hadn't really had time to argue about it, so he was in the passenger seat.

"Stay in the car," I said as I got out.

"Mm," he said, which was not a yes.

Dan was in the office talking to a woman of indeterminate age in a light-blue uniform top and black polyester pants. She had a head full of blond curls that looked like a giant scrubbing pad, tied up in a pink-and-blue bandana. Her face had the kind of sharp lines that some women got at sixty but some bar girls got in their thirties, so she could have been anywhere on the map.

"Mr. Ames," Dan said. "This is Halyna."

"Hi, I'm Ben Ames," I told her, offering a hand to shake. She took it but did nothing else to suggest it was a pleasure to meet me. "I'm a private investigator."

"Yes, Mr. Diallo has said this."

That was the voice of Eastern Europe, somewhere—the best I could do for placing her accent.

"Did he tell you what I'm investigating?" I asked.

She pressed her lips together. "The girl."

"Yes," I said, "the girl. Have you been the one cleaning her room?"

"Yes, since Thursday. There is no one there, I think."

"I agree," I told her. Dan was behind his computer, pretending not to listen. I resisted the urge to give him a friendly wave. "Was she there the first night, Thursday?"

"She uses the soap. But not the bed."

So it was like I'd thought: checked in, went out, never came back.

"And she hasn't been in the room since then? As far as you can tell?"

Halyna shrugged. "Nothing is different. Bed is made. Towels are dry. Garbage is empty."

It wasn't new information, but it was firing my nerves anyway to have my suspicions confirmed. If I could get Luna to confirm that the autopsy showed something out of line, strangulation or strange bruises or a body that was too far along, that would ice the cake.

"One more thing," I said to Halyna and was immediately grateful that she had probably never heard of Columbo. "The little card in her room, the one where people say that they'd like to stay an extra night, did you ever have to replace it?"

Halyna looked at the ceiling. One of the cops I'd worked with had insisted that people who did that were about to lie. In my experience, some people needed to look at something neutral to remember little details, like they were playing back a video. Also in my experience, most people who thought they could tell when someone else was lying were full of shit.

She looked back at me before answering, and her expression was uncomfortably confused. “No,” she said. “No.”

I didn’t blame her for looking disturbed. The conclusion, so obvious that she’d seen it already, was that the re-up cards that had been going into the little mailbox from Kim’s room hadn’t been from Kim. And they hadn’t been from her room. That meant someone had taken blank cards from somewhere else—maybe another room, or a maid’s cart, or the office. And that somebody was somebody who had to be, at a minimum, hanging around the hotel. Maybe even someone who worked there.

It also unnerved me, to be honest. I liked catching bad guys, but I didn’t like knowing they were in striking distance, especially when I didn’t know who I was watching for. It was an added chill to know Jess was here, maybe in the car but maybe not, and not taking this as seriously as he should.

I thanked Halyna and Dan and answered Dan’s question about whether I had heard from the police at all. I hadn’t, but had he? No, he had not. We traded uneasy looks before I thanked him again and went to the car.

To my surprise, Jess was where I’d left him. His head was back against the seat, but his eyes were open. He didn’t move when I got in. I told him what the maid had said, and he just breathed with a slight wheeze. He might not even have been blinking.

"How is there a suicide note with her signature?" he said when I was done.

"Say some guy puts a gun to her head and tells her to sign. He doesn't know what her usual signature looks like, I'm thinking. Is she gonna sign the usual way?"

"You'd have to assume she wouldn't. If you were the guy with the gun."

"I'm going to ask around anyway, see if anyone saw or talked to her…."

"You think she went into the bar?" Jess asked. He looked at the door of the hotel bar like he was thinking of going in there to find out. I held up a hand.

"Just stay put and I'll find out," I told him. "Do not leave this car."

He looked like he'd have been happy to argue if he hadn't been too tired to move.

I went back into the office, where Dan was still at his computer but Halyna had gone, off to clean up after more people or their ghosts.

"Sorry, one more thing," I said. "Is the person who runs the bar around? I'd like to talk to whoever was on staff Thursday night."

"Yes, you will want to speak to Derek," he told me. "He is the manager, but he is often working there."

"Is he there now?" I asked, taking a step toward the pub door.

"No, no, he closes in the afternoons," Dan said. "He sometimes stays here, but he is at his trailer today."

"Okay, I can meet him there," I said. "Where is his trailer?"

Dan pointed toward the back of the hotel and up. He was grinning, the first relaxed expression I'd seen on his face.

"Up the hill. Long way. The road had a rock fall… rockslide?"

I nodded. "Rockslide, right."

"Yes, so you can only walk. This is why he will stay here some nights, if we have the room."

"Up the hill."

"Long ways."

"Got it," I told him. "When do you expect Derek back today?"

Dan raised a hand, flat in front of him, and tilted it this way and that. "Six, maybe, if he will be serving dinner. Later if not. When summer is over, the restaurant is often closed. Until winter he keeps his own time."

"I'll check back later," I told him. "Who else do you have working here?"

"Myself, Marie, Halyna. In the summer we have another maid, but she has been gone two weeks. Derek is the owner for the restaurant, so he does not work for me."

"Anyone else?" I asked. "Pool cleaner? Repair person?"

"We hire these people when we need them," Dan said.

"Okay," I said. "Thanks. Oh, there is one other thing. I know I keep saying that."

If he'd noticed, he was too polite to show it. "Yes?"

"Do you have Kimberly's signature on anything?"

"Yes. All of our guests sign a guest agreement, for damages and so forth. One moment."

He pulled a stack of papers from behind the desk and went through it once. Twice. Three times. He frowned and shook his head. He tried the filing cabinet along the back wall and spent some time fine combing that. Finally, he turned to me with his hands spread.

"I do not know what happened," he said. "It should be here, with all our current guests. I thought it might have been put in the storage cabinet, but it is not there either."

I glanced around the room. There were no obvious security cameras. They didn't have to be obvious, though.

"Do you have security cameras in this room?" I asked.

"We have never had trouble," Dan said. I felt for the guy. Running his own place, not some franchise, he'd had the option to trust people, and he'd taken it. It would have been nice if that could have worked out for him.

# CHAPTER 13

JESS WASN'T in the car when I got back, but he was near it, sitting on a tree stump and breathing with his eyes shut and his mouth slightly open, like the mountain air was a wine he was judging. No mask. He looked up when he heard my steps.

"How'd it go?"

"It was affirming," I told him. "The maid doesn't think anyone's been in that room since sometime Thursday. Hasn't had to make the bed, change the towels… and she didn't have to replace the room rebooking request card. Not even once."

"Oh," Jess said. "Shit."

"Yeah, and if you think that makes the staff look suspicious, you're gonna love this. They had a piece of paper with her signature on it, but it's missing."

Jess stood like he was about to charge into the office. I cleared my throat, and he sat back down.

"Okay, you have to go in there and get their security recordings! What if they record over them every few days?"

"They don't have cameras," I told him. "I think that office is a dead end. Dan and Marie and the maid are the only year-round employees. The bartender owns the restaurant, so he's not technically staff, but I have to think he's in and out of that office at least a few times a day. Hell, I don't know. Maybe anyone in this town can slip in and out without being noticed."

"What about Dan and Marie?" Jesse asked. "I can tell you've taken a liking to them, but realistically, you have to suspect them, right?"

"I don't think a woman dragged Kimberly up the trail to the waterfall," I said. "Actually, I can't see Dan doing it either. Kim wasn't tiny, and he is not a big guy."

"I guess we should meet the bartender."

"Dan says he'll be opening at six tonight."

"Oh," Jess said, cutting himself off with a yawn. "Sorry. Ah, what are we doing in the meantime?"

"You're sleeping," I told him. "I'm going around town to see who remembers seeing Kim. I'd especially like to know who was seen with her."

"Hmm." It was a non-committal sound, but he looked straight-up unhappy.

"What hmm?"

"We just... we don't know why someone would kill her," Jesse said. "Doesn't knowing why it happened help you figure out what happened?"

"That's kind of a TV thing," I said. "Courts don't care about motives. Juries sort of do, but legally the job is to prove that someone did it. If you can prove they did it, you don't have to show why. It doesn't matter why. I mean, if you're saying it's self-defence or something, maybe it matters. But the basic facts—this guy did it and I can prove it—they stand regardless of motive. Can we continue this in the car, where you can rest?"

I offered a hand to pull him to his feet, and he took it. Once we were settled in the car, he started to blink sleepily. Still, he had questions for me.

"So as long as you got the guy, you'd be okay with not knowing why? You don't want to know whether it had to do with her coming here in the first place or if it was just… the worst luck?"

I thought I would until I opened my mouth to say it and my gut told me I was wrong. "I think," I admitted, "I would really like to know."

He nodded and relaxed against his seat, like I'd taken a weight off him somehow. "Go on. Learn things."

I COULDN'T say I met everyone in Dead Man's Flats that day, but I gave it my best shot. I started by leaving a message on Luna's voicemail, and a text and an email, asking her to look into the autopsy if she had any contacts who would help. Then I wore out some shoe leather going to every public building the town had to offer and any private building that would open the door.

Kim had been noticed by a few, though no one had seen her past Thursday night. She hadn't gone out of her way to draw attention or make new friends. If she'd arrived during the summer rush, I doubted anyone would have remembered her. As quiet as the town seemed to be now, I had hope.

I hit gold with three construction guys on a break, smoking next to a square industrial building they were either putting up or taking down. Mid-twenties, all of them, with restrained mullets and grey sweatshirts under work overalls. One raised a hand as I approached, and I was surprised the other two didn't do the same, like images in a row of mirrors. As I got closer, I saw small differences. More stubble on one, Oilers sweatshirt on the far left guy—that was a bold move in Flames country. They weren't actually triplets. I just didn't have a connoisseur's eye for the type.

"You Sherlock?" That was from the one who'd raised his hand. I told him I figured I might be, and he waved me over. "I hear there's a detective in town asking people about that girl that died over in the park."

"You know anything about her?" I asked. I showed them Kim's picture on my phone, and all three leaned in to squint at it.

"Oh yeah," the one with the stubble said. He had a thick rural Ontario accent that took "oh" halfway to "ooh," the way Americans thought everyone in Canada talked. "That's her."

Oilers Sweatshirt nodded. "Yeh. We saw her when we was in the bar on… was it Thursday?"

"Thursday, yeh," Stubble confirmed. A closer look at the two of them and I thought they might be brothers, both out from Ontario. Didn't explain the Oilers gear, but maybe they'd done time in Fort Mac when they'd first moved west. There were a lot of displaced rig pigs wandering the province after the COVID oil crash, looking for whatever work they could find.

"You talk to her at all?" I asked. They looked at each other before shaking their heads, but it didn't seem like they were getting a story straight.

"She was at the bar," Stubble said. "Never saw her go to a table."

Oilers nodded. "Yeah, she was rocking that stool all night."

"Did you see her talk to anyone?" I asked.

The guy who'd waved me over snorted. "Caught herself a real piece of work. Poor kid. I nearly went over there to shut it down, but you know. None of my business."

I watched his face go from amused to worried as he finished, his brow sagging into creases. "You don't think he did something to her?"

"Do you?" I said. "You sound like you know the guy."

He screwed up his face. "Not really. I did some work up at his parents' place, and he was hanging around."

"Little Rich Bitch?" Oilers said. "What the fuck would he be doing in Dead Man?"

"I dunno. Noah pointed him out," Stubble said.

Oilers looked incredulous. "I woulda remembered."

"You were in the can."

"When was that?"

Before this could turn into a one-hour debate about who was in which can when who said what, I decided to bring things back around. "Was she talking to him for a long time? Do you have any idea what kind of conversation it was?"

"Hour at least," Noah said. "They were in the bar when we got there, and they left right before we did."

"Wait, she left with him?" I said.

"Yeah, she must've been into him," Noah said. "He must not have been acting like himself."

I told myself not to get too excited. Just because Kim was last seen leaving the bar with an asshole, that didn't mean I'd cracked the case. One step at a time.

"What's this guy like?"

"He's a kid," Noah said. "Eighteen, nineteen? He got kicked out of U of C, so he's living at home. Supposed to be doing school online, but he spent the whole time I was there playing video games and jerking it."

"How do you know?" Oilers asked. "Were you watching him?"

"Gettin' some video for you," Noah said. Ah, the hilarious gay jokes. Too bad I couldn't let them go on all day.

"Why was he kicked out of U of C?" I asked.

Noah shrugged. "Probably some shit with a girl? He's a creepy fucker."

"Do you have reasons for saying that?"

Noah shrugged again and took a pack of cigarettes from his pocket. "Stuff he said. The way he talked about girls."

He offered me a cigarette. I shook my head. "No, thanks. Can you tell me where I can find this kid? His name?"

"Ethan McCann. Lives up by Banff, right outside the park. Hang on."

He set his cigarette down on a rock near his feet and started to scroll through his phone, talking as he went. "They had me building a solarium on the back of their house. The dad's some kind of business swami, hosts retreats in Banff. I think the mom works at the Centre. They had a goddamn harp in the living room. I shit you not."

The Centre being the Centre for the Arts, where Jess had performed without mentioning to me that he was in my backyard. That didn't seem like a worthwhile thing to add to the conversation, so I nodded instead.

"Here." He turned his phone to me to show me an address in a text.

"Thanks. I'll take the spelling on that last name too."

I handed him my card, and he passed the text on to me, plus the last name. I thanked him, and he took a drag on his cigarette before responding, "Fuck that kid. Round him up, Sherlock."

I WAS on my way back to the car when my phone rang. Lunes was up early, given the schedule she was trying to turn around.

"Ames Investigations," I said, because it annoyed her when I didn't greet her by name.

"Honestly, Ben, if you won't look at your phone, you might at least assign ringtones."

"You can do that?"

She snorted like an irritated horse. "Do you want to know how the autopsy went?"

"God, yes," I said. "Kent burned his bridge over there. You were my only hope."

"I don't think burn is what Kent did to that bridge," Luna said. "Unless he has a medical problem I don't know about."

I leaned against a bollard and looked at the mountains. They had nothing to say to me.

"What happened to Kimberly?" I asked.

"She seems to have died from a blow to the head. That could have happened during the fall. It could have been before. One thing they did say—she doesn't seem to have been dead for significantly longer than twelve, twenty-four hours. She fell in the cold water, so of course that makes things tricky. Both the cold and the water."

So she'd been alive all weekend? I considered how much I'd rather she'd been dead than trapped and dying, or about to die.

"She couldn't have died any earlier?"

"She might've been kept somewhere else, as long as that place was cold."

"For a few days?" I said. "A weekend?"

"I would not rule it out."

My tense shoulders dropped, and I started to fully breathe again. "Okay. Anything else?"

"No sign of sexual activity. Alcohol, possibly, but that's also produced by the body after death. If she was more than forty-eight hours out, it can't be relied on. Since you're so interested, she was not obviously pregnant, though it could have been early days. And that's really all."

"Thanks, Luna," I said.

"No problem. Oh, there is one more thing. Dunno whether it matters, but it might."

"Tell me and we'll see."

"Britt—do you know Britt?"

"I'm out of the loop," I said. "She did the autopsy?"

"Yeah. She said the cops basically told her this was a suicide and not to stress about it, and then she said it was so different from last time."

"Last time?" As I spoke, I wandered toward a wagon someone had propped in front of one of the motels. There were skeletons in it, slightly better than Halloween decorations but not good enough to fool anyone. "What was last time?"

"Last summer some teenager jumped off a cliff in the backcountry. The RCMP thought it was a murder, and apparently this was a bit of a thing, because no one in the area liked tourists hearing about murder in the hills. Rather bad for business. But the RCMP were quite stubborn about it, as frankly they should have been."

"If they thought it was a murder, yes."

"It turned out not to be, though. There were people across the gorge who saw her jump. There was no one around her. They weren't getting cell service, and it took them a few days to come out of the woods, so no one knew."

Huh. "The cops probably regretted being stubborn."

"They wouldn't have capital, would they? To be pushy?"

"They shouldn't need it. They're the police. Hell, they're the Mounties."

"Well," Luna said, "I wouldn't be confident about this death, if it were me."

"That's more helpful than you may think."

"How's my patient?"

"Asleep."

"Take care of each other."

I thanked her again and stretched until something in my lower back popped. Too much driving, and I'd missed a few days at the gym.

Were the RCMP leaning toward suicide because they'd bet wrong before? Because they didn't feel like they were in a position to rile up a bunch of rich resort owners after they'd done it for nothing on such a similar case? Did someone know this would be a similar case? Had they chosen to do this, to use the falls to drop Kim's body, because they remembered what happened a year ago and thought the RCMP might not dig too deep if another girl wound up at the bottom of a cliff?

That might be another reason to consider a local for this one. Someone who'd know what had gone on around here the summer before. That kid the triplets had told me about might fit the bill.

JESS MADE a liar of me by being awake when I got to the car, looking at his phone.

"How's social media?" I asked as I got in.

"Murdering civility one post at a time," he said. "How did the hunt go?"

"Might be on to something," I said. "She was in the bar Thursday night, and she left with some guy. The locals say he's a creep about women."

Jess sat up and dropped his phone to his lap. "What kind of a creep?"

I gave him the details, including the mother's possible connection to the Centre for the Arts. Jess knew people there. "Can you look into it?"

"Yeah, but what do you need to talk to the bartender for? Shouldn't we follow the lead before this guy gets away?"

"We don't need to wrap this up before the commercials," I said.

Jess gave me a dark look, and I rubbed my eyes. The day was getting long, and one of us hadn't been napping through half of it.

"Okay, okay. Go talk to the bartender." He pointed at the bar entrance, where I could see a yellow glow seeping out around the door. "The lights went on in there about half an hour ago."

"Right," I said. "Good. And Jess?"

"Yeah?"

"Stay in the car."

THE PLACE was about what I'd expected. Dark wood with long tables against the walls and small round tables in the middle of the room. Easier to move if they ever hosted a band. The place didn't smell of urine or sour beer, and on a related note, there were no video slots.

The music was more restaurant-loud than bar-loud, which would make it easier for me to ask qucs-tions and hear the answers. Nautical Disaster was playing, ringing in the unpopulated pre-dinner room. A little too apt.

I stepped around the menu, which was written on a whiteboard in black marker. No cartoons or fancy letters, just the information that Pat's was serving shepherd's pie, Caesar salad, and something called the Dead Man's Burger. Ask about today's dessert.

I didn't know who the hell Pat was, but Derek, I assumed, was the mountain behind the bar.

Six three or four and about as ripped as anyone I'd seen in real life. He had buzz-cut dark hair and a navy T-shirt that had no choice but to be tight. His deep tan might've been natural, or it might have some help from chemistry. This was also true for his muscles. It wasn't easy to get to that size without an assist.

I doubted he played for my team, which was a shame because he would've had a line-up down the block.

He didn't notice me at first, focused as he was on typing something into his phone. After about a minute, he set his phone down and strolled to my end of the bar.

"Sorry about that," he said. "Just posting today's specials. What can I do you for?"

He was smiling in a charming but impersonal way. I placed my card on the bar. "I'm a private investigator. Do you have a few minutes?"

He picked up the card and gave it a good look.

"Wow," he said. "A real life PI? That must be a pretty wild job."

"It's mostly asking people questions," I told him. "Making lists, crossing things off."

"Well, if you've got questions for me," he said, "it'll have to be quick. I've got some food prep to take care of before it gets busy."

"I understand," I said. "I should ask first… at the hotel, they said the owner's name was Derek?"

"You're lookin' at him." He offered a handshake, which I accepted. He pressed too hard. "Derek Bellevue."

"And were you working here this past weekend?"

"Yep," he said. "Don't have a lot of staff around for the shoulder season."

That checked out. Australians went back to Australia. College kids went back to school.

"I'm looking for a missing woman," I said. "I think she stayed in Dead Man's Flats this weekend, so you may have seen her."

I'd been opening with that all over town, and most people had corrected me. Missing? Did I mean the girl who died? The construction guys had gone there before I'd even had a chance to ask them anything. Derek shrugged.

"I see a lot of people on the weekends," he said. He saw me glance at the empty room and added, "It's busier later in the week. And I just opened for dinner."

"You might have noticed her," I said, taking out my phone. I showed him a photo of Kim, and he nodded.

"Oh, sure. The girl in the fifties get-up. She was in here on Thursday. At the bar. You say she's missing?"

Was he the only guy in town who hadn't heard about the dead girl under the falls? I doubted it. So what game were we playing here? I decided to skip his question and offer my own. "Did you see her talking to anyone?"

He leaned on the counter. Folksy. This was how the guy played up to tourists, easy-going and gosh-darned glad you'd stopped by. Not a bad performance, but I could see through it because I was the wrong audience.

"Yeeeah… blond kid. He bought the drinks. He kinda liked giving the orders, I think. Saying what the lady will have, you know what I mean?"

"Did they come in together?"

"I think he was here when she came in. Yeah. I think she decided to sit beside him. No accounting for taste, am I right?"

"You are," I said. "Did they seem to be each other's taste?"

"I guess so," he said. "They pretty well closed the place, and they left together."

Did they, now?

"Closed the place means…."

"We close at two, Thursday to Saturday," Derek said. "Last call's at one. Rest of the week, we shut down around midnight in the summer and ski season. Watershed the rest of the year."

My confusion was obvious enough that he explained.

"When we've got more staff in here than customers. This time of year, that means it's just me. We'll probably close pretty soon after dinner tonight."

"Gotcha." I wished I had a photo of Ethan McCann so I could show it to Derek and confirm we were talking about the same guy. "You said this kid was blond. Anything else you remember?"

"Can I check on something on the stove? I'll be right back."

"Of course."

Television would have you believe that people take five during questions because they have to throw a gun in a river or check on the people they have tied up in the basement. I have never known this to be the case. I wonder whether people are uncomfortable with the topic, and why. But I also know people really do have things on the stove sometimes. Sometimes they have to go to the bathroom.

In this case, I thought Derek probably did have something on the stove, and I welcomed the opportunity to look around the bar with him in the kitchen. In particular, I was looking for a security camera. Just because the hotel didn't have them didn't mean Derek couldn't have installed one on his own.

I checked out the usual angles and locations and didn't find anything. If he had cameras, they were well hidden. I doubted that because part of the idea behind cameras is for people to know you've got them. Hell, a good percentage of the cameras out there were hollow plastic dummies, maybe with a battery and an LED so they'd look a little more real.

Derek returned, wiping his hands on a dish towel. He saw me standing in the middle of the room, eyeballing the corners, and dropped both the towel and the folksy routine in a heartbeat.

"Looking for something?" he asked coldly. Everything about him, his face, tone, and the set of his broad shoulders, said I had better not be.

"I was wondering whether you had security cameras," I told him. "Looks like you don't."

"Never needed them," he said. He relaxed a little, but it was still obvious why he'd never felt he needed security cameras. A robber with any sense would take one look at that granite face and try next door instead.

"Fair enough," I told him. "If there's no footage, I guess your description of the guy is all I've got. Do you remember anything about how he looked? Anything distinctive, like a tattoo?"

He folded his arms and leaned against the back wall of the bar. "He did. Some bullshit from a video game. Here." He pointed to the inside of his left wrist. Good enough. If the kid had a tat, I could get a photo and check back with Derek. If he didn't, he was the wrong guy.

"You didn't happen to see either of them around here after that?" I asked. "The next morning, maybe? They mentioned in the office that you take a hotel room sometimes."

Derek nodded. "Yeah, yeah, sometimes. I went up to my trailer all last week, though."

"So you live in a trailer up on the mountain?" I asked. "Like camping all year?"

He laughed. "Ah, no, man, it's all built out. I got power and running water and all that. There used to be a road up there, but we had a rockslide last year, and no one's gotten around to clearing that out yet. I can walk it in the summer and get a snowmobile up there in the winter. Keeps me in shape."

It was hard to tell how much appreciation he wanted regarding the shape he was in. I settled for a nod.

"I went home after I locked up," he said. "Didn't see anyone hanging around. Is that everything? I'm gonna have people in here any time now."

"That's it," I told him, and pushed my card closer to him. "Thanks. And please give me a call if you remember anything that might help."

"Will do," he said and put my card into the back pocket of his tight jeans. I followed it with my eyes, but it was a reflex. My heart wasn't in it.

# CHAPTER 14

JESS WAS on his phone when I got back to the car and made a "just a sec" gesture at me when I reached for the door. I walked a few feet away and looked west, toward Banff. The sun was still up, would be for a few hours, but there was a tinge to the light that wouldn't have been there a few weeks earlier. Even so early in September, you'd never mistake it for summer.

I went past the car to the middle of the parking lot. I had phone calls to make, one to each of my clients, and I wanted to be sure no one was listening from around a corner or behind some stand of trees.

This part of the investigation was always hard to talk about with clients. I wanted to give the impression that I'd made progress, because I had and because I wanted them to know I was doing my job. But I didn't want to share theories or, worse, give them false hope.

In this case, at least I was able to report a few facts. I'd found Kim's car. I'd found her hotel and spoken to people who'd seen her. Emma and Lauren both seemed satisfied with that progress. Emma told me I was right that Kim would have had her satchel with her, and her phone, and probably her laptop. Lauren confirmed for me, reluctantly, that Kim could have gone off with someone she didn't know. Specifically, a good-looking guy. She wouldn't normally, but she might. She had at least once before.

She didn't ask, though I'd thought she would, why I had questions about Kim's tendency toward one-night stands.

I mentioned the sheet of doodles I'd found. Did they know of anything Kim had been thinking about, maybe a decision she had to make? They both said no but asked to see the doodle. I told them I'd take a photo and send it along. I wrapped things up by saying I'd get back in touch as soon as I knew anything more.

I didn't actually plan to call unless I had something rock solid. They had enough on their minds and didn't need me stringing them along.

ACROSS THE lot, the car door opened and I saw Jess leaning across the driver's seat. His phone had been tossed onto the dashboard.

"Sorry," he said as I approached. "That was supposed to be confidential."

I got in and shut the door behind me before saying, "So spill."

He laughed. Slight hoarseness. No cough. "I called a friend who works at the Centre for the Arts."

"Oh. That's convenient."

"The more convenient thing is she owed me a favour. Anyway, she has the whole story on this kid. His mother is furiously disappointed in him."

"So he did get expelled from U of C?"

Jess thought about that. "It was suggested he not come back. He got caught buying liquor for some kids."

That needed context. I'd booted for friends, back when I was newly eighteen and their birthdays were a few months away. It would have been rude not to.

"His buddies?"

Jesse shook his head. "No. It was gross. Fifteen, sixteen-year-olds. All girls."

"Yikes," I said.

"Yikes," Jess agreed. "So his mother decided he should go back to Banff and do some growing up before he tried college again."

"Sent him home to be creepy elsewhere."

"Yep."

I snagged Kim's drawing from Jess's front jeans pocket, ignoring the look he gave me, took pictures for my clients, and put the drawing into my jacket pocket. Then I gave my phone the address I'd gotten from the construction worker and headed for the highway. Jesse was silent until we were back on the main road.

"What about the bartender?"

"What about him?"

"He could have carried her up the trail."

I touched a hand to his forehead. He swatted it away.

"I'm fine. Why are you looking at me like that?"

"She left with someone," I reminded him. "While he was tending bar. In front of a roomful of customers."

He looked so much like he was going to say something that I kept my eyes on him longer than I should have while driving. Finally gave up and looked at the road. Silence continued.

"I can talk to all of those customers," I said, "if I need to. But I have a feeling I won't need to."

"Yeah. Fair. The kid does sound like a creep."

That, my nerve endings told me, was a performance of some kind. Not a lie. Just a carnival mask on a stick, speaking to me from a few inches in front of the real Jess.

"I don't know anything yet," I said. "I'm going to talk to him."

"Hmm."

"It does bother me that he's not staff. It would have been harder for him to get Kim's signature and the blank re-up cards. But he could have a buddy who works there, or maybe they don't watch that office too closely."

"I saw Dan leave when you were talking to the bartender," Jess said. "In a car. And Marie took some trash out to their bin by the road. She didn't lock the door."

"There you go," I said.

I glanced over and saw Jess on his phone, flipping through photos. He stopped on one of a blond kid with a highly punchable face, standing in front of the beer stand at some outdoor event. A Fringe, maybe? I thought I could see the corner of a tent.

"You think he smirks on purpose," Jess said, "or you do think his face just does that?"

I shook my head. "Not enough data."

"I was wondering if he'd be big enough to carry Kim. You think? Kind of stringy, but he's tall and his shoulders look broad."

"I'll ask him to sling a couple bags of flour over his shoulder and walk around with them."

"I would love to see you ask him that and not explain why."

"He probably wouldn't have flour sacks around anyway."

"I wish you had a gun."

"It's amazing how fast you've gone from a gun-hating liberal to wanting me to shoot a child."

"He's not six years old. And he maybe killed someone. You're not scared?"

"I've talked to a lot of asshole college students."

"Yeah, but for what? Vandalism? Drugs?"

"Assault," I said. "Yeah, that kind of thing. Not generally murder."

"If someone did something really bad, wouldn't they do pretty much anything to get out of it?"

"Depends," I said. We were nearing the turn-off to the ultra-rich homes west of Canmore and a few clicks outside the park gates. I slowed to watch the signs. "Do you know what people did when they were in the World Trade Center on 9/11?"

He shook his head. "Jammed the fire exits? Ran for the elevators?"

"Sat around," I told him. "A lot of people took time getting their purses and coats, going through their desks, anything other than admit what was happening was happening."

"So you accuse someone of murder and they start organizing their sock drawer?" Jess said. "Jesus, his family lives close to the park. Are they in the park?"

"Just outside," I said, showing him the map on my phone. "Suspects think they can deny it or redirect me. Even if I convince the cops to arrest them, they'll get a good lawyer. It's hard for people to believe they're in big trouble."

"Especially if they have money," Jess said, as if he didn't. To some extent, he always had. Not that he'd grown up as rich as he was now, but being dragged all over the world by a big-deal business executive was not privation. Not in a financial way.

We turned onto a road that snaked northwest, staying just this side of the park boundary, and the orange glow of houses started to come through the trees. Overgrown log cabins, like they'd been hand built by a pioneer family of giants. One had a For Sale sign out front with an asking price, no doubt to avoid time wasters. Slightly north of two million. Jess gave a low whistle.

"Go half an hour east and you can get twice the house for that," Jess said, as if he had an intimate knowledge of real estate prices along the Calgary-Canmore-Banff corridor.

"Go five minutes west and you can't buy one at any price," I pointed out. He nodded.

"Yeah, I get that. They're jammed in here, though. You'd expect more privacy for what you're paying."

That was good news for me. The houses really were nestled close, and most had large windows in all directions to take advantage of the supposed wilderness. It wouldn't be too hard to find people who knew about their neighbours' comings and goings. What time the McCann kid got home, or had he maybe stayed at the hotel? Whether he'd had anyone with him.

THE MCCANN residence had a triple-car garage and a winding path of paving stones leading from there to the house. Solar lights on stakes were placed around the stones, but it wasn't dark enough yet for them to turn on.

The house itself was mostly dark, with a few lights visible toward the back. If it hadn't been for the floor-to-ceiling windows along the front, I wouldn't have seen any lights at all.

"Okay," I said, turning to Jess.

Before I could follow up on that, he said, "Stay in the car?"

"Yes. But I'll call if I'm going to be more than… let's say twenty minutes. If I don't call and I don't come back, call the cops."

His eyes widened. "You said you weren't scared."

"I'm being cautious," I told him. "I would have been fine doing this without you, but since you're here, you might as well earn your keep."

He didn't look reassured. "And I tell them… what? The truth?"

"Yeah," I said. "If it comes to that, you'll have to. No reason for the cops to show up otherwise."

"Okay."

"And then you wait," I said. "In the car. You don't ring the doorbell or sneak around the back of the house or whatever else occurs to you."

Jess cocked his head. "You know I'm not five, right? You don't have to talk to me like I'm five."

I gripped the steering wheel with some force. Enough that Jess probably noticed my knuckles turning white.

"I apologize," I said. "I did not mean to talk to you like you were five. I meant to talk to you like you were impulsive and had a poor grasp of your limitations."

And you're loyal, I didn't say. Yes, he'd walk out on me and not pay the rent and not talk to me for years, but I was still pretty sure he'd fight a rampaging elephant for me if the need arose. He'd get trampled to death, but he'd jump right in.

He was giving me a look I couldn't read. Not angry. Not even annoyed.

"My mistake," he said. "Good luck in there. Give a shout if you need me."

I left the car and went up the walk, feeling like I'd had circles run around me in some way I could not begin to understand.

The front doors were heavy wood and windowless, never mind that your door was the one place where having a window might be useful. Assuming you'd want to know who was on the other side before you opened it. I rang the bell, which did not have an intercom or an obvious camera, and waited. It wasn't long, less than a minute, before one of the doors opened to reveal the punchable face from the photograph standing on the other side. Sneering a little, eyes red and narrow, in need of a haircut and wearing pyjama pants like they were actual pants. The top was a U of C sweatshirt, which had to take some balls to wear around his parents and made me think they probably weren't home.

"You're not fuckin' Skip," he informed me.

He was waiting for SkipTheDishes to bring him food. From Canmore, probably.

"They deliver out here?" I said.

"I have an arrangement."

He said it like he was a mafia boss who was having fresh lobster flown in for his casino. It was not hard to see why my construction buddy hated him. I was halfway there myself.

"You've got dinner coming, so I'll make this quick," I said. "Are you Ethan McCann?"

He really, actually said, "Who wants to know?"

I wanted to say something smart, but in fact the smart thing was not to antagonize the guy before I'd even gotten in the door. "I'm Ben Ames," I said instead. "I'm a private investigator from Calgary."

I showed him my ID as I spoke. He glanced at it, making a show of not caring. Most people were at least a little bit curious when a PI showed up at their door. I was pretty sure he was too. Tough to say whether he was trying to look innocent, though, or whether he just wanted me to know he was too cool for school.

While he was looking at my ID, I looked at his left wrist. A mess of circles and barbed lines was there, black and bold. Fairly new.

"Cool ink," I lied.

"You a gamer?" he said, raising his eyebrows in disbelief.

"No, just like the design."

"Whatever," he said. "Why do you want to talk to me?"

"I've been hired to find a missing person. I think you may have spoken with her last week."

He chewed on that for a few seconds. He didn't seem to be panicking, just thinking. I eyeballed him while he made up his mind and decided that he could probably have hoisted someone Kim's size if he'd had to. He'd have felt it in the morning, but he could have done it.

Finally he stepped away from the door to let me in. I followed him and pulled the door not quite shut behind us.

On the inside, the house was aggressively woodsy. Thick pine framing. Leather furniture. Plank wood flooring and a stone fireplace running up to the high ceiling, with the famous harp standing between the fireplace and a grand piano. As I took a few more steps in, I could smell cheap weed and lots of it. No wonder the kid was eager for food.

I glanced around for anything that looked like it might have been Kim's. You wouldn't think someone would leave that kind of thing out in the open if they'd been involved in a crime, but you never know.

There wasn't much out of place in this house, which made sense. They would have a maid, and you couldn't go far from what the interior designer had created. God help you if you bought one book too many for the carved driftwood floating shelves.

As I followed the kid to the back of the house, it occurred to me that I had no idea what Jesse's house was like. He didn't do interviews there, so no reporter had breathlessly set the scene by describing his furniture and kitchenware and the framed sales awards on the walls. My guess was that Jesse used his house as working space, for writing, and that it didn't look enough like a sex dungeon to fit his image.

Ethan had made a mousy little nest in a solarium, and a video game paused on a big screen. Scuff marks on the floor said he'd dragged the screen in from the living room. It didn't seem like the kind of thing you'd keep in a sunroom.

He settled himself, and I went through the routine, showing her picture and giving her name. Did he recognize her?

"Met her at Pat's on Thursday. Fuckin' cock tease, man. I'm warning you. Do not waste your money. I bought her two Duvels and a fuckin' fancy whiskey and a plate of mixed appies that she fuckin' hoovered."

"Sounds like you spent some time talking to her?"

"Yeah, you know, I figured she was fresh blood, and she asked about the tat 'cause I guess she's a gamer."

He put that last word in quotes. I reminded myself that punching his punchable face would not have been helpful.

"So the two of you left around what time?" I said.

"Last call. One?"

"Then what?"

"I went to her room. She blocked me at the door. Can you fucking believe that I dropped a lot of cash on that bitch? Did she think I was paying to hear her talk about fucking Shag-all and her fucking jackoff art?"

"Did she say why she was in town? Maybe show you some drawings?"

"She said she was on a fucking—what'd she say—cusp. And she was drawing something the whole time."

I showed him Kim's drawing, and he confirmed it was the work in question.

"So," I said, "what did you do when she declined your advances?"

He huffed and chip dust sprayed from his thin lips. "I left. I'm not fucking stupid. The whole bar saw me leave with that bitch."

My stomach clenched. Some guys, way too many of them, might have done bad things to a tipsy girl who was alone in a motel. But fewer would have put it to a stranger that way, that the reason not to rape someone is you've been seen with them.

"Where did you go after you left?"

"I drove around some. It was too late to start over in another bar. She wasted my whole night. She could've at least sucked my dick."

I looked around at the nest of chips and weed. I didn't say anything. After a half minute or so, he got tired of the silence.

"What the fuck is this?"

What were the odds that he hadn't heard about the death in the park? Maybe not terrible, if he'd been here all day, playing video games and ordering food.

"She's missing," I said. "Her sister hired me to find her. Did she say anything to you about where she might be going, what her plans were?"

This was his chance to pawn it off. Say she'd planned to meet some other guy, or that she'd sounded suicidal. He shrugged. "Nah. We talked about the game. She said a bunch of boring-ass shit about art."

"You were the last person to see her," I said, hardening my tone. That woke him up a little. He opened his eyes all the way for the first time since I'd arrived.

"You don't know that. I never saw her after, like, one."

"And then you drove around. Did anyone see you? You talk to anybody?"

"Just the RCMP."

That was not something I'd expected to hear. "Excuse me?"

"I got a fucking ticket, okay? I was speeding"—another word in quotes—"like anybody goes the speed limit. And the cop threatened to make me take a breathalyzer. That gash is always up my ass."

I tried not to picture the actual logistics of that.

"She didn't, though?" I said. "You got a speeding ticket?"

"Yeah. At, like, I don't know. Two-thirty?"

"You have the ticket around here?"

He snorted.

"Yeah, right. Like I'm gonna leave that around for my parents to find. I paid it, okay?"

"Right," I said. "Okay. You don't seem like you're short on cash. I can't figure out why you'd be drinking in Dead Man's instead of Canmore or Banff."

"Banff fucking sucks," he told me.

"I get you. So why not Canmore?"

He shrugged. I wondered whether a broken collarbone would put him off the habit.

"My mom's shitty friends all drink there. Bitches narc me out."

That checked out. His mom's shitty friends probably did drink in Canmore. They probably put away a lot of ice wine and chocolate cocktails.

"Weren't you worried about rolling in drunk at 2:30 a.m. last week?"

"My parents are out of town. Dad's at some fucking conference."

Leaving him with at least one car and a big empty house. And no one to confirm when he'd come home. I'd have to ask the neighbours about that one.

"If you remember anything she said about her plans, or anyone you saw her with, call me."

He took my card and looked at it like he wasn't sure what it was or what he was supposed to do with it.

He didn't say anything else or move to get up, so I figured I'd be showing myself out. I took advantage of that to look around a little more, ducking my head to see under furniture. I thought about asking to use the washroom, but I didn't think it was worth it. I wasn't likely to find her bag or phone sitting on the back of the toilet. If it turned out that he was lying about the speeding ticket or when he'd gotten home, I'd have to try to talk the police into getting a warrant for the place.

I closed the door behind me when I left and checked my watch. Well under twenty minutes.

"So?" Jess said once I was back in the car. His phone was off and on the dash. I thought he might have been staring at the front door of the house the whole time.

"He confessed. I brought in a judge for sentencing, and he'll do twenty to life in Kingston."

"Hilarious."

"You sounded like you expected answers."

I started the car and turned back down the road to the highway. I could ask the neighbours about Ethan's comings and goings later, depending on how the ticket played out.

"I saw him let you in," Jess said. "You talked to him."

"Yeah. He says he left with her at one, left her at the door to her room, and drove around alone until the RCMP pulled him over to ticket him around two thirty. I'll stop by the detachment and see whether they can confirm it. I should probably catch them up anyway."

"What was the kid like?"

"A sack of shit," I said. "Lousy attitude toward women. Used the word 'gash.' Not sure whether he's violent, though."

"Anything else?"

"We could check his record," I said. "The Mounties won't be able to share that officially, but Kent can look it up."

"I bet it's gross," Jesse said, reaching for his phone. Because he had Kent's number and somehow I had forgotten that. It didn't ring more than three times before I heard Kent answer, though I couldn't quite make out the words.

"Hey," Jess said, and after a pause he laughed. "Yeah, I'm hoping he knocks something off his fee. Look, Ben says you can check someone's record."

Another pause. "Oh, crabby. Bit my head off because I asked him how it went with the suspect."

"I did not bite your head off," I objected.

"He says he didn't bite my head off. Yeah. No, exactly. I was thinking the same thing."

"Give me that fucking phone."

Jess ignored me. "I'll tell him. Yeah, I'll text you the details on the guy so you can check his record. Give my love to Frank."

He tossed his phone onto the dash and gave me a disgustingly satisfied smile.

"Kent says it might take a while. He also says I need to feed you. I think he means actual food."

"Kent could mind his own business."

"He could," Jesse said, "if we let him. Anyway, he's right. You barely had breakfast, and you had rabbit food for lunch."

"If the vegan mobs that follow you could hear you now," I sighed.

He swatted my arm. "Half a salad. You're not eating. You know this."

It wasn't the first time I'd been off my feed during a murder investigation. I usually didn't realize it at the time. Something about the importance of the work or the immediacy of the danger made me want to keep moving and keep myself wrapped up. Less talking. Less food.

"Okay, fine. After we talk to the Mountie."

CONSTABLE MAYBE-MCKAY was still on shift when I walked into the detachment, still alone behind the desk. The difference this time was that I had invited Jess to come in with me. Without his mask.

"Hi there," I said. "You may remember me from earlier."

She looked up, a little bleary and a little "what trouble is this guy bringing" and then froze. Blinked. Blinked again.

I'd told Jess he could lose the ball cap and own up to being himself, which he'd looked askance at but not actually questioned.

"This is—"

Her face turned cherry red as she cut me off. "I know. I mean… uh… I have… I'm a big fan."

An actual *fan* fan, apparently. Not one of the many people who liked the music, liked the style or ethos or whatever he was selling. Someone who'd have had a poster on their wall. And she did look young. Young enough that he'd been part of high school for her.

She wiped a hand on her pants and offered it to Jess.

"I'm Nicole McKay. Constable. Constable McKay."

Jess shook her hand and gave her something between his own smile and Jack's as he told her it was nice to meet her too.

"I thought you were sick," she blurted. "I had tickets. I-I'm sorry, that's your business."

"I'm really sorry," he said. "The venue will refund you. I've got pneumonia. My doctor said I couldn't do any more shows. Ben and I went to school together, and I thought sleeping in his car would be more interesting than sleeping in a hotel room."

Constable McKay seemed content with the explanation. Jess did look tired. And pale.

"I realize this must be weird," he added, and she laughed. Genuine but shaky. It was interesting how close this excitement was to fear.

"He's mostly been waiting in the car," I told her. "Look, I have a question for you. Did you give a speeding ticket to a kid named Ethan McCann around oh-two-thirty on Friday?"

That got her to look at me instead of Jess. "Who told you that?"

"Ethan McCann," I said. "Because I accused him of having been the last person to see Kimberly Moy alive."

"Why would you… how did you wind up talking to him?"

I told her. About Kim's car and the construction guys and the bartender saying Ethan and Kim had left together. I left out the part where he'd called her a gash.

"I don't know why you didn't give him the breathalyzer," I said in conclusion. "I promise he was drunk."

"You think I don't know that? Of course the little shit was drunk. I drove him home, and I thought he was gonna puke all over the back of my car."

It was funny how everyone seemed to think of him as a little shit when he was nearly as tall as I was.

"He was so drunk you drove him home, but you didn't insist on a breathalyzer?" I said.

She shook her head. "His mother has all kinds of clout around here. Actually his father, but she's the one who swings it. I give him a ticket he can pay online, make him walk up the highway to get his car the next day? Fine. His parents never hear about it. I run him in on a DUI, suddenly I've got lawyers in here and reporters on the phone, and my boss wants to know what I'm doing with my time."

"That's the job," I told her. "I used to do it."

"Yeah, I looked you up," she said. "So you know sometimes you don't get to do the job."

I wanted to give her a speech about how you did the job no matter what. You found a way. But I had resigned instead of finding a way to do my job, and Jess was standing right next to me, well aware of that.

"How much trouble is he?" I asked instead.

"Phew… a lot. Do you guys want coffee or anything? We have muffins in the morning, but they're long gone."

Jess opened his mouth. I gave a light slap to the side of his arm.

"I'll have coffee. He's hydrating and will have water."

She looked at Jess and raised her eyebrows. "He's pushy, hey?"

Jess laughed. "Always has been. Water would be great, though."

While her back was turned, I gave Jess a look that told him exactly how cute I had not found that.

McKay poured a mug of brown paint stripper for me and found a bottle of water in a bar fridge for Jess. For herself, she took a Diet Coke from behind the desk.

"My stash," she said. "Sorry. Not even Jack Lowe gets to have it."

Jess laughed with more joy than I'd heard since we'd reconnected. I wasn't sure what it was about being treated like a normal person that was so appealing to him. Maybe it was that he wasn't, that she was making a note of it. You're special. You're very special. Just not Diet Coke special, wink-wink.

Or it could have been that he'd always loved sass.

"The McCann kid is a creep," she said. "Hangs out by schools. I mean, he is the goddamned worst. He's creepy in bars. He doesn't like being told no. He gets hostile, verbally abusive. He scares people, and I think they're right to be scared. As soon as I heard a girl died out by the falls, I thought of him."

"What?" Jess said. "I thought you were calling it a suicide."

"We have a suicide note. The autopsy is inconclusive, and this other stuff you're bringing me about footprints and disappearing invoices, that's not going to buy me much. We're going with non-criminal until we find out otherwise."

"You're not going to find out otherwise," I said, "if you refuse to investigate."

"I am investigating! I was all over Canmore today, asking if anyone saw her. I told people I was making sure it was non-criminal, tying up loose ends. If I'd started in Dead Man's, I would've got to those construction guys myself. And Derek."

"Well, now you know," I said. "She left the bar with McCann. There's over an hour not accounted for between them leaving and you giving him that ticket. Bring him in. Get a warrant and search his car."

"I can't go charging in like that. Throwing accusations around, getting his parents all fired up, pissing off the business community. I'd get shut down."

"You're leaving potential evidence unsecured," I reminded her.

"If she died Thursday night, he's had days to clean out that car and any other place he needs to. He probably did a shit job, but he's not going to redo it unless we spook him. Until you rolled out here, McCann didn't know anyone was thinking of it as a murder."

"I never said she was dead," I reminded her. "He didn't correct me."

"Well, he'll figure that out soon enough. He's stupid, but he's not that stupid."

"He is that stoned," I said, but she had a point. I'd put him on notice that people were sniffing around.

"It'd be easier if you'd stop stirring the pot, no offence. I follow this little asshole around a lot anyway, so he won't think anything of it if I'm up in his business."

"I can stay away from him," I said. "But I'd rather work with you than not at all."

She ran a hand over her hair, like she'd forgotten it was in braids and had meant to run a hand through it.

"Okay, okay. Let me think about it. You might be of some use."

"Put that on your business card," Jess told me.

"Fucking put it on yours," I suggested. He flipped me off, without malice.

"Like college days again, hey?" she said.

"I'll check in with you tomorrow," I said. "We're about to shut it down for the night anyway. Sicko here needs to be in bed."

"It was… really surreal to meet you," she told Jess. "Um, take care of yourself. Get better."

# CHAPTER 15

BACK IN the car, Jess picked up his phone and started typing.

"Checking socials?" I asked.

"No, I'm making a note to send her something. Signed merch. She'll realize she didn't ask in about an hour or so."

Was that kindness or protocol? I couldn't tell, and I thought maybe Jess couldn't either.

"You discombobulate people."

"So much so that they might forget to be cagey with you."

"Like it says on your business card," I told him. "You may be of some use. Let's get dinner."

I GOT food from the pseudo-British place and parked in a day-use area along one of the back roads. It was empty, and we didn't see anyone along the way. Jesse shook his head.

"A lot of places, you can't go to a park without seeing other people. You can't go anywhere without seeing other people."

"Yeah. Those places are not for me."

"Ben Ames, Hermit Detective."

We moved to a picnic table, and Jess sat on top because why sit where the Man wants you to sit? He took one more look around to make sure there was no one to see, then took off the ball cap and ran a hand through his hair. So there he was with the mountains behind him and the sun starting to set and the wind catching his hair a little, and he was about the most beautiful thing I'd ever seen.

He would probably have been up for sex on the picnic table, but it was a bad idea for all kinds of reasons. Splinters not the least of them.

"I could stay here forever," he said. He was looking at the mountains, which was a relief because I didn't know what he'd have seen on my face.

"You'd freeze eventually," I told him. "Or you'd be eaten by bears."

"Been *there*."

I could never tell whether he knew how fucking impossible he was.

"What do you want first?" I asked. "Conversation or food?"

"Both," he said, turning to me and reaching for the paper bags in my hands. "What are you thinking?"

"Constable McKay is going to look into this," I said, "and I am going to lie low. You will continue to be along for the ride."

"And we're sure it was the kid."

I looked at him. He was staring at the food like a guy who needed to be looking anywhere but at me.

"Jess?"

"Uh-huh."

"Is there some reason you don't think the kid did this?"

He was setting the food out. Very tough job. Took his full concentration.

"Jess."

He set down the foil packet of naan that he'd been unwrapping. "You're going to be mad."

Not a prediction, in my experience, that had ever been wrong.

"What have you done?"

"Nothing. I just… when you went to talk to the bartender? After Marie took the garbage out, I went into the hotel office. To see if someone could."

I was in Ontario for a second, some town outside Toronto, pulling Jess and his guitar off an old steel bridge he was trying to climb. High as hell and convinced it would make a great shot for the socials. His band cheering him on. Seeing if someone could.

"Was I unclear about you staying in the car?"

He was back to sorting out food. Shoved a plate of butter chicken and rice in my direction. I let it sit.

"Jess. Was I unclear?"

He looked at me.

"Don't you want to know if some rando could walk into that office and go through files? When Marie left, I figured it was a good chance to check that out. I thought it would help."

"If you thought it would help, why didn't you tell me?"

He had a plate on his lap and was poking dal with a plastic fork. Poke. Poke, poke.

"I knew you'd be mad."

"So why are you telling me now?"

He pressed his lips together and set his plate on the table.

"Because I could hear your conversation with Derek. I listened."

"Of course you did. I'm surprised you didn't stroll right in."

"I don't like Derek. I know you want to climb him like Everest, so maybe you didn't notice, but there's something wrong with him. I think he's a bad guy."

"He's a good old boy. I don't like those much better than you do. But this is a world full of shitty people, and most of them aren't murderers."

He was doing that thing again, where he was close to saying something and didn't. So still he could have been a painting. When he did finally open his mouth, all I got was "Okay."

He pushed the food toward me again, and I considered that Kent might have had a point about my mood. No harm in eating something and seeing whether it changed anything. He picked up his plate and made most of the food disappear. He didn't say another word until he was taking the empty plates to the dumpster, disappointing the crows that had been watching our meal from the sidelines.

"Are you completely sure," he said, "that you don't want to bag that summit?"

A joke. I took it as an olive branch.

"Nah. He's covered in oxygen tanks and abandoned tents. It's a mess."

Jess laughed. "Shame to ruin a national treasure like that."

"Is just one of the things people have said about you."

He laughed harder, until he coughed, and sat at the picnic table to recover. The wind had picked up and was tossing his hair around. He was shoving it behind his ears, only to have it creep out again. I'd carried elastics for him back in the day. He never seemed to have one, and it was something I could do.

Then his smile went, another of his sudden weather changes.

"What if he lied, Ben? What if Kim went back to the bar after she got rid of the creep?"

"Why would she do that?"

"I don't know, but how did that drawing wind up where you found it? She drew it at the bar. You found it under the coat hooks, right, like it fell out of a jacket pocket? But you didn't find her coat. She must have gone out again."

Jess, goddamn it, had a point.

"Okay. Fine. She might have gone out again. That doesn't mean she went to the bar, though."

"Maybe other people would know whether she did?" he said.

"I could ask around. But I don't like it. That bar is Derek's paycheque. He'd have an aversion to shitting where he eats."

"You don't know that. Maybe he has—what'd you say about me?—bad impulse control. Could we see whether he's been in trouble before? I could ask Kent to check."

"Yeah. Okay. No harm in that."

Jess nodded. His eyes were darkening with the sky but still green. Deep and determined, like a ten-storey wave.

"Ben. Don't just say no, okay? When you talk to Derek again, I want to come along. It'll put him off balance. I might be able to get him to slip up or—"

"Stop talking." My voice was even and quiet, the way it got when I was trying not to yell, and I could see from Jesse's face that he remembered the tone. "Have you confused this with a game of some kind?"

"You think I'm not taking this seriously?"

"You want to talk to a guy you think is a murderer and try to get him to slip up? So he gets to choose between going to prison or throwing a B-lister off a mountain?"

"Wasn't I a national treasure a few minutes ago?"

"We're in Canada," I told him. "And I'm being generous."

That was nasty, and I didn't even mean it, but that seemed to be the mood I was in.

"Oof," Jess said, with a smile that he didn't mean. "I thought you said people don't assume they're sunk because a detective shows up. They think they'll get a good lawyer. Didn't you just say that?"

"For fuck's sake, Jess, there's a difference between asking some general questions and actively trying to get them to implicate themselves. If you roll your eyes again, I will put you in the trunk of the car and leave you there until I'm done for the night."

He sat up and hugely, deliberately, rolled his eyes.

I slammed my hands onto the table on either side of him. The table shook. His eyes snapped wide open. I put a hand over his mouth. I might have been rough about it.

"Fucking try me!"

I took my hand away. We stared at each other. He was breathing hard. Angry. Thinking. It wasn't impossible that he'd swing on me. We kept staring. He cocked his head, and I knew he was about to speak.

I slammed the table again.

"Which fucking superhero do you think I am? That bartender has me outmatched. You want to taunt him so you can see what I'll do if he goes after you? Because that would be hot for you? Or because taking care of you is everyone else's job?"

The idiot looked like he might say something. I kept going before he could.

"Is it my job to save you, Jesse?"

"Of course not."

I leaned in close, so close that I could feel him breathing against my face. Short, quick breaths. "Or are you trying to destroy whatever small part of my soul you left me by getting yourself killed on my watch?"

His eyes were bright with something ugly, and he was controlling his breathing, taking exactly the same time to inhale, hold, exhale. And again. We stared some more.

"If you wanted me to have a heart," I told him, "you shouldn't have fucking incinerated it. You selfish, brutal, conceited piece of shit."

Crows called to each other. Something small moved in the brush. The sun was finally down. Jess's mouth was turned like a cartoon frown, a thing I'd rarely seen from him. He had to be completely miserable, and I didn't think he even knew he did it.

He said, "Okay."

My head rolled back. I looked at the stars, which were crowding us. So many, so bright.

"Jesse…."

"I did hear you," he said.

I looked at him again.

"I'm sorry," he told me. About what, he did not say. "I didn't mean to—"

"No, it's… you get to. You get to say things, okay? Just, uh, the whole alpha male thing, saying you'll lock me in the trunk…."

"Mmm-hmm."

"Please don't say that. I have… it's a problem for me."

His expression said we'd be leaving it at that.

"Sorry," I said.

"No, I get it."

We were silent again, but it wasn't bad. It was just quiet.

"I could check the bartender's socials," Jess said. "Bellevue? The French spelling?"

"Yeah. Do that. I'll call Kent. And I need to check something in the bar—the freezer."

Jess lay back on the table. "Women in freezers," he said.

"I know it's a cliche. But when people are trying to cover something up…. Jess, bodies rot. They stink up the joint. Sometimes a freezer is practical."

Jess made a face but said nothing.

"There's also Kim's stuff," I said. "Everything we didn't find in the hotel room."

"You think he kept it? Like trophies?" Jess asked.

Everyone thought they knew all about murder.

"Like tossing them in a dumpster around here would be risky," I said. "So maybe he's gonna wait until the next time he goes into the city. He should have thrown them over the falls with her but, you know. Live and learn."

"Nice," Jess said.

"Just how it is. Best way to learn is to keep doing something."

He blinked. "Man, that is a dark idea."

He sounded haunted by it, in fact.

"It's why they're easier to catch after the first one than the tenth. They don't know what they're doing yet."

KENT WAS still at my house when I called, hanging out with Frank. He would be happy to run a check on Derek Bellevue in the morning.

He asked whether I'd eaten. When I said I had, he told me to be careful and to call if I needed anything. It was unnerving. I told him I was fine, because I'd sooner have drunk toilet-bowl cleaner than suggest I was worried about anything.

He said my boyfriend had left a T-shirt on the bathroom floor, and it was a great shirt. Could I please ask Jack where he'd bought it so they could be sexy twins?

I told him I would not.

WHEN I got back to the table, Jess held up his phone. "No Facebook. No Instagram. No LinkedIn. He mostly uses the Twitter account to announce when his restaurant is open and what he's serving, like he was doing when you went in there. Either he uses fake names or he is not a social media guy."

"It's the number one sign that a guy is running from his past," I said. Jess cocked his head and waited. I sighed. "No. I'm talking shit. Look… I'm open to ideas about how I'm going to get a look at his freezer."

"Wait until he's gone and pick the lock?" Jess shrugged.

"I am not allowed to break the law."

"Do it while the place is still open," Jess said. "Look, the front door of the hotel has been propped open all day. I need to duck in, find a fire alarm, pull it, and get out. Very low risk to me, and it'll clear out the bar. We can park around the corner. I'll go back, take the car up to the highway and wait with the doors locked. I know it's technically illegal to pull an alarm like that, but I'd be doing it, not you."

"I cannot endorse that," I told him. Jess sighed dramatically.

"If you're going to insist—"

"I cannot endorse that. I can't suggest it. It would be a problem if I knew you were going to do it. In fact, we should agree right now that you are not going to do it at—" I looked at my watch. Ten minutes should give us enough time. "—eight thirty."

Jess grinned. He still looked sad, but the grin was real. "Wouldn't dream of it."

"Thank God for that."

SOMETIMES A plan can go off perfectly and still leave you disappointed. I stood in the kitchen under red emergency lights looking at a freezer that was far too packed to have held a human being, even one half of Kim's size. I gave it a look regardless, for blood or hair or a scrap of clothing, but I knew I was wasting my time.

I wasn't sure how long I had before the Canmore Fire Department showed up, so I got out of there fast, through the back door to the alley. A Dodge Ram was parked there, a dark-blue standard-cab long box with a white fibreglass cap. On impulse, I paused to look in the windows and stopped dead when I saw a pair of bolt cutters lying where I'd told Jess they wouldn't be, right in the middle of the bed. I didn't know this was Derek's truck, but there it was, right behind thc restaurant. Easy enough to find out for sure.

I took a picture of the tire tread while I was there. I didn't think anything I'd gotten from the trailhead parking lot had been clear enough to be useful, really, but it was no trouble to get a tire photo in case I could make a match.

I took the alley past the rock-piled road up the hill and around the back of the pseudo-pub until I found the side road to the highway, where Jess was waiting with the car. He'd kept to the side, in the shadows. The lights of the approaching fire trucks played over his face like he was on stage.

He jumped when I let myself into the car. He was still in the driver's seat.

"Sorry, do you want to drive?" he said. I shook my head.

"No, you drive."

On the way to Canmore, I told him what I had and hadn't found.

"Bolt cutters," Jesse said.

"I don't know that's his truck," I said. "And a lot of people have bolt cutters. This isn't Toronto. People have all kinds of tools."

"Would he have another freezer? Maybe at his trailer?"

I shrugged. "I guess he has outbuildings and power up there, so maybe."

"But you'll go? You think it's worth checking?"

"Maybe," I said. "I still think it's the kid. Last one seen with her. Had a motive. Has a history. But I can check out Derek."

Jess's grip on the steering wheel was tight, and I thought I saw tears in his eyes. He said nothing.

"I'm not going up there in the dark, though," I said, "or while he's home."

"You sure aren't," Jess agreed.

"I can go tomorrow at lunch. He'll be in the restaurant."

"I'll be in the car."

I didn't say anything. He looked straight out the windshield the whole way back to the hotel.

I LOST the coin flip for the shower. When I got out, Jess was in a T-shirt and boxers, sitting on the floor next to our hotel room's floor-length window and looking at the mountains. They were suggestions in the moonlight.

"I'd offer a penny for your thoughts," I said, "but I know most people pay more."

"You can have the friends and family discount," he told me. I went to the window and sat next to him, not touching. Looking at the mountain-shaped holes in the sky.

"Are we friends, Jess?"

He wrapped his arms around his legs and rested his chin on his knees. Like he was drawing into a shell. "I have to tell you some things."

"You don't."

"I want to."

I put a hand on the floor between us. "Okay."

He took one of those deep, voice-trained breaths that seem to go on forever. Then he said, "You saw the antidepressants."

"Yes."

"I started those last year. I should have been on them since… I don't know. Before we met. But I didn't know that."

"I remember when you'd take to our bed," I told him. "When I saw the pills, I thought about that."

"It wasn't just those times," he said. "Every gig, every party where I was there to be seen and meet people, it was fucking endless, and I was so tired, Ben. I was running on this… crazy determination to get the record contract, like it would all be okay if I landed that. But you have to project this energy all the time, like you're already a star. And you're fucking exhausted. So what do you do?"

"A lot of drugs," I said. I felt gut-punched, a dull sickness spreading from the center of the pain. I'd thought he was partying, having a shallow, stupid, irresponsible good time.

"Whatever works," he said. "I did whatever worked. I was never addicted, you know. It wasn't a problem to quit, as long as I didn't have to be… him."

"Do you really think of it like that?" I said. "Like he's not you?"

He nodded. "It's like a role in a play. And it's one of those roles that drinks your blood. Jack has a presence. You need to feel it when he walks in the room. I have to keep pouring energy into that or the lights go out."

"What do you think of him?" I asked.

Jess looked at me, his head still resting on his knees. "I think he's a very effective machine."

"That's no way to live," I told him, and he gave me a lopsided smile.

"Better him than me."

I reached over and pushed his hair back gently with my fingertips. He looked me in the eye and said nothing. Didn't move.

"I'm sorry," he said, when I took my hand away.

I'd waited forever to hear him say those words. I'd thought it would be vindicating, or that I could stop being angry or finally stop loving him. Those last two things—I'd figured they'd go together.

He raised his head and looked out the window.

"I was awful to live with. You don't have to tell me. I lived with me too. I know you think I was living it up the last year we were together, but it was the opposite of that. Everything in my life, every person I talked to, everything I wore, everywhere I went, everything except for you… it was all my job. When I came home, that was the only place I could be lazy and weak and sad and scared, so that's what you got. I gave you the worst of me." I could see tears starting, his head tilting back to try to keep them from falling, these little things he did and had always done. "I'm so sorry, Ben. That was not what you deserved."

I could have said damned right or asked whether he thought saying sorry was good enough, which were both things I'd imagined saying if he ever apologized. Here, now, both felt wrong.

"I didn't know," I said instead. "You're right about what I thought. I had a lot of opinions about your behaviour. I could have once, maybe, taken ten seconds off from judging you and asked how you were doing."

He huffed out a little laugh. No cough. No excuse to put my hand on his back. "I would have said I was fine."

"I'm still sorry," I said.

He turned to me like I'd fired a gun. That startled. Eyes wide. Still with the shine of tears. "I didn't leave you. I know I did, but it wasn't like I was trying to get away from you."

"You left me for Jack Lowe," I said. "You left me for a million strangers. Do not say you didn't leave me. You asshole. I distinctly remember you breaking my heart."

Jess tilted his head. He was dangerously close to crying now. "Yeah, well. Mine too."

What could I say to that? He'd chosen the music over me, but he'd talked about it from the day we'd met, how he was going to write and make albums and tour and play for people who knew his songs. He'd been married to that idea. Didn't mean he hadn't loved me, but we'd always been playing around on the side.

"You got what you wanted," I said. It came out harsher than I'd meant. He blinked slowly and let the tears fall.

"It's not like I stopped loving you," he said. "It's not like that at all."

We sat with that for a while, looking at each other. The moon was very bright. What had Bowie called it? The serious moonlight. Jess liked that song.

"I hate to keep harping on the actor," I said finally, and he laughed like I'd thought he would. Like he'd found a way to go ahead and cry.

"Do you really care who I was dating, or pretending to date?" he said. "I didn't love them. I wanted to sometimes. You know?"

"I know," I said. I did.

"Matt wanted an Oscar. His people decided he needed to look a little edgier so he could get Oscar roles, and my people were down because, you know."

"Family friendly gay."

"It was horrible," Jess said. "Like, everything about it. You know Matt is… *that's* an A-lister. He's another kind of famous from me. The shit I've been pulling here with the mask… he couldn't do it. Those A-list people have to go to these insanely expensive resorts and private islands just to walk around outside. It's not luxury. It's a trap."

"When you were dating that guy, I couldn't go anywhere without seeing a picture of you and him," I said. "I might have been a little ratty about it."

"Paparazzi. Man. I don't really have that, you know. I have people wanting to take a picture with me or ask me stuff or just… I don't know. I don't exactly know what they want. And some stalkers. Everyone has those."

I wanted to offer to wring the neck of anyone who was stalking him. It would have been my pleasure. But that would have been more of the alpha male stuff he'd objected to earlier.

"Mostly the weird stuff is when I'm touring. Some people wait years for me to come to town. That's when I need a locked-off hotel floor. The whole paparazzi thing? I only had that when I was with Matt. We had people mobbing us so we couldn't make it from a hotel to a car, that kind of thing. I get that a little after a show—people wait outside—but this was everywhere. Like people are…. You remember that movie with all the telepathic alien kids?"

"Unfortunately," I said.

"It's like that," he said. "Like they all get some signal and they turn toward you. It is seriously creepy. And they're people, Ben. I like people. I don't want to be scared of them."

"Be a cop for a while," I said. "You won't like people so much anymore."

He side-eyed me. "I wondered if that was part of why you quit."

I shrugged. He smiled to himself and looked out the window again.

"Did you really quit everything?" I asked. "I thought you weren't drinking because you were sick."

He unfolded and leaned back against the wall, letting one leg slide forward. I thought, of course people want pictures of you.

"I told you, I'm not an addict," he said. "I can have whatever I want."

"But you don't."

"I try not to be in situations where I need it to survive."

I leaned against the wall next to him. "That sounds like your whole career, though."

He took one of those deep breaths. "Not the whole thing. The touring, maybe. I thought I'd go to bed after the shows, hang out in my room, but now the internet thinks I'm a fucking ego monster who thinks he's too good for his band, so that may not be working out."

I put a hand on his arm and pressed it gently. He was warm from the shower but not sick warm, the way he had been.

"How many weeks of rehearsals did you do for this tour?"

His brow creased. "A few. Why?"

"You have a high opinion of yourself. Of course you do. You're successful and famous and people blow sunshine up your ass."

He rolled his eyes. "Apparently not everyone."

"I didn't say your opinion was unwarranted."

"But I'm an ego monster," he said. "I'm stuck-up."

He didn't say conceited. He very deliberately did not say my words.

I pressed his arm again. "Jess. You like you a lot. You always did, and then you got this job of yours, which didn't help. But anyone who rehearsed with you for weeks and says you're some kind of snob who thinks he's too good for other people is an idiot or an attention-seeking troll."

He looked at me from under his hair, like he was all of a sudden shy. I took my hand away, and he wrapped himself up again, his arms around his drawn-in knees.

"Matt Garrett is not a nice guy," he said. "He's… who Derek reminds me of."

I glanced at him. He was staring out the window. I moved between him and the damned window so he was looking at me by default.

"Jess. What happened?"

"We got into a fight," he said. "Like, an actual, physical fight. Backstage before one of my shows."

"What?"

"You heard me." He lifted his head a little and looked at me from under his hair. "He wanted sex. I wasn't into it. He got grabby and I shoved him, and it ramped up from there."

"He…." I was seeing Matt Garrett from a dozen films, punching out the bad guy. Throwing people into walls. Some of that was Hollywood magic, sure, maybe even stunt doubles. But the muscles were real. "Jess, that guy has almost a hundred pounds on you."

"Tell me about it," he said. "He's real good at not getting people in the face, though. He must get into a lot of backstage fights."

"Jesus."

Jesse was tougher than he looked and tenacious in a fight, but that didn't give a guy twice his size the right to knock him around. Especially when it was a fight over whether Jess was going to put out for him.

"I think I might kill him," I said.

Jess barked out a laugh. "I considered that. I gave up on it only recently."

"So you charged him with assault and battery and then…."

"Ha," Jess said. "Can you fucking picture that? Yeah, no. I told Gia, and she got me out of the deal."

"Quietly," I said. "To save your brand."

"Gia offered to courier a knife to me," Jess said. "So I could cut his dick off. Then she asked whether I wanted to press charges before or after I did that."

I stared at him. "So why the hell didn't you? I mean, press charges. Or, fuck it, both."

"Like my manager pointed out, Matt could ruin me. His fans could straight up murder me, Ben. I say this as a crazy person: some of those people are crazy. You don't have a gun, but Matt does. He has bodyguards and his own gun."

Jess was trying to tell me that it was for self-defence, that Matt's life was scary. All I could see was a huge guy throwing Jess around, and now that guy also had a gun.

"My best-case scenario," Jess said, "would have been them making my life impossible for years. And I didn't put up with all of that pretending and having to kiss him and smile at him in front of the cameras just to burn it down by admitting it was a con job the whole time."

I lay my head against the cool glass of the window. "You need to quit."

"I fired that manager," Jess pointed out. I stared at him.

"A whole... what, three years after it happened? What in the fucking hell did he do to make you fire him now if that wasn't enough?"

"He suggested I date another actor," Jess said.

I took a deep breath. "I assume you have his address," I said.

Jess pulled at the carpet, splitting the strands. "Stop it. He's fired."

I wanted to point out that firing him was not even close to enough, but I kept it to myself. It had to be obvious, right? Even to Jess?

"Matt's fucked up too," Jesse said, like I cared or wanted to hear it. "You think this job has made me, what, extra conceited? Selfish? Out of touch? Used to getting whatever I want? What do you think being an A-lister has done to him?"

"I do not think selling more records would make you commit sexual assault."

He sighed. "It wasn't exactly like that. He grabbed and I said no, and he wasn't used to hearing it. I lost that fight, and he didn't... you know, press the advantage. He walked away."

"Every time you make an excuse for him, I get closer to cutting his brake lines," I said. "He had better not cross my path."

"He wouldn't," Jess said. "He won't. You don't winter in Dubai."

So that was why Jess was so hell-bent on Derek being the guy, even though everything pointed to McCann. Not just that Derek reminded Jess of Matt Garrett, but that this was a Matt Garrett within reach. Someone Jesse could confront. Turn in. It was like getting himself arenas full of screaming crowds to stand in for his disapproving parents. This was the kind of magic Jess did, thinking it would make everything right.

"This guy did a real number on you, didn't he? Not just that one night. Did he scare you before that? What did he do?"

Jess sighed.

"Ben, look… I didn't tell you this to get you riled up. I wanted you to know how I wound up on antidepressants."

"A doctor thought you needed to be medicated because some asshole grabbed you backstage at your own show?"

He sighed. "This is why I didn't tell the guys in the band why I was hiding in my room."

"What, because you didn't want them to know what happened with Garrett?"

"No, dumbass, because people have an attitude about depression and they have an attitude about meds. Like you. You think you don't, but you do."

"What do you mean?"

"I'm not on meds because something bad happened to me once and I was too lazy to do something real about it. I'm on them because I have had depression for years."

"You might be overly sensitive about this," I suggested. The look he gave me made me raise my hands in surrender. "Or I have an attitude. I'm sorry. Go on."

"I was the one thinking about my brand," he said. "I was worried about ruining it. And then I started thinking about how one reason I couldn't press charges was my brand, you know? Because I had that bad-boy reputation and the sex thing. Jack Lowe is always in the mood. He's not a killjoy, and he is not a snitch."

He slid down along the carpet until he was lying on the floor, staring at the ceiling.

"And I really was doing a lot of drugs and all of that. I woke up places not knowing how I got there. I had bruises I didn't remember getting. I woke up with people I didn't remember. That's all true. Once I—"

I winced and patted his leg along the boxer's hem. "Can we assume I get the picture?"

"Sorry. I just… you know, I got myself fucked up enough to do my job, and then I did whatever people do when they're fucked up. So I started thinking about whether I was happy with that."

"And you weren't."

"I should have asked you," Jess said, without any bite to it. "You could have saved me a lot of therapy."

"Do you feel better now?"

"I would have been way more fucked up about cancelling the shows and all this bullshit on social media if it had happened a year ago."

"Then that's good," I said. "You're good."

He shrugged. It was a strange brushing sound of his shoulders against the carpet. "Work in progress."

I lay on the carpet beside him, and we looked at the ceiling together. A wolf howled, and he startled, then smiled. "This place."

"I invited you out here when we were in school," I reminded him.

"I was dumb."

More silence. Then, "Shouldn't there be a bunch of wolves? He's not all alone, is he?"

"You want to put him on Tinder?" I asked. "Get him a date?"

"He might prefer Grindr. Don't assume."

I took his hand. There we were, lying on the floor, holding hands.

He said, "I never stopped loving you. I don't know if I was clear about that earlier."

He said, "I mean, I still love you now."

"I got that," I said calmly, like I wasn't shoving words past the heart in my throat.

"Okay," he said. "Good."

"You broke my heart," I said.

"Yep."

"I wouldn't be so pissed about it if I were over you."

His hand tightened on mine, but his voice was casual as he said, "Probably not."

"I mean, I still love you now."

I could see his smile from the corner of my eye. "What?"

"I said I still love you now."

"I'm sorry, I didn't quite catch—"

"I barely remember you. Who are you again?"

He laughed. He didn't cough.

"How long do you think you're still sick for?" I asked. He turned his head to face me.

"Luna says I'm not contagious anymore."

I blinked. "When the hell did she say that?"

"When I called her," Jess said. "When you were in the shower."

The heart in my throat started pounding. I was sure he could hear it. I was sure the wolf could hear it in the hills.

"You…." My voice was higher than I liked. I cleared my throat and tried again. "You're very sure of yourself, aren't you?"

He rolled to his side, toward me. "I hear that I have a high opinion of myself," he said. "But I also hear it might be warranted."

I rolled toward him in turn, put my hand on his face and ran my thumb along his cheekbone. He felt like silk, like always. "Let's find out."

He took my face in his hands and moved in for a kiss.

I'D LIKE to say I took it easy on a guy who was recovering from pneumonia, but that had never been our style, and we'd been apart way too long.

I grabbed a ponytail's worth of his hair while we kissed, not pulling but drawing him closer. My hand under his shirt, against the small of his back, did the same work.

He put his hands on my chest and let out a little sound that made every second I'd spent at the gym worthwhile.

He was stronger than you'd think, all that running around on stage with guitars for hours a night. At one point, he managed to flip me onto my back. My fault for being distracted, trying to get a hand down his boxers.

He straddled me, and I sat up to get close again. I was kissing his jawline when he put his head against my shoulder and I realized he was shaking.

I put a hand on his face and looked at him. "Jess? You okay?"

His eyes had that teary brightness, but he nodded. "I've *really* missed you."

I leaned forward until our foreheads were touching and stroked his face. He sighed, and we kissed some more. Then he put his head on my shoulder again and I held on.

"It's okay," I told him. "I've got you. Everything's okay."

I kept saying it until he was still and quiet against me. I almost thought he'd fallen asleep, but then he straightened, grabbed the front of my T-shirt in both hands, and kissed me like we were a mile underwater and I had the last of the air.

IT WAS the middle of the night, nearly three by my watch, when I woke from a nightmare that was fading fast. Jesse was at my side, his head on my chest and an arm slung across my stomach. We hadn't bothered to put our clothes back on after. We'd barely managed to move to the other, less messy, bed.

"You okay?" he asked sleepily.

"Yeah." I kissed the top of his head. "Sorry. Was I talking?"

"Mmm. Not really. Noises."

He was moving his fingers in soothing little circles. He was good with those hands.

"I forgot to mention something," I told him.

"What?"

"If you break my heart again, I will resent it."

I could feel his smile against my skin. "I won't, then."

"I will seriously not forgive you."

He stopped smiling. "I know."

"You're not exactly forgiven now," I added.

"Yeah. I figured. But I do plan to stay."

He couldn't one hundred per cent promise that. He could get cancer or something. People left in all kinds of ways.

"I might still tour," he said. "Not big tours. A few cities at a time."

"Just come back when you're done."

"Mm-hmm." He yawned. "Frank'll miss me."

"He'll be lost without you," I said.

He raised his head to kiss my shoulder and the side of my neck before settling in again. "Poor Frank. I guess I'd better come home."

# CHAPTER 16

WE DIDN'T have to be in a rush to leave the hotel in the morning, since I couldn't climb the trail to Derek's trailer until he opened his bar for lunch. This was, as Jess put it, "a damned shame," but we managed to entertain ourselves.

We barely got packed up and out of there by the 11:00 a.m. checkout time, and breakfast still needed to happen, so the plan was for Jess to lie low in the car while I checked us out and grabbed some food from the "Open Till Noon!" breakfast room.

It was going fine until I approached the car and found Jesse surrounded by what could only be called a pack of wild dogs. Or, if you were Jess, fans.

I hung back. I'd never seen this, not right in front of me. He'd taken off his mask and ball cap, and why not, since he was busted and everyone had their phones up for pictures.

I realized I might as well move closer. I saw Jess notice me and quickly look away before anyone realized he was focused on a particular person.

He was trying to talk to a middle-aged blond in a sweatshirt and jeans while a half-dozen others shot questions at him or tugged at his shirt, which was loose fitting and made of a thick, dark-blue peau de soie that felt like water. I didn't think Jess would be too pleased if someone tore it.

People were shifting around to get selfies. It had to be suffocating.

"You don't look sick," some girl in black lipstick observed. It wasn't quite true, but he was looking better every day.

"Antibiotics," Jess said with only a hint of an edge. She narrowed her eyes and took a picture. Someone shoved a crumpled copy of *sCene* at Jess, and he signed it. I wasn't sure where the pen had come from.

I looked at my watch. We couldn't stand around here forever.

"Okay, show's over," I said.

Jess gave me a "please don't do this" look.

I put on my cop face and stance and moved people away from both Jesse and my car. Some people asked me who I was. Pictures were taken. I considered the odds of Jess talking to me anytime soon if I took even one person's phone away.

Goddammit.

I put my head down, the way famous people did on TV, and plowed through. I could see Jess waving and telling people he had to go as he moved efficiently to the passenger side. That was what experience did for you. He made it look effortless.

He gave me a deeply unimpressed look before picking up his phone to see what the interwebs were making of this encounter. He didn't even notice how nice I was being, looking behind the car and making sure I wasn't running anyone over as I pulled out of the lot.

“Everyone wants to know who my new boyfriend is,” Jess said, holding up his phone to show me Twitter.

“They’ll know as soon as they run my plates,” I said. “They were taking footage of my fucking plates.”

“Yeah,” Jesse said. “They’ll do that.”

I looked over my shoulder to see whether we were being followed. Nothing so far, but I saw a few people booking it and thought they might be heading for their cars. I sped up. If they saw us take the exit to Dead Man’s Flats, this whole plan would be sunk.

“You were supposed to keep your head down,” I said.

Jess sighed. “I’m sorry. I should’ve known it would happen eventually.”

“This is a problem for me, Jess. I can’t have my face all over social media.”

“You spend that much time undercover?”

“I stake people out,” I told him. “And I don’t need the whole world knowing where I live.”

He leaned back and shut his eyes. “Yeah. I get that.”

I realized as I fishtailed down the exit ramp that there wasn’t a lot he could say.

This was his life, and mine, if we were really back together. We listened to the radio without speaking. Small plane had gone down in BC. The corn maze east of Calgary was staying open later this year. The lottery ticket was still unclaimed.

Once I was reasonably sure there was no one behind us, I drove to the road that went up the hill where the rockslide had been. I could see Derek’s truck behind the bar about a block away.

There was room to park at the foot of the road, so I stopped there and looked at Jess. He was watching me and looking almost as tired as he had the night he'd arrived in town.

"I guess we didn't think about the practicalities," he said softly.

Being with Jess was one thing. I'd never really wanted anything else. But we'd had a normal life before, mostly. People hadn't mobbed him, and they hadn't cared at all about me. Being Jack Lowe's boyfriend was a completely different situation.

Had we jumped into something that was never going to work?

"Thank you," he said.

"For what?"

"For checking into Derek just because I don't like him."

"I check out leads. It's what I do."

He turned his face away. I couldn't tell whether he'd closed his eyes.

I kissed the back of his hand and got out of the car.

THE HIKE up the road wasn't bad. The rocks and shale and dirt were tricky sometimes, but a fair amount of the road was still visible, and it was possible to follow the pavement most of the way. Not in a car, or even on a motorcycle, but by foot you could do it if you were able to step over the odd boulder as you went.

It took me about fifteen minutes and might have taken less if I'd been familiar with the route. I tried to imagine it with Kim on my back, dead weight. Even for someone Derek's size, it would have been tough. This wasn't like the path to the falls. The hill was steep.

If she'd been beside him, though, a little drunk and laughing at the stumbles as she went… that could have worked. Okay, a lot drunk. Those beers she'd had were no joke, especially with a whiskey. But still. She could have made it, especially if he'd helped her over the rough bits. She might have held on to his arm. Like he was a gentleman.

She'd probably have been happy, thinking she was going to get laid, one of those special out-of-town hook-ups that you remembered fondly forever. Or told stories about forever, depending on how it went. Friendly, good-natured Kim with her honest social media and "whatever the hell she wanted" fashion sense. Even if Derek wasn't a murderer, which he probably wasn't, he was a thousand miles beneath her.

But say he'd done it. Since that was why I was climbing this hill, it was worth thinking about. What would Derek have wanted with her, anyway? Sex, sure. That was a good bet. Kim wouldn't have been everyone's type, but she'd been cute enough, and a lot of guys cared more about availability than type. But if he'd killed her… why? Because it had gone bad? Maybe she'd changed her mind and he hadn't liked it, like Matt fucking Garrett. Except worse.

Or maybe this was just what Derek did. If so, Kent would probably dig something up.

I was taking deep breaths for the exercise, and the smell of spruce and pine made it feel like a wholesome stroll in the wilderness. The wind was starting to pick up, carrying off the warmth from the sun. That suited me fine after the hike. I had almost managed to convince myself that I was enjoying nature when I made it to Derek's trailer.

It was a tidier scene than I'd expected but still pretty low-rent. The original fifth-wheeler was bookended by sheds, one flush against the front of the trailer and the other a few feet from the back. In front, a rickety sunroom ran along most of the trailer's side. It was full of patio furniture and empties and a rusted tire rim that was probably used as a firepit. Nothing that would get any worse if the roof leaked in the rain.

Power lines were attached to the trailer and the back-end shed from a pole along the former road. I doubted that the power company knew anything about it.

I went around the outside, looking in windows, to start. That wasn't illegal. I wasn't death on the idea of picking a lock and lying about it, but there was no harm in starting with the law-abiding part of the tour.

Through the small mud-splattered window of the shed with the power line, I could see a snowmobile, along with some tools and jerry cans and an oblong white thing in the back that could have been a freezer.

Thc little shed was built of plywood, and the door was another sheet of this stuff, all of it stained with something to seal it. The door was shut with a padlock that was, to my surprise, hanging open on the hasp. Burglary was not a big concern halfway up a mountain, it seemed.

So I let myself in. It was too dark to see well, even with the door open. I reached for my phone and… dammit. I'd been distracted enough to forget my goddamned phone. I could live without it, and I sure didn't plan on calling the cops while trespassing, but it would've been nice to be able to take some pictures or use the flashlight.

I had a business-card LED in my wallet, and that would've helped if there'd been anything to see. Just a shed and a freezer, both well past their best days.

I nudged the chest freezer open with my elbow so as not to make or disturb any prints. The freezer was nearly empty. That wasn't a crime. Mine was too. My flashlight, carefully sent around the inside, showed stains and cracks but nothing suspicious. Nothing that looked like hair or fabric or blood.

Maybe I should've started back in on the kid. Constable McKay thought he'd already done his clean-up, but maybe not. Maybe I was giving him more time to ditch evidence. Time to work on his story. This was a thing that had been easier as a cop. Having more than one suspect, following up on everything at once.

I wasn't surprised to find the sunroom open. The trailer, on the other hand, was locked. Sort of. The fifth-wheeler was an ancient thing, nineties or worse, and the door handle was one of the aluminum levers with an inset lock that you saw on trailers from that time. Those locks weren't popular anymore, largely because you could pick them with almost anything—like the Allen wrench I kept next to the flashlight in my wallet.

The sunroom rattled in the wind like it was going to tear free of the trailer and go flying across the mountainside. The wind was stronger now and gusting to something that made it hard to breathe when I faced it. I hunched my shoulders against it and focused on the lock.

I felt a little bad that Jess wasn't around to see this. He would've been delighted that I was being naughty, for one thing, and also that I was finally behaving like a TV detective. But I only felt a *little* bad, because when it came down to it, crime was always better without a witness.

The trailer was about what I'd expected. Blond wood panelling, a pop-up side with a dinette, a pop-up roof with a sleeping loft, and everything designed to either hide dirt or wipe clean. I flipped the lights on with the side of my arm and looked around.

At first I thought there wasn't anything to see. It was tidy, especially for a bachelor pad. A leather jacket was lying on the bed, and a box of saltines was on the kitchen counter. I stepped farther in and saw something that didn't look right—a billy club in the sink. It was sitting in a drying rack. Who washed and dried their fishing clubs in the kitchen?

I turned, slowly, to take in the rest of the space. The dinette had two lights in sconces above it. One of the sconces looked as if it had been glued back together, and not well. I looked closer—for blood or black hairs—and found none. This trailer predated the internet. The sconce could've been broken anytime. It wasn't promising.

But I was here. No point doing half the job.

I started going through the place, back to front, opening every cabinet and door. Looking in the oven and the half-height fridge. Nothing. Nothing. Nothing. I straightened and tried to think. The wind howled around the buildings, whipping branches against the trailer and dropping pine cones onto the roof. The sunroom creaked. It was unnerving, as if the place was going to fall apart. I told myself it had to have survived worse.

What was I missing? It seemed impossible that someone, especially someone as vivid as Kim, could vanish into this trailer and leave no sign. I sat on the edge of a dinette bench and looked around for what I might've missed. There was a scuff on the edge of the counter, but that had too much dirt rubbed in to be new. That damned billy club in the sink. A bit of paper sticking out from under the sugar canister.

I hadn't noticed that before. It was barely out of reach from where I was sitting, so I went over there and lifted the canister.

It was a lottery ticket.

The draw was last Wednesday. Not a quick pick. The numbers were three, five, eight, thirteen, twenty-one, thirty-four. Why did those numbers seem familiar? Was it… what about all those stories on the news? The ones about the unclaimed jackpot from the ticket sold in Calgary. For last Wednesday's draw. Had any of them said what the numbers were?

Three, five, eight, thirteen. Was that it?

Three. Five. Eight. Thirteen. Twenty-one. God help me, it sounded so familiar. I could almost hear the newsreaders' voices.

And then I could hear Jess in my head. One plus one is two. Two plus one is three. Three plus two is five. Five plus three is eight.

And eight plus five was thirteen.

Five, eight, thirteen, twenty-one, thirty-four. Going around like a spiral. Like a snail shell. Like the paintings on Kim's wall.

*"Everything's a Fibonacci sequence."*

The ticket fell from my hand.

She won.

She won the lottery.

She found out Wednesday night. Every Wednesday's Winsday, like the commercials said.

All the news stories. The ticket bought in Calgary. Unclaimed.

The drawing. College for her niece and a trip around the world on one side. All those eyes on her, like she was prey, on the other. She was on the cusp, she'd said.

Oh Jesus. She won the lottery.

My fingers were numb, but I managed to grasp the ticket and pick it up from where it had fallen to the counter. I turned it over. It was unsigned.

I was looking at millions of dollars on a chipped and dull countertop, still half-tucked under a tin sugar canister that had been around far longer than I'd been alive. In the hovel of a guy who had nowhere else to go and not much further down to slide.

Did you kill for a lottery ticket? For a million dollars or more, people would. Killers would. But you couldn't cash it. There were so many ways you had to prove it was yours. It wasn't killing for money. It was killing for scrap paper.

Why would you do that?

Was he enough of an idiot to think he could say it was his all along? Holding on to it even now because maybe, maybe there was a way to make this all pay off?

I looked around the trailer again. My parents' camper, when I was a kid, had featured a similar dinette. The table had come down and rested on the seat to make a bed, sort of. The seat backs had gone down to make a mattress and… you could store pillows and blankets in hollow benches of the seats. That was storage space.

I put the cushion from the nearest bench onto the table and ran my fingers along the front of the bench until I found a small notch, and pulled.

Before I even looked, I smelled the cologne. Lying on top of a grey army blanket and a winter parka was a black satchel with a Japanese luck cat on the front. At least Jess had put me on the right trail. At least Ethan McCann wasn't ditching the satchel in a pond somewhere. I had to feel good about that.

Didn't I?

I took a piece of paper towel from the kitchen and used it to handle the satchel. Kim's wallet was inside, with her ID. A laptop and a phone. I pulled out one of her credit cards. She hadn't signed that either.

I sat on the scratched lino floor and put her satchel down in front of me.

I took out her phone, but it was dead and the sim card had been pulled.

The laptop had been hit with something, like a hammer or, hey, maybe a billy club. I tried anyway and blinked in surprise when the thing binged softly and lit up. Goddamn.

It was password locked, of course. Too old or cheap to be opened by touch or facial recognition. Just a password. Could be anything. I shut my eyes and pictured Kim's room, her psyche splashed on the walls. The sequence.

I tried it.

Nothing.

I tried a few of the numbers in pairs. Nothing. I had to be careful. These things had only so many tries before they locked. I closed my eyes again. The wind sounded like it was in the room with me. I could feel it seeping through the cracks between the panels, cutting at my arms like a chilled knife.

Emma. The niece. Her favourite person. Carefully, I typed MEbird.

I was in.

The desktop was Kim and Emma, smiling, twin smiles in the sunlight by a lake. No windows open, but the browser was running, so I pulled it up and looked at the search history.

*What do you do if you win the lottery?*

My hands shook a little. I accidentally closed the window and had to bring it up again. She'd done a lot of searches. She'd been a good student. How did you claim your ticket? What was it like? Were people's lives better after?

She'd looked at stories about people who'd lost it all. People who'd lost family and friends. People who'd been robbed. People who'd been killed for their money. No one had been stupid enough to kill for the ticket, the piece of scrap paper, but wasn't there always a first time? Wasn't there always a first guy who was that desperate or drunk or dumb?

Did people know you had to prove where you'd bought it, who you were, that they checked security footage against the time and date? Not everyone knew, it seemed. No one had told Derek.

Maybe he'd seen it in her purse, or maybe, inhibitions soaked in booze, she'd leaned forward across the bar after everyone else had gone.

*"Do you want to know a secret?"*

My breakfast pitched in my stomach, and I regretted it, regretted everything I'd eaten for days. I swallowed hard. I shut the computer and shoved it into her satchel.

The wind howled. It was deafening.

I couldn't walk out of there with the evidence. I'd broken in. But I could put the evidence where Derek might not find it if he got the idea to destroy it. If I'd made him nervous.

I couldn't hide the satchel or the computer. I put them back. But the phone neatly fit between the top of the kitchen cabinet and the ceiling. He wouldn't find it, even if he noticed it was missing from Kim's bag.

The last thing was the ticket. I went into my wallet and pulled a receipt from the gas station in Dead Man. I tore the time/date stamp off, trying to make it look natural, and put the receipt where the ticket had been, with the edge sticking out. He'd think it was the ticket if he glanced at it, checking that it was where he'd left it. I'd paid cash. There was no path back to me.

And the ticket? I looked around. Somewhere safe and flat and invisible.

There was shelf paper in the cupboard by the sink.

I couldn't picture Derek neatly trimming floral paper to keep his cupboards extra clean, so I guessed that it had been there when he'd bought the place and he'd never thought about it. It would never cross his mind to peel it up.

And that was it. The wind howled, and the sunroom screeched, and my stomach pitched again. I could not be sick in here. No one could know I'd been here.

My hands were cold and shaking. I stumbled outside.

"Mr. Detective," Derek said.

I turned to see him standing beside the trailer, tight T-shirt and jeans and a windbreaker. A gun in his right hand.

Watery cold, like ice cubes were melting inside my skin. For all I'd told Jesse that guns were for losers, for all my lecturing about how people thought they could talk their way out of trouble, I knew Derek had other plans. He hadn't shot me yet because it wasn't as easy as people thought, especially if you hadn't done it before. But he was gearing up, and he'd get there soon.

I was in very bad trouble.

"It's funny… I wasn't worried when I saw a strange car at the bottom of this hill," he said. "Then I posted my lunch menu to Twitter. You will never guess what I saw."

I got it in one. Jess… and me… and my car. Which I could've parked anywhere—around the block, out by the highway—but I wasn't used to people knowing it was mine.

"I found her bag," I said. "That's it. It doesn't prove anything. She came up to your trailer. She left on her own. Now you're holding a gun on me because I trespassed. You've got a story you can sell."

"Shut up," he said. That was bad. That meant he didn't want to talk. On the other hand, he was still getting his nerve up to kill me. It was taking him longer than it should have. Maybe there was a weak spot in his psyche that I could work on.

He'd seen the car, though.

He'd passed the car on the way up.

Had Jess seen him? Had he called the cops?

Or….

Jess, asleep in my car. A gunshot sounded like backfire coming from an alley. No risk, not really. Not if you were already thinking you'd have to shoot another guy. And maybe we were standing here, now, both waiting for that next shot because he was cruel enough that he'd wanted me to know.

Everything mapped out like I had laser beams and rulers and string. How it had to be. Where his eyes had to go. How long I'd have. I'd never been that clear before, not about anything.

He was an amateur, standing too close, watching my face and not my center of gravity.

Distracted by a sound in the trees, some paper caught in the wind.

I dove for him.

It was not a graceful fight. Most aren't. I needed to knock him down, give myself a chance to pull the gun away. I moved between his hands, for his center.

He went down, and we rolled. Threw one-handed punches and kicked, and the gun went flying, of course, somewhere neither of us saw. I was impatient, trying to put him down quickly so I could go find that gun. I missed him reaching behind him with his free hand.

The next time I knew where I was, I was on my hands and knees in the pine needles and scree. My head felt like it was hosting a gang fight, and I tasted acid. I'd thrown up as far as my mouth. I had an idea that there was something I needed to do.

I saw Derek scanning the ground, hunting for something. The gun. I needed the gun.

I lunged, throwing punches. Finesse was not an option. It hurt to open my eyes, so I was keeping them a crack open. The big blurry thing was making me hurt, and I wanted to make it stop. That was the closest thing to a plan I had.

Things cracked and broke and split. We spat and swore and yelled. The yelling tapered off as we got tired. Or we ran out of things to yell at each other about.

Or our heads hurt too damned much. Even in my confused state, it was starting to dawn on me that I was in trouble. I was starting to feel something more than the adrenaline, something like drowning. Panic.

And then, cutting through the howl of the wind and the howling in my head, there was a sharp spitting noise. A shaking in the earth and the air. My head felt like someone had drilled a hole in it to let the wind out. A gunshot.

Things happened out of order after that. I heard a voice. I felt Derek getting off me. I saw, through swelling eyes, the shadow of him moving away. I winced as the light he'd blocked hit my face.

"Get away from him. Now."

After a second or two, I knew it was Jesse.

Not dead.

Jess had found the gun. Unless he somehow had his own. He didn't. Did he? I couldn't remember. And I was missing something now. More talking.

"…Ben! Are you okay?"

I made a noise of some kind and started trying to sit up. My stomach let me know that was a terrible idea, and I made another, less agreeable, noise.

"Just roll onto your side," Jess said. "Onto your side. Roll."

The big blur a few feet from me moved, sending another whirl of nausea around my stomach.

"Don't even think about it," Jess said. The blur stopped.

Time passed. I don't know how much. My left eye was nearly swollen shut, and my head was all knife edges and fire, but I slowly put the rest of me together. Jess had climbed the hill. Really? With pneumonia?

We were waiting for the police, and I knew because Jess had said that to Derek. "The police have been called. Try any more bullshit now, you're digging yourself deeper."

"He did it."

That was me. It came out of my mouth, which was so close to the rest of my aching head that I regretted saying anything.

"I sort of figured," Jess said.

"Jack Lowe is holding a gun on me," Derek said. "Jesus Christ. Fucking surreal."

"You're probably imagining it," Jess said. "Sit down."

The bulk beside me slouched back to the ground. I hadn't seen him start to stand.

"Should've shot you on the way up."

"I didn't tell you to talk."

Jess sounded good. He'd climbed the hill, with pneumonia, but he sounded like he'd stepped out of a limousine to see whether Montreal was ready to rock.

"...cut-rate Marilyn Manson," Derek was saying. I'd missed something again.

"Shut the *fuck* up," Jess said.

"It's him, Jess," I said. "It's him."

"I got that," Jess said. "Just... take it easy, okay?"

"He has the ticket," I said. I really don't know why I said that, because I hadn't intended to let Derek know I'd found that ticket. And Jess wouldn't have any idea what I meant. But I spit it out like it was vital, like saying it was the last thing I had to do before I died.

Jesse glanced at me. Bad form. Amateur.

"Eyes," I said. Jesse's back straightened, and he looked scared for a second. He'd forgotten again that it wasn't a game. He fixed his eyes on Derek.

"Down," Jess said, like you would to a disobedient dog. Derek shifted subtly. He'd barely started to rise that time.

"What do you mean, he has the ticket?" Jess said.

"Fibonacci," I said. Jess didn't look away from Derek, not completely, but his attention shifted, and it was enough. Derek saw an opening. And I saw Derek, a second too late.

He was on Jesse in that second, knocking him to the ground. Jesse's right arm, the one with the gun, flew back.

This is what I knew, about the only thing I knew: if Derek got the gun, Jess and I were dead.

No other thought could have been enough to make my concrete limbs move. I rocked to get going, then lurched toward Derek. I'm sure it wasn't pretty, but I cleared the distance.

I could have sworn it took a hundred years to get there. In that time, Derek had given up on trying to pry the gun from Jesse's hand. Guitar, piano; Jess had more strength in his hands than people would think. I flew into Derek, but I heard a snap, and I heard Jesse yell.

My momentum bowled Derek over. I got some good shots in, I think. I had the element of surprise. But that evened out pretty fast and left us rolling on the ground like before. It didn't even hurt, really. I felt like I was made of static, like I was crackling and shifting. Difficult to hit but likely to blow away in the next strong wind.

The gun fired again and brought me back to myself.

We stopped, and in the sudden stillness with the shot still echoing from the mountains, Jess said, "Break. It. Up."

He didn't sound good anymore. He sounded like he was holding a scream behind his gritted teeth. But he was by-God loud. I moved away from Derek, and he let me go. Hands and knees, dried pine needles digging in my palms, my head hanging. When I did look up, through a rivulet of blood that was winding past my good eye, I saw that Jess was sitting on the ground, pale, his right hand caught between his knees and the gun in his left. Shaking a little, but not so much that Derek was likely to rush him again.

"You okay?" I asked him.

"This guy has assaults," Jess told me. "And a peace bond. Kent called to say. You left your phone."

He shoved the words out a sentence at a time, then clenched his jaw again like it was the one thing keeping him together. Whatever magic his voice training had done for him, it was over. He sounded like he had pneumonia and then some.

"Could've waited," I told him softly. "Could've told me later."

"Thought you'd need your phone."

I still didn't hurt. That was a bad sign. Slowly, I shifted until I was sitting beside Jess, my arm against his left shoulder.

"I can take the gun," I told him.

He didn't say yes or no. I put my hand on the gun. He didn't do anything, didn't even tense. I took the gun into my own hand and aimed it at Derek.

"Don't move," I told Derek. Now that I was really looking at him, I realized I hadn't needed to tell him. He was sideways on the ground, right eye as fucked up as my left, and I didn't see any intention to go anywhere.

We sat for I don't know how long. Crows fought in the trees down the hillside. An orange-and-black caterpillar shuffled by. We waited. Jess wheezed and gasped. Luna had specifically said he shouldn't climb mountains.

I said, "She won the lottery, Jess."

I said, "He thought he could cash her ticket."

I said, "He didn't know you can't. He killed her for scrap paper."

That last thing, as I said it, I sounded funny. Almost like I was crying.

"He killed her for *paper*, Jess."

Jess leaned into me.

"If he'd killed her for a million dollars," he said softly, one painful word at a time, "would that've been better?"

He passed out when the police arrived.

WE TALKED later, in the hospital. When I had it together, and he had oxygen, antibiotics, and Luna on the phone, mad as hell at both of us. McKay had expressed some thoughts too when she'd shown up on the hillside. She'd specifically told Jack to take care of himself and me to lie low and what the hell was all this?

I told Jesse what I'd found as he lay there sucking in hospital oxygen like it was his whole job and like it still wasn't enough. He was so pale I thought I could see through him in places. He's sick, a doctor had said. Like Luna had said the first night, with the special meaning doctors gave it.

I was stupid for parking so close to the trail. How hard would it have been to park somewhere else? I wasn't used to being recognized. But I could get used to it. I needed time to get used to it.

He kept breathing. I kept thinking he'd stop, the fucking quitter, the prince of midnight moves, but he didn't.

Constable McKay stopped by to check on us after Jess had drifted off. Told me that Derek had confessed almost immediately, the way truly horrible people did when they figured they had no choice and might as well get the satisfaction of bragging about what they'd done. That was fortunate. Derek had confessed to me under duress, and I'd tampered with evidence in his trailer. If he'd realized that any half-decent attorney, even a legal aid lawyer, could have thrown out that confession and everything I'd found on his property, the cops might have been up a creek. But Derek was not that smart.

McKay left a gift for Jesse on the nightstand. A Mountie quarter. Her lucky quarter, she said. I didn't know whether to laugh or cry, so I did neither.

The nurses tried to move me back to my room after the constable left, but they found it too difficult, and I fell asleep next to his bed with my head on Jesse's arm. The not-broken one. Until the orderlies came and made me go, I stayed.

IT WAS nice for October. The sky was bright blue, the sun felt warm, and there hadn't been enough snow to pull the leaves from the trees.

We stood at the top of Quartz Falls, next to Emma and Lauren. Kim's friends had sent us, in a way. They'd put an inukshuk there, with Kim's bird symbol painted on it, and Emma and Lauren had called us when they'd decided to visit on Thanksgiving. Did we have time? Did we want to come?

Jess had pinched the bridge of his nose and called it "some well-meaning cultural appropriation" when he'd seen the inuksuk on social media, but to Lauren he'd merely said, "Yes, thank you, and when can we meet you there?"

We'd seen them a few times since Derek's arrest. They'd come to see us in the hospital, and of course there'd been Kim's funeral.

The lottery winnings went to Lauren and Kim's parents, who had promptly given most of it back to Lauren, and to Emma in a trust. Lauren had insisted on not just paying but ridiculously overpaying me, no matter what Jess and I said. So Jesse took the money he'd intended to pay me and used it to send some poor kids to art camps, and then we all tried our hardest to forget where any of that money had come from.

Jess liked Emma, who made a lightning-fast transition from awe at his presence to mocking his hair. Maybe he was going to teach her guitar, if she still cared about it in a month and hadn't moved on to the next thing. And if she and Lauren didn't decide, as they well might, that being around us was too painful a reminder of how their favourite person had died.

We'd been talking about this and that along the trail but stood in silence when it became clear that this was a moment for Emma and Lauren alone. I put an arm around Jess, and we headed back toward the car.

"I have to go to New York next week," he said once we were far enough away. "It's only for a few days. You can come if you want."

"I have to finish something up for a client. Can you tell them you'll go later?" I asked. "Or you could tell them to go to hell."

"It's a non-optional trip."

"Ah."

ZZGold had eventually backed off. Jess said he'd decided the controversy had done more for his single than Jesse's promotion ever could. I thought it was also possible that he'd remembered Jess had something on him, but that was a sore point for Jess, so I didn't bring it up.

Jess's label, on the other hand, had not appreciated learning from the newspapers that Jess had been recovering from pneumonia by running around the mountains chasing a killer with his once and future boyfriend—and getting his wrist broken in the bargain. They'd taken care of the blowback and leaned into the hero and new boyfriend aspects of the story, neither of which thrilled Jesse. He was even less thrilled by the petty chores they'd seen fit to assign him, from ghost writing for hacks to singing backup for… well, more hacks, at least in Jesse's view. But he was trying to take it with grace.

He laid his head against my shoulder. "The internet will say we've broken up."

"How long until they get bored with me?" I asked. "Like what's her name, Matt Damon's wife?"

Jess laughed. "I don't know. I'm way less famous than he is, but you're a lot more interesting than his wife."

"You don't even know her," I chided, and he laughed again. It gave me a chill, and I pulled him closer.

Jess had told me some things about Derek after we'd gotten out of the hospital. Things Derek had said while I'd been too out of it to understand. Jess hadn't understood at the time, either, but he remembered.

Derek had been furious, going on and on about rich people, people who didn't even want the things they had, and he had nothing. People dangling a fortune in front of him. Laughing at him. People who thought they were better than him. Thought they deserved things he didn't.

He'd asked me if I thought Kim had laughed at Derek. Say he'd asked for the ticket. If you don't want it, give it to me. And she'd laughed, thinking it was a joke. Who would say something like that and mean it?

I'd told him I'd bet on it. Laughing at certain people was as lethal as kissing a cobra.

I didn't say how much it surprised me, with Jess and his sense of humour, that he'd never met one. Lucky guy.

KIMBERLY MOY, who in a way had brought us back together, was happily in heaven if you believed that kind of thing. She was a newborn baby somewhere if you believed that. I believed she was gone.

I'd dreamt of her in the hospital, while I slept with my head on Jesse's arm.

In my dream, she'd checked her phone and screamed in joy instead of terror. She'd run back into the restaurant and bought drinks for her friends. She'd called her sister and said that Emma's college was taken care of. She'd never come to Dead Man's Flats. I'd seen her face on the news, local lottery winner, and pissily thought it should have been me, though I'd never bought a ticket and never would.

And then she'd walked into my hospital room, where I was lying for reasons I didn't understand, and she'd put a hand on my leg, just below the knee.

"It's directions for spirals," she'd said and was gone.

Keep Reading

for an Exclusive Excerpt from

*The Man Who Lost His Pen*

Ben Ames Case Files, Book #2

by Gayleen Froese

# CHAPTER 1

A LOT of people would have loved to be where I was. Standing in the wings of a grand old theatre, watching a rock star do his soundcheck for that night's show. A secret space where you could see the real Jack Lowe. No filters. Just light, draped like silk over him and the piano, playing up the sheen of his ice-white shirt and the deep blue running through his newly dyed black hair.

I admit, there was nothing wrong with the view.

Where I was, at the edge of the stage, the light was sparse and sliced by rows of curtains. People were milling around onstage or gathered at the tech booth at the back. The only person near me was a hedgehog, a woman with short hair in spikes, bulky headphones, pens bristling out of her vest and cargo-pants pockets, and a battered low-end Samsung in her hand.

She was texting someone while she talked to someone else, and I didn't think she'd noticed me until she said, "You must be the boyfriend."

"That's on my driver's licence," I said. "Most people call me Ben."

She laughed, quick and sharp. "Sorry. I didn't mean to treat you like the little wifey. I'm Vic." Vic offered a fist and I bumped it.

"No worries. What's your job around here?"

"Assistant director," she said. "Stage manager. Flunky. Hey, aren't you a detective? Aren't you that guy?"

I didn't know for sure what she meant by "that guy," but I'd caught a murderer and made the news a year before so I figured that might be it.

"I could be. Do you need a detective?"

She looked me up and down. Mostly up. She was barely the height of my shoulder. In the dim light, her face looked almost as dark as Jess's hair. Or Jack's. Always the stage name onstage.

"Can you find me a decent sound tech? Your boyfriend's right. The guy does not know how to mic a piano. They forced us to use the house staff and—oh, shit, excuse me."

She slipped farther into the shadows to take a call. I could only hear her side, and it didn't tell me much. A change in the schedule. An unexpected addition. Her response could have been summed up as "Go to hell, but fine." She was scowling and fiddling with her horn-rimmed glasses when she returned.

"Trouble?" I asked.

"Not your kind," she said.

I nodded. "Too bad. I'd love something to do besides stand here."

When I'd said that, I'd had no idea that we were a few hours away from a murder. There was no way for me to know. But I would definitely, before the night was over, feel like an asshole for saying it.

Vic bustled away, onto the stage where she had a word with Jess, then up the aisles to the soundboard. Jess tilted his head back and looked up into the light grid as if it had some kind of salvation for him, then spun the piano stool around and stood. He couldn't have seen me with the light in his eyes, but he smiled at me anyway. He had a lot of practice at that, smiling at people he couldn't see. Also assuming people were where he'd left them.

He gave me a real smile once he was close enough to actually see me. I put my arms around his waist and kissed him. He leaned back a little, a thing he did when he was tired or frustrated. Like a metaphor in motion: Help me. I didn't think he knew he did it.

"Everything okay?" I asked.

"Did it sound okay?" he asked, clearly meaning it hadn't. I gave him my blankest stare. "Right. Sorry."

He took my hand, and I followed his lead through the backstage labyrinth to the green room. That surprised me. I'd thought he might want to sulk in his dressing room like a musical Achilles, but apparently he was up for socializing.

The halls did nothing to reflect the glamour of the theatre's foyer or auditorium. They'd never been fancy and hadn't been kept up because they weren't expected to impress anyone. The concrete walls and floors were crumbling in spots, and the off-white walls were farther off white than they'd been to start with. Bare bulbs overhead were in cages to keep them from being shattered by stacks of amps or incautious double bass players.

The paint was missing here and there, always in rectangles that I assumed had once been signs holding the theatre's name. It turned out that the fur trader turned entrepreneur and patron of the arts whose family name and money had gone into the place had been, as my friend Luna had put it, "a true ass bag," and the theatre was in the process of finding a less embarrassing title. True Ass Bag Theatre was not under consideration.

It was The Calgary Theatre until someone sorted the name thing out.

The green-room door was propped slightly open to save people the trouble of swiping their cards to get in. If I'd been on the security crew, I'd have used the door to go inside and lecture everyone in the room, then shut it myself, but the crew was nowhere to be seen, and it wasn't my job. I settled for pulling the door shut behind me and kicking the empty pop can that had been holding it open under the nearest couch.

I'd been in a few green rooms, thanks to Jess, and there seemed to be two kinds. One was everything that wasn't a bathroom or the actual stage. A dressing room, a hang-out, a warm-up space. People would be packed in, wearing whatever amount of clothing was convenient for them, and about half would be sitting on the floor because the make-up tables didn't leave room for enough comfortable chairs.

This was the other kind.

It was a big rectangle with a lot of tables and chairs, little clutches of couches scattered around, and a kitchenette at the far end. Real food would show up there later, but for now, it was home to a Keurig and a basket of pods, mugs, water glasses, cans of pop, and a bowl each of fruit and granola bars. Not, Jesse had told me, the kind of spread you'd expect at most shows—it was more what you'd see at a cheap convention—but this was a charity show, and economizing was only appropriate. Next to the kitchenette were doors to two unisex washrooms. These, too, had bare rectangles where signs had once been, so I guessed they hadn't been unisex until recently.

The night's line-up was written on a whiteboard next to the door, along with You are in Calgary, Alberta.

If I ever needed that kind of reminder to know what city I was in, I'd hope I was being professionally supervised. Then again, that was probably what road managers were for.

"Oh my God, it's you guys!"

A gangling tower of a person with wavy black hair and a sloppy grin rushed at us full speed and hoisted Jess off the ground. Jess laughed and returned the hug. I stood to the side and waited for them to get over their musical-theatre-kid dramatics.

Thom Cross had been in the same music program as Jess in university, and they'd been in the same cast a few times—*Hedwig*, *Evil Dead*, others I'd tried to forget. I wasn't a musical-theatre guy. Now Thom played keyboards for a pop/roots/country rock band that should have been called We Can't Make Decisions but was instead called the Brennan Murphy Twist. Or the Twist, to people with less time to kill.

He set Jess down and offered me a handshake instead of a hug. This wasn't a snub. He'd known me as the criminology student who dated Jess, and killjoy had been my brand at the time. I shook his hand and gave him a friendly smile to show I was both human and happy to see him. Thom had always been a good guy.

"I love the new album," Jess told him. "I love that it's an album. It's like a concept piece about… I don't know, man. Not rednecks…."

"It's more the whole subsidized housing thing," Thom said. "Brennan and Reiss both lived it as kids. I mean, Brennan was in the UK, but still."

"Not my world," Jess said. He sounded ashamed of it and probably was, though he hadn't touched a cent of his parent's money since high school. He didn't like the corporate raiding they'd done to earn it.

Happily, Thom didn't seem to remember or care what Jess had come from.

"Seriously," he said. "The rest of us are so boring it's boring. But Reiss and Brennan do the writing, so whatever, right? It's their songbook."

If Thom resented this state of affairs, it didn't show. I'd never known him to resent much of anything for long. He parked his narrow back end on a table—to hell with chairs—and regarded Jess and me.

"It is amazing to see you guys. Like, both of you. Together. What was it? Seven years in the wilderness?"

"We were together for about three and a half years," Jess said, "and apart for about seven. And then together for… just about six months now."

Thom raised his hands palms up, like they were the sides of a scale, and moved them up and down.

"Four years… seven years… pretty close. In a few years, it'll be like those seven years never happened."

"It won't," I said automatically. I glanced at Jess to see whether that had stung. He seemed okay.

"It really won't," he confirmed. "Those years mattered. I needed that time to get my shit more or less together."

"And turn into Mr. Big Time Rock Star," Thom said with a grin. Jess shrugged like he was trying to dislodge that from his shoulders. Then as I watched, he pulled some of that rock star to the front. The charisma, the cool, the easy charm. Jack Lowe smiled.

"I don't know, you're getting pretty big time yourself. What did they call you on *The Current*? Canada's Rock Chroniclers?"

"Yeah, it's cool," Thom said. "It's like we're starting to get respect, you know? Not just sales."

"You deserve it," Jess-as-Jack said. I looked at his shoes. Expensive, of course, but not one of a kind and not what he intended to wear on stage. I stomped on his foot. Like the pro he was, he did not make a sound. His eyes widened a little, but he didn't look down. Instead he looked up at me. The glare he gave me was pure Jesse Serik.

"Are you thirsty?" I asked politely. "After sound-check? We should grab something for you to drink."

"Oh yeah, do that," Thom said. "Then I'll introduce you to the guys."

He loped off to said guys, who were on couches around a video game, while Jess and I went to check out the beverage selection. Jess limped a little, which was dickish because I did not step on him that hard.

"So, Stompy, mind telling me what I did?" he asked as he picked through the cans.

"Thom wants to talk to *you*. Not Jack. Most of the people here would prefer to talk to you, I think. Save Jack for the stage."

"Oh, so I was supposed to tell him that I'm not sure about rock-star business and maybe I'm downsizing my career, or maybe I'm just destroying it or, fuck it, maybe I already have? Those were pleasantries we were exchanging. No one wants to know how you really are."

"That's catchy," I said. "They should make that the name of the show, instead of A Big Night for Mental Health."

"The name sucks," Jess said.

"It does," I allowed. "Is it me or is there no booze here at all? I don't care. It's just weird."

Jess laughed, loud enough that a few of the room's scattered artists looked our way.

"Oh my God, did I not tell you? What this is?"

"A fundraiser for the Cross Canada Society for Mental Health?"

"Yeah, yeah, that," he said, waving it aside with a hand. "But we're all… mentally interesting. That's why they invited us. We've all been open about having a mental illness. They're super excited about me because I just started talking about it in October. Even if depression is pretty fucking vanilla."

"I still don't see why…?"

Jess cocked his head and waited.

"Oh," I said. "Addiction."

"It's not like people couldn't have brought their own," Jess said. "But it's a gesture, I guess."

Considering how famous Jack Lowe was for doing all the drugs, preferably in bunches and while drunk, it had taken me a while to concede that Jesse wasn't an addict per se. If nothing else, the past six months of him living with me had shown that he really could take or leave the stuff. What he did was use whatever he could get his hands on to be Jack Lowe, who radiated energy like a forest fire and needed about as much fuel to keep going.

He'd been trying to stop doing that for about two years. The last six months had been easy because his broken arm had kept him off the stage. I was curious about how it would go here, at his first show in the new year.

He grabbed a Coke Zero and I found a Sprite hidden toward the back. The logo always reminded me of my mother, who had spent many Saturday nights winning at canasta with a lemon gin and Sprite at her elbow. It gave me a small pang when I realized that I hadn't seen her in a year. I made a note to visit her in Kelowna. Maybe I'd even take Jess along.

"See her?" Jess said, pointing his chin toward the far end of the room. Three wispy women were sitting around a small table with mugs of tea, looking at their phones. They had identical pink cotton-candy hair and outfits made of watermelon-coloured leather, velvet, and tulle. If you put them in a huge chocolate box, they'd be in danger of a giant coming along and eating them.

"I see three hers. Or I'm seeing triple."

"The one closest to us. Ash Rose."

"Is that her name or the shade of her hair dye?" I asked.

"Her name and her band's name," Jess told me. "Anyway, she's borderline. I mean, shit, she's got borderline personality disorder—or is living with—I need to look that up before I go on stage. Like, am I a person living with depression?"

"Say you're an indolent drama queen. That should be fine."

"You're a riot," he told me. "Never go near a live mic. Also, all mics are live. Seriously, Ben, help me out here. You've got the psych degree."

"Criminology degree. As you well know."

"You took a lot of psych classes."

I sighed. "Living with BPD should be fine. If you overthink this, you will put your foot in your mouth. Or you could ask her."

"Yeah, but I need to know what to call myself, not her. I'll say living with depression."

"What kind of music do they do?" I asked. "Ash Rose."

"Shoegazer," he said. "Or dream pop. They're kind of retro. It's really layered, and I didn't see a synth rack that could handle it backstage, so they're probably using backing tracks tonight. I bet they'll just do vocals. It's easier to get them off the stage in a hurry that way too. They've only got—" He looked past me to the whiteboard. "—twenty minutes. Looks like they're on from eight twenty to eight forty. That's not too bad, actually. I've only got forty-five minutes, and I'm the headliner."

"If I were to say the word shoegazer around them…?"

Jesse frowned.

"Risky. You could say nu gaze. No, better to go with dream pop."

I would have made fun of him over all the linguistic dancing, but I'd been a cop for a few years, and I had in fact completed a lot of psychology classes. I knew words could make any situation a lot better or worse than it otherwise would have been.

"Hey, you guys wanna come meet the band?"

Thom was back, already putting an arm around Jesse's shoulders to lead him. Jess went without complaint, though I knew he wasn't wild about being dragged places. I tagged along.

I'd seen enough of the Twist to have an idea about who was who. The two string beans on the couch, both at least as tall as Thom, were guitarists—one a lead guitarist, the other a bass player. I couldn't have said which was which, and in fact apart from one having a blond shag and goatee and the other a matching set in dark brown, they might as well have been the same guy. They were playing the same video game as we approached, either shooting reptilian things while wearing battle armour or being reptilian things and breathing fire on the guys in battle armour.

"Connor, Charlie, this is Jesse and Ben. We went to school together."

Connor and Charlie each raised a hand in greeting without looking away from the screen. One of them said, "Hey." Jess grinned and gave them a "hey" back.

The other two were on a couch sidelong to the screen, one holding an acoustic guitar and the other a notebook and pencil. I wasn't an expert but it looked like songwriting to me. They were watching with amusement as Thom slid the fact that he'd turned up with Jack Lowe past their oblivious bandmates.

Brennan, the namesake and lead singer, put down the notebook and stood to offer Jess a hand.

"Is it Jesse or Jack?" he asked, his Geordie accent bending the vowels and chopping off the hard end of Jack.

"Jesse, offstage," Jess told him, shaking his hand. He didn't ask for Brennan's name because he didn't need to any more than I did. I never got used to meeting people this way, and it was even stranger when Jess was involved because then everyone knew one another without having met.

"This is Ben," Thom added. "We all went to school together."

"Good to meet you," Brennan told me, and we shook hands. "This is Reiss."

That was fair, since even casual fans of a band didn't always know the name of the drummer. Reiss set his guitar on the floor and leaned forward to shake hands with both of us. He didn't speak.

From my perspective, he didn't have to say anything to bring value. He had ridiculously large ice-blue eyes, straight features, and dark hair that spiralled to just past his shoulders. The guy could have been on the cover of *GQ* or an extra on *Vikings* without looking out of place. It didn't hurt that he had drummer's muscles either.

Brennan couldn't match him for looks, with eyes and a nose that were a little too round and a sandy brown tousle on his head, but he had a lead singer's charisma, and I felt like returning it when he gave me a smile. Reiss, on the other hand, did not smile. He had, a little, when the video gamers ignored Jess, but now he just seemed wary.

"I saw you once back in the day," Brennan said to Jess. "A long, long time ago. A student production, in fact. You were playing Hedwi—"

"Oh God no!"

Jess flushed. I leaned against the back of the gamers' couch and settled in to enjoy it. Jess rarely got embarrassed enough to blush. It was a good look on him.

"I'm so sorry you saw that," he said while Brennan laughed. "I was at least a decade too young to play Hedwig. I had no way into that character."

Brennan patted his shoulder.

"University shows," he said. "Nothing to be done about it. Everyone is the same age. But I will tell you, even then you had a huge voice and so much control over it. I remember thinking you'd be a star."

Jess laughed. "Well," he said, "I was there, and I know you're being kind. But I'll take it."

I had also been there, and I didn't disagree with anything either of them had said about the show. Except that I hadn't known Jess would be an actual star until the day I'd seen him fronting a band of his own.

"Why did you even go?" Jess asked. "You didn't know Thom back then."

"I like *Hedwig*. I see it whenever I can. I'm interested in how people stage it." Brennan turned to me. "Are you a singer too?"

Jess managed, barely, not to laugh. I managed not to throw my drink at him.

GAYLEEN FROESE is an LGBTQ writer of detective fiction living in Edmonton, Canada. Her novels include *The Girl Whose Luck Ran Out*, *Touch*, and *Grayling Cross*. Her chapter book for adults, *What the Cat Dragged In*, was short-listed in the International 3-Day Novel Contest and is published by The Asp, an authors' collective based in western Canada.

Gayleen has appeared on Canadian Learning Television's *A Total Write-Off*, won the second season of the *Three Day Novel Contest* on BookTelevision, and as a singer-songwriter, showcased at festivals across Canada. She has worked as a radio writer and talk-show host, an advertising creative director, and a communications officer.

A past resident of Saskatoon, Toronto, and northern Saskatchewan, Gayleen now lives in Edmonton with novelist Laird Ryan States in a home that includes dogs, geckos, snakes, monitor lizards, and Marlowe the tegu. When not writing, she can be found kayaking, photographing unsuspecting wildlife, and playing cooperative board games, viciously competitive card games, and tabletop RPGs.

Gayleen can be found on:
Twitter @gayleenfroese
Facebook @GayleenFroeseWriting
And www.gayleenfroese.com